The Overnight Palace

Janet Marie Sola

Spotted Owl Press

Ashland, Oregon

Copyright © 2014 by **Janet Marie Sola**

Spotted Owl Press
47 California Street
Ashland, OR 97520
www.spottedowlpress.com

This is a work of fiction. Names, characters, places, and incidents are a product of the author's imagination or are used fictitiously. Locales and public names are sometimes used for atmospheric purposes. Any resemblance to actual people, living or dead, or to businesses, companies, events, institutions, or locales is completely coincidental.

Book Layout © 2014 BookDesignTemplates.com
Cover Design by BookCreatives.com

Library of Congress Control Number
2014912703

The Overnight Palace/ Janet Marie Sola. -- 1st ed.
ISBN 978-0-578-14509-9

For my mother, who taught me
so much about courage.

All journeys have secret destinations of which the traveler is unaware.
—*Martin Buber*

Prologue:
A Lake in Rajasthan

I move across our room and open the French doors that lead to the tiny balcony. A gust of wind from the lake blows in and the long white curtains billow in response. They look like the ghosts of veiled women. I step through the doors. Two stories below me, the dark water laps against the stone walls. The moon floats on the surface of the lake. The night is a mirror.

Then, in the silence, a thud. Then another. Sahil must be reviving. I turn to look, but he hasn't moved. There's the sound again. Muffled. Insistent. *Thud. Thud.* The sound is coming from the other side of the double doors that lead to the hallway. *Thud. Thud. Thud.* Then another sound. Sharper this time, a cracking sound, a hard object butting against wood. The sound of a rifle butt. No, the sound of two rifle butts. It's the most sickening sound I have ever heard. I can't move. I stare at the door where the sounds are coming from.

The curtains billow again. My mind stops in mid-thought, freezes, then slides through a narrow bright opening to another dimension, a dimension where everything rational, everything civilized has been left behind, like so many silly customs, and what is left is very clear. The hunter and the hunted.

I press my palms together to stop shaking. The henna patterns I thought were so beautiful look strange now, nonsensical swirls and whorls. I try to connect something of what I am doing at this moment to the woman who came here a few short months ago, maybe a little naïve, maybe a little overly romantic, but a nice woman, surely, a nice educated woman with a life and friends and a career—surely that's a description of me. Will I ever get back to her? Will I ever get out of this room? Will I ever get out of India?

PART ONE

SARASWATI

Saraswati, goddess of the arts, is often pictured playing her lute by a river, her black hair streaming down onto her white sari, her swan vehicle nearby. One calls on her to release the flow of creativity necessary to achieve freedom.

CHAPTER ONE

A Mysterious Painting

Even with the dry wind blowing through the open window on the overnight train headed north, I can't shake off the memory of the ashram I've just fled. I can still feel the sweat running down my back and pooling at the base of my spine under the white polyester tunic and pants I had to wear there. I can still hear the chanting of hundreds of voices, two notes over and over again, all day and all night. I can still see myself, knees extended, fidgeting on the hard marble floor, sure that I alone among all the devotees was not flowing in the stream of divine love. I wanted to flow, I really did. I wanted to heal. I wanted to cry. I even just wanted to breathe deeply. But I was stuck. Every gesture, every breath, was a struggle.

A calm sanctuary, a place where your wounds will heal and your heart will open. That was the picture my friend Jason had painted when he proposed we make the journey from California all the way to India. It would help me, he thought, recover from the shock of my failed relationship. Jason needed solace too. His lover had died of AIDS a year earlier and he was still in mourning.

And so we traveled to the other side of the world, to an over-decorated pink temple in the jungle. But after weeks of sitting, sweating and chanting, with no enlightenment or serenity on the horizon, I felt trapped. And yet, just like my bad relationship, I was afraid to leave. Even though I longed for adventure, I was afraid of being alone. I was afraid, period.

I would probably still be at the ashram except that an unexpected thing happened. A woman there, her blue eyes rimmed in kohl, presented me with a gift. It was a ticket she couldn't use, she told me, to a city called Udaipur, situated on a lovely lake in the desert state of Rajasthan in the northwest of India. Jason thought it was a sign that I should go out on my own. He would catch up with me later. Maybe.

And now here I am, the train rumbling along beneath me, headed to this mysterious place. A storybook India, the guidebook on my lap tells me. A land of elephants and palaces and gypsies. The home of the fierce and noble Rajput race, propagated by the sun and the moon. A desert state bejeweled by lakes.

I love these words, *propagated, bejeweled*. I have always loved words, maybe too much. There is a life waiting for me that is more urgent, more beguiling, than what I can find in books. I believe that. With my finger, I draw a question mark in the dust film of the window. I see now that its shape suggests the *om* mark. Perhaps the universe began with a question: What will I be? And the answer is another question, and another and another in an unfolding forever. The wind is turning cooler and the night blacker. I shiver. I am forty years old and I have never traveled alone before. I'm exhilarated. I'm terrified. I'm heading north, into the desert, into the unknown.

The family sitting across from me is asleep, a softly snoring white-bearded patriarch, a woman in a dark sari and an old cardigan, a child with a scarlet dot on her forehead, wrapped in her mother's arms. The little girl opens her huge eyes and gazes at me. I smile at her. She continues staring as if I'm an alien being. I smooth my almost-new linen travel skirt and try to sleep.

We arrive in Udaipur the next morning. During the brief journey in an open three-wheeled taxi from the train station to the guesthouse, there is a moment when I first see the Rajasthani people, swaying through ancient streets, wrapped in the flaming colors of the sunset, looking back at me with their eyes of fire.

I am here to find the courage to step out of my middle-class, middle-aged skin and into a culture that traces its ancestry to the sun. There are secrets here, and I want to discover them. I write this in my journal as I wait for breakfast in the courtyard of the guesthouse on the edge of the lake. Am I being overly romantic? Maybe. That's what my ex would have said. The ex of the "failed relationship." The ex who dumped me, and unceremoniously at that.

To be honest, at the moment I feel like a prisoner again, with all the promise of the exotic culture outside these thick walls still eluding me. I've been stuck here for two days now. "The ladies cannot be leaving the premises," the manager tells me again, a smug smile on his pockmarked face. "Much mischief in the street today. Much danger. This is better you stay in safety, madam."

Why do you call me madam? I want to say to him. Maybe I am forty, but can't you see I'm an adventurer and a poet, and in no way the kind of fussy, proper woman associated with that title? But I don't say it. Not out loud. I simply sigh and resign myself to another day in the hot, fly-plagued courtyard. The other guests shrug and settle down to wait for breakfast under the scattering of shade from the courtyard's lone tree.

The official excuse for all this constraint is the festival of *holi*, usually a benign rite of spring where, I've been told, people dash about merrily and throw dust in all the colors of the rainbow at each other. But there have been reports of violence between Muslims and Hindus in faraway towns like Mumbai. And even here, in this seemingly tranquil city, a rumor has gone around that some young Indian women were grabbed and molested.

The manager assures us he is erring on the side of safety, but I wonder if he is being overly dramatic. He lifts his chin to the waiter who is serving breakfast, and soon I and the other guests are brought omelets and black coffee and *toastbutter-jam*, as they pronounce it. The flies swarm around my plate. The waiter tries to chase them away, to no avail. I look at my fellow guests. Each of us has our own little fly cloud. There's the silent German couple—he lean as a stick, she stout as a globe and wrapped in a sari of some metallic material she wears as if it's armor. They pretend they don't even notice the flies as they eat, a sign perhaps that they've been here for a while. Then there are the two young English fellows, swearing and swatting as they recount tales of how some taxi driver tried to cheat them out of a few rupees, the equivalent of a few cents.

Finally, face lifted to the sun, is the woman who looks as if she might have been a model. Long blond hair, huge sunglasses. She brushes her own fly cloud away with casual disdain and returns to her copy of some scandal sheet with a tearful Indian actress on the cover. Without looking up, she turns to the Brits and says in bellowing American English, "No mistake about it, dudes. They're all out to cheat you."

I smile at them, but inside I'm seething. Their cynicism and arrogance are getting on my nerves. Can't they see the beauty and magic of this culture around them? Did they come here just to complain and act as if they are great white gods dispensing their precious rupees to the native ingrates? I want to say, you traveling Philistines, don't you know that the people here are descended from the sun and the moon? Don't you know they are fierce and beautiful? Don't you know that their painting, their culture, their palaces, their souls—especially their souls—are far more complex than yours?

I know I'm being snooty, but I can't help it. By the time I've finished my breakfast, I realize that hanging out in this place with my fellow travelers for another day instead of in the streets and bazaars filled with the exotic beings who live on the other side of the wall—well, it's more than I can stand. I take my coffee, my books on the history and culture and poetry of Rajasthan, and climb two flights of stone stairs to what has become my retreat since my arrival, the rooftop.

It's lovely, with a pergola that offers protection from the sun and overlooks the lake. All around me the city creates itself in the brilliant sunlight. A wash of white and honey-colored buildings flows over the hills that circle the lake. Graceful minarets reflect themselves in the glassy stillness of the water. In the lake's center, a shimmering white palace seems to float on the surface like a lotus blossom. I feel myself drifting back and forth between my books and the vision unfolding in front of me. The lake was born, legend has it, because once upon a time a gypsy built a dyke on a stream for his cattle to cross over.

Three or four hundred years ago, Rajput princes and princesses, when they weren't fighting each other in to-the-death feudal wars, created the fairy-tale palaces and artificial lakes and arched bridges that surround me. It's all exquisitely sensual and incredibly romantic. It's everything, to be honest, that was missing from my own life back in California. I surrender to the heat and close my eyes.

Thwack. Thwack. Thwack. Slowly, I become aware of a rhythm, a constant soft percussion coming from somewhere beneath me. I shake off my lassitude and look over the edge of the roof. And there, on the lake's shore, women, hip high in water, are slapping their ropes of laundry on the stone steps that lead into the lake. They're beautiful, their gauzy veils shielding their faces from the sun, their midriffs bare and glistening above wet sari skirts, their arms lifting and slapping, lifting and slapping. There's the thwack—and the echo of the thwack. *Thwack. Echo. Thwack. Echo. Thwack. Echo.* The sound, deep and seductive, translates in my head as *Come. Out. Come. Out. Come. Out.* But then another inner voice, much higher-pitched, chimes in. *Watch. Out. Watch. Out. Watch. Out.* I try to shut it out. That's the voice, I remind myself, that I came here to silence—squeaky, cautionary, always full of the-worst-thing-that-can-happen scenarios.

The women call to me once more *Come. Out. Come. Out.* I make up my mind. I will go out, the so-called danger be damned.

I retrieve my camera from my room, pick up my shoulder bag, and turn to catch a startling glimpse of myself in a tarnished mirror. I see a pale, worried-looking woman in a stiff beige linen skirt and a large straw hat—definitely someone who should be addressed as "madam." Someone who reminds me of the woman I thought I'd left back home. Reliable, loyal, cautious. A bit bookish. A woman who had stuck with a job she didn't like for years and with a man who didn't like her for even more years. It's a woman I would like to take a vacation *from*, I think, rather than *with*.

I take off my hat, pull off the band that ties my hair in back—my plain brown hair that I wouldn't mind being a little blonder—and change into something bright blue and silky that I picked up in a market in the town near the ashram. I look again. I attempt a tentative smile, then a bigger one. Much better. The face of an adventurer and poet. Someone who isn't afraid to feel the sun on her face even if there are a few tiny lines just beginning to show. Someone who is ready to plunge into the waiting world on the other side of the wall. I slip back through the courtyard, and, when no one is looking, I push open the heavy wooden door that leads to the street and steal out. In the distance, on the next hill, the golden dome of the city palace glows in the afternoon sky.

The cobblestone streets twist through warrens of lovely old buildings adorned with latticed wooden windows and arched doorways. Women float by dressed in saris the colors of dreams—saffron, lime, orange, melon, hibiscus. The men wear the same dazzling colors on their heads in the form of huge turbans. They look like flowers and mushrooms in an enchanted garden. The smells are different at every turn. I try to separate out the flavors—curry, charcoal, musk, patchouli oil. People behind the walls making food or love.

Around a corner, children play near a water pump, hanging from the handle. They don't quite have the strength to pull it down, so I help them. When the cool water starts to spurt, they squeal with delight and splash each other, then me. "Help," I say and put up my arms in mock defense, which makes them laugh and splash harder. I shake the water droplets off my head. They imitate me, shaking their heads too. I'm feeling something I haven't felt for a long time—pure joy.

I wave goodbye and follow the street as it winds up the hill, away from the lake, then dips into a tunnel under a phalanx of medieval buildings, a cool stretch out of the sun. The tunnel opens on to a busier part of town, and soon I'm in a square, lined by long rows of open stalls selling clothes, trinkets, newspapers, snacks. The square is thronged with revelers. Young men run around throwing colored powders into the air with great flourish, like Tinkerbells of the east. The dire warnings of danger seem greatly exaggerated.

Two young boys, their skin and clothes pink and blue and purple from the powder, are perched on a stoop in front of a dress stall. They shout at me to take their photo, putting their arms around each other and grinning at the camera. I oblige them. Then I take a photo of the tailor behind them, yellow turbaned and fat, sitting on the floor of his stall. He looks like a big caterpillar. His legs are contorted in front of his body in a way that allows him to use one foot to push the treadle of an antiquated sewing machine. A little further on, a vendor is selling bracelets encrusted with a handpainted design and tiny mirrored cutouts. I buy two of them and put them on my wrist.

A pair of teenage girls, their long braids woven with flowers, approach me. One of them giggles with one hand over her mouth and with the other tosses rainbow-hued powder in my direction, sprinkling my face and arms. A thrill goes through me. I'm no longer an invisible outsider, the cautious American tourist. I'm part of the mysterious world of Rajasthan. People are pouring into the streets now, a river of color and sound and movement. I'm feeling the rhythm of the crowd, gliding through it like a dancer, neatly side-stepping motorcycles and bicycles, waltzing around clusters of multi-hued girls and boys.

As I turn a corner, I slow down to step around a reclining humped-necked cow, munching on a plastic bag, so thin its white hide looks like a sheet draped over its jutting shoulder blades. So I'm not in a dream. This is real, part of the vast pulsating scene where exuberance and misery exist side by side. I want to do something to help, but what? As I'm standing there pondering this unanswerable problem, my gaze travels up to a tarnished sign on a wall that says, in English, "Miniature Paintings of Old India." I remember finding them fascinating in some long ago art history class.

A stout man appears in a doorway, the round belly under his white shirt a fat mountain compared to the hungry, craggy peaks of the cow's shoulder bones. When he sees me eyeing the sign, he extends his arm in a flourish. "Welcome to my shop. Very nice painting here," he says. "Very old. Come, I show." I hesitate for a moment. I don't have money to spend on paintings, and I don't want to leave the spectacle of the street, and yet I find myself drawn in.

"Yes, OK," I say. "But I only want to look." I follow him into a small courtyard, centered by a fountain gone dry. Off to the side, in a small room revealed by a partially open curtain, a slender man wearing a white turban sits on a cushion. His back is toward me, and he is bent over a miniature canvas. He holds a paintbrush in one hand while he taps a rhythm on the floor with the other, as if he's bored, as if he's been doing this forever. His hands are striking, dark and fluid and experienced, as if they belong to someone very old. Abruptly, the proprietor crosses to the alcove and pulls the curtain shut. "Please come to my shop," he says, as he opens another door off the courtyard.

I follow him into a dimly lit room. The hypnotic sounds of a classical raga float down from a boom box on top of a tall cupboard. After the brightness of the street, it takes a moment for my eyes to adjust to my surroundings. The walls are bare. The only pieces of furniture are a few large cupboards and a counter covered by scratched glass. There's a smell of dust and old things in the air that reminds me of the attics of my childhood. A tingle goes through me, as if I'm a little girl about to unlock a trunk full of secrets.

The proprietor places his hands on the counter, then looks up at me from heavy lids, and says, dramatically, "Very fine paintings I show you, American lady." Well at least he didn't call me "madam." From somewhere he fishes up a box and shoves it under a rusty lamp.

One by one he pulls out the miniature paintings and displays them in the circle of yellow light. A young woman plays the lute in a night garden. A man waits outside in the rain while his presumed beloved looks on scornfully from her window high above. An extravagantly dressed girl primps in front of a mirror being held for her by maids. There are scenes of the god Krishna and his milkmaids. Scenes of tiger hunting and of great battles on painted elephants. Some are crudely done, others very skillful. And yet I'm disappointed. It's obvious to me that the paintings are not old. They are bright, fresh, newly minted copies of famous old miniatures, made, of course, for tourists like me, probably by people like the turbaned painter I had seen on my way in.

"Do you have anything old?" I ask him.

"These old," he says, gesturing to the pictures on the counter.

"Do you have anything older?" He looks puzzled. "Very old. More old. Most old."

His eyes gleam. "Ah," he says. "I have one you are liking very much." He turns around, unlocks the cupboard, and removes a single painting. He places it on the countertop, positions the light over it, and carefully pulls back a tissue overlay as if it were a delicate skin. In the painting, a figure swathed in blue from head to toe—it's impossible to tell if it's a man or a woman—sits cross-legged under a tree edged in gold and stares out at a small fire. At the shrouded figure's feet, a lion reclines, its maned head resting on supine paws. Each tree leaf is a precise jewel, the column of smoke a thick braid in the sky. There's something about this painting that makes me want to gasp or sigh, but I know that would drive the price up. "Hmm," I say.

"Perhaps one hundred year old." The shopkeeper lowers his voice. "See, very, very old writing." He turns it over to show me that it's been painted on the back of a manuscript page covered with a finely wrought script in a mysterious language. "This artist is great master. This is from old book. Look. Very nice color. Blue is lapis. Coming from Silk Road on high mountains. Gold is true gold."

He moves it back and forth under the light to better show off the glint of the gold edgings. It might be old, it might not be. But it's beautiful. The brushwork is very fine, the colors are exquisite, pale, the shades of a desert dawn. But that's not what attracts me. I'm enchanted by the expressions of the shrouded, meditating figure and its lion companion. Both seem to look inward to their own thoughts and yet outward to each other and the landscape around them. There is a shared understanding between the meditator, the lion, the tree, the fire—and even the desert backdrop with its parched hills and hazy blue sky—that says something like "the great adventure of life is simply being." The painting seems to embody the elusive thing I'm seeking. Transcendence. Transformation. I'm not even sure what to call it, but it's a place beyond the fears and anxieties that I want to leave behind. It reminds me of something I can't quite call up, almost like a memory that hasn't happened yet.

"I give for twenty thousand rupees. Very good price, very special painting." I can't quite do the math in my head, but I know this is a ridiculous sum, representing weeks of meals, lodging, and transportation. He must have seen the admiration in my eyes.

"No," I say, "not possible." I shrug with feigned disinterest. I've never been good at bargaining, but I think I'm catching on.

"If you have US dollar, maybe two hundred dollar."

"Maybe fifty dollars."

"Not possible. Very old. Gold is true gold. Maybe one hundred dollar. That is best. You are from America. You can sell for many hundred dollar."

I try to be tough. "I don't want to sell. Final offer—seventy dollars."

"OK. OK. Eighty dollar." He sighs as if this is causing him excruciating pain.

I turn away, unzip the money pouch tucked inside my skirt, and pull out the appropriate bills. Yet even as he wraps it for me in cardboard and string, I know that I've probably first, overpaid, and second, overextended myself. I have months to go before my return flight home, and a continent to cross to catch it. I'd come within a millimeter of cancelling my entire trip due to cold feet, so at Jason's suggestion I did something to insure myself against such future panic attacks. I booked my arriving flight in the south of India, in Madras, near the ashram, but my return flight—with an open date—from Kathmandu in Nepal, thousands of miles away. Jason did the same. That way, as he pointed out, we couldn't turn around even if things got strange. Now that I'm on my own, with a long way to go, I have to be careful to make my money last. Still, I tell myself that beauty, that special kind of beauty that feels as if you alone have discovered it, is irresistible. This painting is something that will inspire me forever. The proprietor hands me the wrapped package, urges me to come back soon, then lowers his head over his accounting book.

Back in the courtyard, I squint in the glare of the sun on whitewashed walls. I wonder how long the fountain has been dry. I hold my package close to my heart, relishing the feel of the cardboard, the old string, knowing they protect the painting that will be my companion on my journey. The curtain is now open again and the painter is still there. His back is still to me, the fingers of his left hand drumming, the fingers of his right hand poised over the tiny canvas. A column of dim light from a high window illuminates his enormous turban, which seems to be coming loose. As if he feels me staring, he turns toward me and meets my gaze.

His face does not match the aged look of his hands. In fact, he is young, his eyes are huge and calm, his skin smooth as water, his features finely drawn and sensual. He is almost pretty, except that his dark eyes are overshadowed by eyebrows that nearly meet, which gives him a kind of wild, intense look. I nearly turn away in embarrassment for being caught at staring.

But then I hear myself say, "Look at this light you're working in. You'll ruin your eyes." Immediately I feel ridiculous, like a schoolteacher. I have no idea if he understands me or not.

He frowns as if he's puzzled. "My eyes see you very well," he says.

What a strange thing to say. I feel myself blush. I reach for the sunglasses in my bag and put them on, just for something to do. "Well," I say, "I'm going to enjoy the painting I bought."

"I may look?" he asks.

"Yes, of course." I move to the curtained doorway, carefully take the painting out of its wrapping, and hold it up for him.

He tilts his head and puts his hand on his chin, as if he is thinking very hard about this painting. "Very good." He pauses. "But also true."

I consider this for a moment. So simple. "Yes, true." I nod.

"The painting is very special. What is your name?" he asks.

"Elena," I say, without thinking. That *is* my name, but my middle name, one I've never used before. And now I know what middle names are for—that other identity that is murmuring just beneath my skin.

I want to talk more to this intriguing young man but suddenly another presence invades the space of the courtyard. The proprietor. He has a stiff smile on his face as he puts himself between me and the painter. "Please, you come tomorrow and I show you very many more nice paintings." I already understand the message. The young painter is his employee and has crossed a line by consorting with a customer. The proprietor takes the painting from me, wraps and ties it again, and hands it back to me as he walks me toward the main entrance.

I tuck the package back into my shoulder bag and secure the clasp. Just as I'm leaving, I look back over my shoulder to see the young painter watching me. I give him a quick, covert smile and shrug as I leave. I'm no longer the schoolteacher, but the student being reprimanded. In some way I'm now in league with him. In the street again, I can hear the proprietor's voice, a mounting torrent of Hindi syllables. I cringe, because I know that the painter is in trouble because of me.

The sun is lower now, and the skinny cow is still there, still munching on his plastic bag, casting a long cow-shaped shadow on the cobblestones.

Back in the square, the crowd of revelers has turned into a densely packed throng. There is really no way around it, so I hold my bag close to my chest and plunge in. Immediately, I'm pushed from all directions by people whose eyes are bright with excitement. We're all moving together like one enormous beast. Streams of colored powder are tossed into the air, suspended for an instant before they settle on skin, on hair, on clothes. The crowd thickens by the second. I pull in my shoulders and wriggle along as best I can. The sun is merciless on my bare head. I wish I'd worn my wide-brimmed hat. It would have provided me with an extra margin of space. Still, I tell myself, it's no worse than a packed metro train during rush hour. Then it *is* worse. A trickle of sweat runs down my forehead, slips behind my dark glasses, and glides onto my nose. I dare not even lift my hand to wipe it off because I might not be able to get my hand down again. The air is heavy with pinkish dust. It's hard to breathe.

Then, between bobbing heads in front of me, I see a dark sedan moving up the street, slowly, relentlessly. Like a steamliner plowing through an ocean, it's forcing the crowd to part around it. From the other direction, a bicycle carrying three boys twists through the mob. They're skinny teenagers in Western shirts and jeans, waving their arms in the air. The sedan and the bicycle are headed directly for each other. Of course, they'll miss each other by millimeters. They always do.

But not this time. The car's fender swipes the bicycle. The bicycle goes down. The boys sail up and into the crowd. There's a communal roar of shock and anger. The boys flail around for just a moment, then scramble to their feet and chase the offending car.

The sedan is at a dead stop. The crowd sways and shouts, sways and shouts. I sway too, carried back and forth by the force of hundreds of bodies. Outraged men close in. They jump on the hood and roof, beat on the windows, pull on the doors. The driver, just visible behind tinted glass, pulls a scarf over his head. He doesn't want anyone to recognize him. Then, just as someone starts banging on the car window with a stick, he guns the motor and brakes. The car jerks and a man falls off the hood. The driver keeps at it, braking and jerking. One by one, he shakes off his assailants until they're all gone. He speeds off and the crowd surges forward, carrying me with it. Someone grabs at my camera strap. I twist it free. I keep my head down, hug my shoulder bag, and try to shove through the fray.

I have one thought: I've got to get out of here. When a flock of older women in saris passes by me, pushing through the crowd in a no-nonsense fashion, I see an opportunity. I smile tentatively at them and try to insert myself into their midst. At first they frown at me and close ranks. Then one, whose silver hair matches the silver border of her black sari, gives a little head bob in my direction and steps back to make room for me. "Thank you," I say. I need to learn the Indian word for thank you. I need to know much more about this culture. In another block, we have escaped to a quieter street. I murmur a *namaste* to them when I leave their ranks. They smile at me, with a bit of pity—or do I only imagine it? It doesn't matter. I'm free.

I make my way back the way I came. Everything is calmer now. Stragglers are on their way home, men with their arms around each other, women in wilted pairs. When I reach the medieval building with the tunnel that leads back to my guesthouse, I breathe a sigh of relief. I check for my camera, feel the comfortable weight of my old single-lens reflex. I pat the money pouch under my skirt. Everything is all right. But then something is not all right. The clasp to my bag is undone. My heart sinks even before I know what I'm missing. I thrust my hand into my bag, groping like I'm searching for a wound I can't see. My map and brochures are there. My cosmetic bag is there. My wallet with my cards and identification is there, inside the zippered pocket. But my package with the painting is gone.

My painting is gone. *My painting is gone.* I search for it again and again in my bag, pat underneath my blouse and skirt as if somehow it could have slipped down there and lodged itself in my underwear. Be calm, I tell myself, but there's a flush of panic spreading out to my skin. I force myself to remember my steps. I can see it so clearly, wrapped neatly in its cardboard and string. The proprietor wrapped it. I showed it to the artist. Then the proprietor wrapped it again. I tucked it securely in my bag and turned the clasp. I went from the shop to the crowd to here. That's all. The shop to the crowd to here. The crowd. The moving sea of bodies. The grab at my camera strap. Of course. Someone opened my bag and took it. That's what happened. I will never find it. Never. I retrace my steps, scanning the debris on the streets, cigarette butts, papers, powder packages, plastic bottles, food, all kinds of disgusting detritus. But not my package. It's nowhere. There's nothing to do but give up.

On my way back, I notice another smell among the aromas of spices and incense. Piss. When I finally pull open the heavy door of the guesthouse, the manager takes one look at me—disheveled, my clothes covered with streaks of powder, my hair a sweaty mess—and smiles his smug I-told-you-so smile. I ignore him. As I cross the courtyard, a pair of houseboys are pouring buckets of water over the floor. It sloshes over the stones and runs off into nowhere. The lone tree in the corner is wilting for a drink of water. But they ignore it. This is India, where they water the stones and let the trees die.

CHAPTER TWO

The Night Market

Back in my room, I take a shower to compose myself. My room is cell-like, with just a single bed, a chair, and a small dresser. A small window opens onto the lake. Back in San Francisco, all the things I owned and lived with formed so much of my identity. My city flat with its brick garden and fireplace. Elegant dishes and furniture and pictures and gorgeous oriental rugs. A huge closetful of clothes to choose from. Concerts and opera tickets and most of all (arrogant ex aside), wonderful and supportive friends. I had worked hard to have these things. They made me bigger than I was. They gave me comfort and order. Now there's just me, a few garments and books, and no one to talk to. Not that I'm in a mood to talk to anyone.

Just chill, I tell myself as I change into a long black dress, appropriate for my mood, tie a purple sash around my waist, and head for the rooftop. I get there in time to catch the sun blazing its grand finale over the distant hills. I have company. The silent German couple and the blonde, still hidden behind her enormous sunglasses. They all look so content, as if they have all the answers. In spite of the sense of destiny I felt on my arrival, I now have no idea what I'm doing here. I have a

theory. I've entered a parallel universe where I haven't yet figured out the rules.

The women are still washing clothes in the lake. Eventually,
the *thwack, thwack, thwack* slows, then stops, and they call to
each other and their children. I watch a man on a nearby roof
shake out a length of white cloth and unfurl it like a sail that
might carry him out over the lake. Even in my current state, I
feel the pull of the sheer beauty of this place. The white city on
the hills is melting into gold and then spreading a perfect re-
flection of itself on the lake's glassy surface. A flock of birds,
composed of hundreds of tiny V shapes, appears out of nowhere, swerves over the water, and then, by some trick of light,
is gone. Seconds later it reappears, diving and spinning, as if
emerging from an invisible time warp. The birds are so in tune
with each other that they are one elegant creature. There is no
leader, yet somehow they know the exact moment to turn so
they will all be in unison.

No one, as far as I know, has ever seen a collision between
birds. They undoubtedly have some kind of knowledge that the
bumbling human race, superior as we think ourselves to be, has
no clue about. We push, shove, and grasp, just like the people
in the crowd where I lost my painting. *My lost painting, my
perfect painting.* I can feel the weight of the brown paper package in my hands, like the ghost of an amputated limb. I can see
it as if it were right in front of me. The shrouded figure sits
before the fire. The tree's painted leaves are the notes in some
raga yet to be played. The reclining lion gazes tenderly at the
onlooker.

Suddenly, loss, like a buried root, digs at my chest. Familiar.
Don't you know, a chirpy voice in my head mocks, *what you*

love is what you lose. That's the way it goes. Ha ha ha ha. Better not to love anything at all. When I think of it, all my life, I've lost not just objects, but people, even whole communities. I'd lost the other children I loved, my childhood friends, time after time, when we followed my father to yet another town where he would design yet another dam or bridge. Loss followed me into my adult life. Every love I've had has slipped through my fingers.

I remember that day—what was it, just a few months ago— that Peter said goodbye, after years of coupledom. I was shocked. I was outraged. But even more at myself than at him. There was part of me that wanted that secure, conventional life. Peter was smart. He was a professor. He wrote books. In the beginning he thought I was wonderful. You're such a good listener, he'd say. Or, you've got great eyes. Or, it's wonderful that you love books like I do. I even thought of having children with him as my biological clock's ticking got louder. But I put it off. He was changing. He was becoming rigid. He wanted me to play a role, but I couldn't learn the lines. I felt more and more uncomfortable, more and more like I was trying to pour myself into a costume that didn't fit.

Even so, I kept clinging and clinging, even after he began to criticize everything about me. I tried so hard to fit his idea of what he wanted me to be that I hardly knew who I was. Let's see. Dress: classic and tailored, please. Beige or black. Personality: social and pleasant, but circumspect. Opinions: exactly what his were. Job: professional, the more money the better. My job as a writer and editor for a local arts and entertainment magazine didn't quite fill the bill for his upscale future as far as he was concerned. Not that I loved my job, which was mostly writing puff pieces on galleries and restaurants. When I told him what I really wanted to do was take time off to work on my own writing, the novel I felt I had in me, it pushed him over the edge. "You're irresponsible," he said, slowly shaking his head at me, as if in disbelief.

"I didn't say I was actually *going* to do it," I backtracked. "I just said I fantasize about it."

And then, two months later, he met me as I was pulling up my car into the driveway. He signaled for me to roll down my window. When I did, he leaned over and rested his arms on the frame. I can still see his pitying smile, his reddish moustache twitching as he told me: "I've met another woman. She's a lawyer." That was explanation enough, as far as he was concerned. I should not have been, but I was devastated.

My friend Jason had always told me that I take things too hard. "People come, people go. Things come, things go. You have to learn not to cling." I had known Jason for over a decade, ever since we had worked together for a short time. He was the one friend who was there for me. That day, I drove around in a kind of mild shock, not knowing where to go or what to do. I didn't want to go back to the flat I had shared with Peter.

It was hot that day, and for some reason my car's air conditioning didn't work. I drove by Jason's apartment building. There he was, leaning out of his third story window, head bent and his long hair falling forward from his bald spot. He was working on the plants on his fire escape. Jason was a nurturer. He said it was his lover dying of AIDS that had made him that way, but in truth it was just the way he was. "Come on up," he shouted down when I waved to him.

He poured me a glass of white wine. While he made a vegetarian dinner for us, he listened to my tale of woe. I worked myself up into a rage, then a philosophical calm, then into a fit of sighing, back and forth, always finishing with "What should I do?"

The third time I asked this, Jason nodding as if he really did understand, the room started to shake. "Earthquake," we both whispered. We watched as a ceramic statue fell from a shelf to the floor. The shaking stopped almost as soon as it started. "Thank God it wasn't another Big One," I said, trying to make light of it. "That would be way too much for one day."

The statue was lying in several pieces on the floor. He picked them up and began studying them as if they held the clue to some mystery. "It could be a warning. But I think," he paused in that I'm-going-to-tell-you-something-important way of his, "it's the universe trying to send you a message. You personally."

"Come on. Don't go new age on me, Jason."

"Well, I *am* new age, my dear. But seriously. Look at this." He put the two broken pieces next to each other on the kitchen counter. The statue was of a long-haired woman with a sweet expression holding a lute. "Saraswati," Jason said, bending down and trying to fit the pieces together. "The Indian goddess of creativity, learning, a whole bunch of stuff."

"OK."

"It's a sign."

"What of?" I asked. "That I'm broken and have to be glued back together?"

"That maybe now you're finally free from the obstacles to doing what you want to do. That maybe you should take some time off. Dive into that creative side you've been repressing for so long to be with this . . . ."

"Jerk. No. Asshole."

"There you go. Attitude. It's a good thing."

Two weeks later, I was still walking around in a septic fog when Jason called me. "India," he said.

"What?"

"Healing. For you and for me." He wanted, he explained, to go visit his guru in the south of India. I should go along with him.

India was too vast, too unknown, too frightening. "My idea of travel is sitting at a sidewalk café in Paris, or sunning on a beach in Hawaii," I told him. "Someplace pretty, but safe. Maybe if I really get my courage up, I could take a singles cruise. Not that I ever want another relationship in my entire life."

"Look, I'm going," he said. "You're not the only one who's hurting." I was embarrassed. His boyfriend had died just a little over a year earlier and I was acting like it was all about me. "Anyway, you won't be alone," he added. "And the ashram is very peaceful."

The more he talked, the more I began to see the journey through his eyes: meditating in a flower-filled ashram, being nourished with an aura of spiritual love. In the space of several weeks, I found myself quitting my job, putting my possessions into storage, and accompanying Jason to the travel agency where we bought tickets to India. After the ashram, refreshed and whole, we would travel together, go sightseeing in fabulous but still vague places—the Taj Mahal, the Buddhist caves, Varanasi—and finish up in Kathmandu, Nepal. Buying our return ticket from Kathmandu, Jason pointed out, was insurance that we wouldn't get cold feet in the middle of our trip and go home.

We arrived in India at midnight. It was a long way from the Madras airport to the hotel, and the driver didn't speak to us for the entire ride. Jason slept next to me as I stared out the window. The night air smelled of rotting fruit and diesel fumes and a hint of urine. In the darkness I could see only flickering shapes: people cooking, squatting, mothering, selling, begging. Thousands of shapes that seemed to go on forever, an epic shadow play. I couldn't see their faces, and they couldn't see mine. I felt invisible, moving in a world made up of the stuff called *maya*—illusion. If I turned away, it would all be gone.

But the next day, Jason, forever upbeat, led me on a quick tour of the very real city, swarming with more people than I ever thought could be on the planet. We were on our way to look for a restaurant, sidestepping the weaving bicycle wallahs with their calf muscles moving up and down like mice under their skin, the men stoking the smoking braziers, the women tending to their children. I almost stepped on a black bundle lying in the middle of the street. Just at that moment, it moved. A second later, a woman snatched it up. I caught a glimpse of a tiny brown face—the face of a newborn baby.

The street, I could see then, was their living room, kitchen and nursery, and I was clomping through it. I tried to find a place for this in my understanding of the world and how it works, what it means, but I could not. It was too big, too incomprehensible. It simply was. Jason and I went to a bank, filled our pockets with change, and gave it here and there, to a child propelling itself with its arms on a skateboard, to a thin young woman holding what looked like her baby brother but was likely her child. Soon, we were surrounded by an agitated, hungry crowd, holding out their hands. Any amount we gave was only a drop in a bottomless bucket of need.

The next day, we took a train to the town closest to the ashram. I again imagined a serene light-filled room where I would join a circle of linked hands. A place where, as Jason kept saying, the chakra of my heart would open and the wounds of my psyche would heal. At the end of a path through thick vegetation, a bright pink temple awaited us. Hundreds of gods and goddesses cavorted over every inch of its surface. India was chaotic, confusing, crazy, and crowded. This seemed to me more of the same. I was soon presented with an outfit of white pants and tunic wrapped in cellophane. This was the required clothing for women; stiff, long-sleeved, and made of polyester. From the moment I put it on, I started to itch and drip.

The ashram was presided over by an efficient and dedicated group of Westerners with a very long set of rules. One of them was that women had to be completely covered up while men could go around in sarongs. The devotees spent most of their time seated on a hard marble floor, waiting for an appearance of the elusive guru. Jason was happy doing exactly this. But the more I sat, the more I chanted, the more I breathed deeply, the more I felt like a failure.

I started escaping to the garden where I could breathe in the scent of tropical flowers. An Indian man wearing a suit with a loosened tie was sitting near a bush bursting with red blooms. Next to him was a tiny woman with a sad, luminous face. The man held out his hand to me and introduced himself and his wife as Mr. and Mrs. Randive. "I am from Bangalore," he said. "I am coming with my wife this long distance to see the compassionate Arushi. My wife is sick. She needs a medical operation. But I have lost my job."

"I'm sorry," I said.

"I came here because I want to ask her to help me get my job back. Do you think she can help me?"

"Yes, yes, of course I do," I lied.

"And you, what do you ask for?"

I paused. "I don't know," I said. He looked so disappointed, I added, "I'll think of something."

"We go to ask," he said. His wife picked a red bloom from the bush and handed it to me with a sweet smile. "For you to give," Mr. Randive said. His wife leaned on him as we walked.

The temple was humming with frenzied chanting. The curtain had been drawn and the woman they called Arushi had appeared. Behind her were several Western men playing sitars. She was resplendent, sitting swathed in pink under an arch of flowers, all roundness, a plump brown face. But it was her expression that was striking, a half-smile floating under black moon eyes. She radiated a combination of the selfless, nonjudgmental kindness of a buddha and the shining self-awareness of a movie star.

Hundreds of people waited in two lines that hugged each wall. One by one, the devotees climbed the steps, then went down on their knees before they reached her. Each laid something at her feet, a gift of some kind. She took each face in her hands and looked deeply into the eyes of each person in turn. This was the fabled *darshan*, or blessing.

"We part here," said Mr. Randive. "You go in this line, for tourists. We go in this line, for the rest of us."

I scanned the room. He was right. There were two lines, and the line for Westerners was much shorter. "This doesn't seem right," I whispered.

"Because you are guests in our country," he said. He smiled at me. "And because we know how to wait."

I nodded apologetically. Maybe he's right, I thought, as I waited my turn to go on stage. We all just get in line for the things we think we need. For some the line is shorter. For some it's longer. Each line is like a little rainbow with a promise at the end of it. For Westerners it's often a rock concert or a latte or a feel good transformation. For Indians like Mr. Randive, it's a cure for his wife, or a job.

As the line advanced, I kept looking for Mr. Randive on the other side of the room, through the crowd. Once I caught sight of him, his hair perfectly combed, his hands folded, his wife in a chair. Each time the line advanced a little, Mr. Randive would lift the chair and move her forward. They would be waiting, I figured, for hours and hours.

Then it was my turn. I did what I had seen everyone else do. I walked on to the stage, knelt, and put the flower Mrs. Randive had given me at Arushi's feet. She reached out her big koala-bear arms. Her head was surrounded by lights from the stage, and her blond backup guys were softly strumming on their sitars. She smiled with her eyes.

"Arushi," I heard myself say, "what I would like to ask is for Mr. Randive to get his job back." She spoke no English and so did not know what I was saying, but that was not the point. When she held my face between her plump hands and looked into my eyes, I felt all my defenses crumble. I felt not like a sophisticated woman, or a world traveler, but just a being who was like every other being. I started to back up on my knees to make way for the next supplicant. But then I knew what it was that I wanted. I inched forward again and bowed to her. "Give me a chance to love somebody," I said. "Give me what Mr. and Mrs. Randive have." She nodded and answered me with the same benign smile, as if it were easy for her to grant my wish.

But the next day I didn't believe any of it. Not really. I didn't believe Mr. Randive would get his job back or that I would find devoted love. A potbellied man from the Netherlands asked me if I would like to share his room, and when I said no, he told me he had asked Arushi for a better physique so women would want to sleep with him.

The whole thing started to seem quite senseless to me. I was hopelessly restless as I sat for hours in my stifling outfit, decidedly claustrophobic in the insular atmosphere, and deeply depressed as I tried unsuccessfully to mend the still tender wounds of my heart with rituals.

"Why don't you travel on your own for a while?" Jason said, when he saw my distress. I shook my head. I had never traveled alone, and certainly never in India, a place as strange as the moon. "There are good, safe trains. Nearly everybody speaks English. You'll be fine. We'll stay in touch by email. And I'll meet you in Kathmandu, if not before."

I thought about it. And the more I thought about it, the ashram seemed to me a sort of spiritual corporation. Cut off from the world, life here was predictable and circumscribed, without the danger or romance I found myself yearning for, in spite of my cautious nature. And then the woman with the blue kohl-rimmed eyes offered me the train ticket. I didn't believe in signs, but it did seem auspicious. It was time for me to make the break. I tried to talk Jason into going with me. But by this time he had found his bliss, and not only the spiritual kind. He had met a man, a kind and handsome New Zealander who he hoped might become more than a friend and help him forget his own grief. He wanted to stay at the ashram indefinitely.

"Remember the goddess who gave her life for you. I think she had a message," Jason reminded me when I was leaving.

"Gave her life for me? Oh, you mean the cracked statue."

"Saraswati. Exactly. Whatever you encounter, remember it's just part of the flow of life," he said. "Let each moment carry you into the next. Don't cling."

And now here I am, sitting on a rooftop in Udaipur, Rajasthan, falling back into my old pattern, clinging again. Clinging to a lost picture, for god's sake, or maybe for goddess's sake, when all around me is all this exotic gorgeousness. The pulse of real life.

A faint sound scratches its way into my consciousness. And something else, the tang of sulphur. I turn my back on the remains of the sunset and see the blonde, looking cool, leaning forward in her chair, striking a match. The blue flame flickers, then burns steadily. She picks up a shiny garment of some kind and holds the match under it. Not surprisingly, it starts to smolder.

"See, I damn well knew it," she says. "They told me this was silk, and it's goddam polyester or something."

I'm halfway annoyed that my thoughts have been interrupted by this silly woman. "Hmm," I say and turn back to the sunset. Undeterred, she pulls her chair closer to me and thrusts the fabric under my nose. "Take a whiff," she says. Obediently, I do. It does smell slightly acrid.

"The burn test tells. If it were silk, it would smell organic when you burn it. They cheated me."

"Did you pay a lot for it?" I ask to be polite.

She names a figure that's the equivalent of about three dollars. "But that's not the point. The point is they try to cheat me because they think they can get away with it. They see this tall blonde and they see a mark. If they're not trying to cheat me, they're trying to come on to me. I'm always getting hassled. Sometimes I wish I weren't blond and gorgeous."

I look at her more carefully. Aside from being blond, part of her problem, I think, could be the way she's dressed. In a country where women cover up, at least from the waist to the ankles, her long tan legs are showing themselves off between short khaki shorts on one end and scruffy boots on the other. She looks as if she's come back from an African safari.

"You always have to have your guard up." She grimaces, snatches the garment back from me, stuffs it in a bag and lights a cigarette.

I give up on ruminating and let myself be drawn into the conversation. "It's been a bad shopping day all around," I say. Once I start talking, I realize how lonely I've been for female companionship. It all comes spilling out, the story of my encounter in the shop, the crowd, my lost painting. "The weird thing is, I fall in love with this painting that embodies, I don't know, letting life be, letting life flow, just letting go. And now here I am attached to this painting."

"Yeah, well all that non-attachment crap isn't what they care about here. Any more than we care about loving your neighbor as yourself." Then she grins wryly, showing off her huge, extravagantly white teeth. "My name's Cathy, by the way. From Chicago."

"I'm, um," I take a second to fix on my new name. "Elena. From San Francisco."

"Cool," she says. "I've got a great idea. Let's head out to the night market. I'm going to take this cheap shit blouse back to the vendor and you can hunt for your painting."

"How would I do that? Look under cobblestones?"

"Well, maybe somebody snatched it and then fenced it. I know people in the market. They can point us in the right direction maybe."

"I don't know," I say. "It was pretty crazy out there before. I think I should lie low."

"That whacky festival they call holi ended at sunset. It's all back to basics. Come on, did you come all the way here to mope?"

"Mope? Me? Is that what I look like I'm doing?" She's right. It's so easy for me to fall back into endlessly stirring the simmering pot of my thoughts. "Well, OK. For just a while. I mean, not that I think I'll find my painting, but I'll keep you company."

"Great, meet you in the courtyard in fifteen," she says as she bounds off.

Once I'm alone again, I look out to the horizon. The city is now wrapped in twilight. A light goes on in a distant window, then another and another, until hundreds are glowing like fireflies in the forest of houses on the hills. I imagine the dwellers of the magical city of Udaipur as they are uncoiling their turbans, loosening their saris, settling down to their spice-laden dinners.

When I meet her in the courtyard, Cathy is still wearing her hot-army-mamma outfit. I don't say anything, but I must have given her a look. "I don't care what anybody thinks," she snaps. "I'm not going to change, and I'm not going to let some crappy patriarchal standard developed to suppress women tell me how I should dress."

"Right on," I say. It seems a little disrespectful of cultural standards, but I've noticed people with chutzpah can get away with almost anything. In a minute we are in the darkening street, Cathy striding and male heads turning the entire way. Except for a kind of aggressive clumsiness in the way she moves, she really could be a model. Next to her, I feel as if, in spite of my efforts, I'm still a "madam" kind of person, a bit prim. I'm glad I'm covered up, but secretly I admire her bravado.

She stops for a minute, and, just before we go into the tunnel that leads to the city proper, takes out a cigarette and lights it. Men pass us. Some of them wear turbans, some wear *lungis*, the sarong-like skirt worn by males that wraps at the waist. Others, usually the younger ones, are dressed in Western clothes, jeans and shirts. But all of them give Cathy a look, not so much of lust, but of wonder.

"I'm getting tired of all the attention," she says, a bit disingenuously I think. She blows smoke out the side of her mouth and smiles. "I know I sound like a bitch, but just wait till you've been here a few months like me. You'll start to go nuts. Just whatever you do, don't get involved with an Indian man."

The idea makes me laugh out loud. "I didn't come here for romance," I said. "I mean, yes, I did. It's the most romantic setting in the world. But not the kind of romance you're talking about. That's the last thing I want."

"Well, I hope to God that's true. My boyfriend's an Aussie. Rich, which is a bonus. I'm going to meet him in Delhi in a few days. You ought to come with me. I'm already tired of this supposedly exotic old stuff. Who cares about old forts and palaces anyway? We could do some upscale clubs, decent shopping."

She lifts her chin and inhales deeply. "Want a drag?" she asks. I shake my head. "So why did you come?"

"I guess . . . ." I struggle for an answer that makes sense. "I guess I want to discover new sides of myself. Maybe to write."

"Hey, you're kidding," she says. She flicks her cigarette to the ground, crushes it with her boot, and we continue on our way. "I'm a writer too. I lived in Australia for a few years before I came here. I worked for the Aussie version of the *National Enquirer*. Good money, going through people's garbage and all that. I went through Mel Gibson's trash can."

"No way," I say.

"Stick with me and I'll tell you the deepest, dirtiest secrets you can imagine."

We both start giggling like schoolgirls as we emerge from the tunnel and find our way to the dense row of shops and stalls. Cathy leads me to one where drapes of brilliantly colored garments hide the shopkeeper. She doesn't waste any time. She brushes the garments aside and immediately goes into full battle mode. "You told me it was bloody silk," she says, pulling the burned garment from her bag and waving it in front of her.

"Silk," says the surprised shopkeeper, who is sitting cross-legged on the floor, looking up at her. "Yes, silk. Very good, very beautiful."

"Silk, my friend, does not melt like plastic. Look at the edge." She holds the blouse up to his face, pointing to the spot where she held the match.

The shopkeeper shakes his head. "You smoke cigarette, then burn. Then you want money back."

"No," says Cathy, "you're the one who cheated me." Her voice rises until it becomes one shrill note that plays against the guttural mumbles of the shopkeeper. People are turning and watching. Suddenly, I'm embarrassed by the whole thing and want to hide.

"I'll be back," I tell her, although she isn't listening, and I float away. Without the white heat of the sun and the press of the crowds, I can relax and watch the parade of life. Here's a group of women from the villages, walking arm in arm, proud of their tight bodices and pushed-up cleavage and skirts of a thousand mirrors. There's a wedding procession, with the bride and groom being carried on a pedestal by four men. She's covered in a scarlet veil glittering with sequins. He looks as solemn as if he were going to his execution. A line of earnest revelers follows them, shouting and chanting.

Then I see a familiar shape in front of me. She's in a different place, but I know it's the skinny cow, which I somehow recognize as distinct from all the other skinny cows in town. Maybe it's her sad, wistful eyes. Tonight she's chewing on a plastic bag again. What happens to these cows at night, I wonder. Does someone lead them home? Do they have owners? They're supposed to be holy, pampered, but they seem more like lost souls. I have to give this cow something to eat, I decide. What do cows eat? Grass. Well, there's no grass, but something vegetarian. Chapatis would do. I quickly cross the street and buy some of the tortilla-like patties from a vendor. The cow gobbles them up with the same unruffled enthusiasm with which she was devouring the plastic bag.

As I'm bending down to feed her, something catches my eye from the other side of the street—a shadow of a hand waving to me. I look up at a young man, eyes glittering in the dark, wearing jeans and a black T-shirt.

"Hello, Mademoiselle Elena," he says. His T-shirt says "Paris" on one line and "Fun City" below it. He's young, lean, and handsome. I don't recognize him. "You are a very kind lady to feed this cow. But they are always hungry no matter how much they eat," he says. He gives me a dazzling smile. I still don't know who he is. He stops smiling, frowns, and squints his eyes. "I have hurt my eyes from painting so much in the dim light," he says in a serious tone. *Oh no*, my own speech. I can't help but laugh.

Now I see the face I saw in the shop earlier today, the serious young painter working in the bad light. The same luminous eyes, the same sculpted features, the same eyebrows that almost meet over his narrow, perfect nose. His hair is thick and dark and cut in an old-style American antihero kind of way, with one lock falling over his forehead.

"You look different. No . . . turban." I roll my hand around my head.

"Yes, I must wear for tourists who come." His mouth twists into a wry grimace.

He is standing quite close to me, but I feel the gulf between us. I am one of those tourists—even though I think of myself not as a tourist but a traveler—that he had to dress up for. I don't know what to say, so I say nothing. On this warm night, so many people are out, drifting by us. I hear the shuffle of their feet on the stones, the singsong murmurs of their voices, a backdrop to this long moment of silence. In that moment, I also hear the echo of history: colonizer, colonized; consumer, consumed.

In the same instant, his grimace turns into a playful smile. I'm being too dramatic. After all, we are not actors in a historical or socio-economic drama. We are just two people.

"Do you enjoy your beautiful painting?" he finally asks me.

"Oh, that. My painting." I shake my head. "I'm afraid it disappeared before I even got to my guesthouse. Maybe someone took it in the crowd. It was very crazy after I left the shop." I twirl a finger in the air to indicate craziness. I must be nervous, because I'm talking with my hands, something I don't ordinarily do.

"Yes," he agrees. "Indian people are sometimes crazy. But steal, no. Rajasthani people are very honest. They do not do this. Your picture is not gold. Not silver. Only a small painting." His English, I notice, is different than most Indians. A different accent, more casual, without the clipped chirping sounds that inflect the language of many English-speaking Indians. His voice is calmer, slower, more sensual.

"Well, I'm very sorry to lose it." I inadvertently let out a sigh.

"Maybe I can help," he says.

"Help?"

"Help find this lost painting."

"How?"

"This man that paints your picture, you see, is a very fine master artist. He can make you another just the same. Not just the same, I am sorry. But very alike."

"But I thought this master painter is no longer on this planet."

"Yes, of course, on this planet." He looks taken aback that I would say such a thing. "He is here on Planet of India. Place of Rajasthan."

"Well, then someone was lying. He told me this was an old painting. Maybe a hundred years old, your boss said. So whoever painted it must be . . . well, dead."

He looks at the ground, then up at me again and directly into my eyes. He is calm, but I can hear the flash of anger, or pride, in his voice. "No. Not my boss. Some days I paint for him.

Some days I do not. If I feel like it or not. He lies, this man. He tells you a lie. To get more money. How much do you pay for this?"

Too much, I think. The whole thing is too much. "I thought you just said Rajasthani people were very honest."

"Yes. But not all. Most."

"Well, it doesn't matter. I can't get my money back, obviously."

"Miss Elena," he says, "I am telling you I know this painter. He is alive. One time, many years ago, he is my teacher. For many years he paints beautiful paintings. He lives in a village not too far away. He is now an old man."

"Your teacher. Really?"

"Yes. I want very much to be a great painter such as this man. So I am telling you this artist is alive. This painting is not old. But it is good." Suddenly he grins. "Like me. I am not old, but I am good."

Yes, I think, he may not be old, but I am, at least compared to him, and it's strange that this young guy seems to be . . . *flirting* with me. Suddenly, the entire conversation seems insane, a microcosm of the whole macrocosm "planet of India" craziness. "Well, thank you," I say. "Nice to see you again. I really must get back to my friend."

"Yes, nice to see you again." He pats the cow on the head and once again gives me his razzle-dazzle smile. "I ask your name but you do not ask my name."

"What is your name?"

"My name is Sahil. Sahil the painter," he says.

"Sahil. The painter. I'll remember. Good night," I say as I walk away.

When I find my way back to the line of shops, I can hear Cathy's voice before I see her. She seems to be shouting in Hindi. How strange. And there, still at the shop, among drapes of clothes for a curtain, and with a glowing bare bulb for lighting, she holds center stage. Now she has an audience. A group of boys has gathered around the front of the shop. They move their heads back and forth between Cathy and the shopkeeper as if watching a tennis match. I politely wave to get her attention, but she ignores me. Finally, I stage-whisper her name, which causes all eyes in the audience to turn toward me, as if I were a new character making an entrance. She glances at me, winks, and gets in one final insult. The shopkeeper throws a blouse at her; she grabs it and leaves.

"Come on," she says, victoriously holding up her new garment. "I think he's learned his lesson. Let's get out of here."

As we walk, she gives me a blow-by-blow account of what she said, what the shopkeeper said, how important it was not to let him get away with anything. I'm about to ask her how she acquired her apparently fluent Hindi, but as we near the tunnel I hear a voice call my name. "Miss Elena." I turn around to see the young painter again. I'm a little surprised and, to be honest, a little pleased. It seems centuries since any man has paid any attention to me at all—except Peter, of course, and usually to criticize me—especially a funny, sensitive, handsome young man.

"I am going this way to my house," he says. "Do you mind if I walk with you and your friend?"

Before I can answer, Cathy says, "Yes, we do mind."

"You don't have to be rude," I mutter to her under my breath.

"Yes, I do. Come on." She picks up her stride. As we enter the tunnel, I can hear her army boots clomping on the cobble-stones.

"Some people come to India, but they do not like the Indian people," Sahil says, still at my side. "They have too much . . . too much . . . inside."

"Too much attitude?" I say.

"Maybe too much anger. Better to leave anger back home."

Cathy is way ahead of us now, probably out of earshot. "Yes, that's true. I don't know her well. I don't understand her anger."

"We should talk of happier things."

"Yes, I agree."

"Do you know the story of this place? Very famous place. Come, I show you." As we exit from the tunnel into the street again, we pause by the massive wall. The nearly full moon lights the wall with a phosphorescent glow. And then I see them, dozens of palm prints of different sizes.

"Go. Put your hand on one," he says, and I do.

My hand is huge by comparison. "They must be the handprints of children."

"Some are children, some are ladies. These ladies wait for the men who fight in war. If the men lose and die, the ladies walk into fire. Then the children follow until all are gone." He hovers his hand inches over mine, which is still on the tiny handprint. "She makes this picture of her hand the very last thing, before she goes to the fire. So the world does not forget her. This is a famous story of Rajasthan," he says.

I shiver. "I'm not sure that's a happier story."

"Come on," says Cathy, who is standing off to the side, waiting for me, pacing and smoking. "Everybody knows this story. Let's go."

"Sometimes sad stories from a long time ago can bring happiness, if they are beautiful. Your friend does not like these stories."

"But I like them." And in fact I do. I like seeing the world through eyes that understand these stories. I like the magic and the mystery. I like him. In fact, I decide, I like him all the more so because Cathy is so boorish toward him.

"Your friend does not speak nice to me. I must go. If you like, I can come tomorrow and I can help you find this master painter. If you tell me the name of your hotel, I can come."

"I don't know. I think I should just give up on this painting."

"Good idea. Give up on the painting, Elena," Cathy says. "It's just a cheap touristy piece of crap anyway."

I bristle. "I guess to you everything here is a cheap piece of touristy crap."

"Whatever," she shrugs.

"Now I remember the name," I tell Sahil. "Lake something. Peaceful Lake."

"Yes, I know it. I can come for you at what time you like."

"All right. How about eleven in the morning?" He smiles at me again before he vanishes into the dark. As soon as he leaves, I know that I didn't agree just to piss off Cathy, but because I'm really looking forward to seeing him again. There is something intriguing about him, something that makes me feel he's the beginning of a story, although I have no idea what kind of story. And then there's the lure of this master painter, in my imagination a sage and elusive artist, the embodiment of the old India, or at least my idea of it.

The streets widen as we near the lake. Here and there the barrier of buildings opens to *ghats*, the steps that lead into the water where people gather and talk, where the women wash clothes in the daytime. Now they are nearly deserted and so quiet I can hear the water gently lapping against the stones. When Cathy and I reach our guest house, we find the heavy wooden gate is locked for the night. "I think he looks a bit like Johnny Depp," I blurt out as we knock. She rolls her eyes at me, exactly the reaction I expected.

The glum face of the manager finally appears. "You ladies are too much running around," he says as we trudge in.

"Sooo sor-reee," says Cathy as she heads off to her room. "You gotta get over the romantic bullshit syndrome," she fires at me as we part ways. "It never has a good outcome."

"You gotta get over the cynical tough-chick syndrome. And you know what, it *was* a really beautiful painting." What did I expect of someone who works for the Aussie version of the *Enquirer* anyway?

Up the stairs, on the rooftop, the night sky is waiting for me. The white palace on the lake is now a ghostly apparition, its ethereal loveliness reflected in a silver shimmer. A city in love with itself. A city that needs nothing from the outside world. And here I am, alive, inside its walls.

CHAPTER THREE

Cathy's Story

The next morning, I dress in a floral cotton skirt and a long-sleeved lavender T-shirt, the costume I deem appropriate for visiting a dignified artist in a traditional village. In the courtyard, I order a cup of tea. It's still early in the day, many hours before my planned excursion. No one is awake besides the shoeless boy who serves as the waiter, but it's already hot. I take my tea and return to the cool of my room.

For company I have my little water pitcher in the form of a copper cow that Jason gave me when I left the ashram in disappointment. The idea was, he explained, that when you put sacred water from the Ganges into the cow's body, she would bless your dwelling, or your bus, or a project you were working on with libations that came from her nose. I don't have water from the Ganges, but I have my tea. I perform a small ritual, filling her belly and letting the tea run from her nose onto the pages of my notebook. Perhaps Saraswati, goddess of the water as well as the arts, will choose to pay me a visit. So far my notebook has been empty.

I sit down to write, but immediately I'm overwhelmed with a flurry of images, sensations, and hazy thoughts that won't translate themselves into words. For inspiration, I pick up a book I brought with me—a small volume of poems and other writings by Indian women. It begins with an ode to joy written in something like the sixth century BC by a Buddhist nun named Mutta, one of the few women who were allowed to join those early Buddhist communities. How wonderful it was, she says, to escape from her domestic chores and her tyrannical husband, into the peace of the sangha.

> *So free. So splendidly free am I*
> *From three binding things set free*
> *From mortar, pestle, and my twisted husband*
> *I have hurled away*
> *All that imprisoned me*
> *Free from death and rebirth am I*

That long-ago poet comes alive in those words. How little has changed. Even then, women sought an escape from drudgery and oppression. I am not a good meditator, but I close my eyes and try to imagine what life might have been like for these women. A shaft of sunlight is pouring through the small window into the gloom of my room. In my imagination, it expands into a rising tide of water that sweeps me out into the lake, where I'm floating among flickering iridescent shapes that might be fish or swimmers. I take big butterfly strokes as I reach out to touch them. But something is holding me back. My arms and legs are so heavy that I can move only with the greatest effort. And yet it seems enormously important that I reach these shimmering things, even if my lungs might burst with the effort. Then I understand. These are the images of my unlived lives. They are beckoning to me, waiting for me, if I can just reach a little farther, be a little braver. The daydream, or vision, or whatever it is, fades. I am again in my dim room with its stone walls, its one glassless window that looks out to the lake. But maybe, just maybe, my expedition to search for the master painter is a beginning.

"Cathy," I say later in the courtyard as I'm waiting for the painter to show up. "I'm curious. How did you learn to tell people to fuck off in Hindi?" I'm a little shocked at that coming out of my mouth. In fact I'm not even angry with her anymore. Maybe she's just an unenlightened being, too full of herself to be aware of the world around her. Not unlike the rest of the cast of characters of Western travelers I've met.

My remark seems to have caught the attention of the others at the table: the surly Brits and the silent German couple, plus other new arrivals—a redheaded woman from New Zealand and a Frenchman, who seems to be on drugs or nursing a hangover. They all look up and squint in the white sunlight that illuminates the courtyard. Cathy takes her dark glasses off and looks at me with what seems like new respect.

"Well," she says, looking at her watch, then at me. "I'd be happy to tell you. But I'm not sure if you have time to listen. Don't you have to leave soon for your date with Johnny Depp?"

I sigh and shake my head. There's no point in explaining. "It's not a date."

"Oh? Excuse me. What is it then?"

"It's an excursion."

"Oh," she says sarcastically. "Hey, anybody want to go to the Lake Palace for drinks this afternoon?"

There are no takers and she picks up a Bollywood magazine and hides behind it. I ask the German woman the time and she, still silent, holds out her wristwatch. My painter friend is late by more than a half hour.

Cathy catches my nervousness and shrugs. "Indian time. Or more generically, third-world time," she says. "I wonder if they all go to the same school—you know, the driving school, the time school, the checking-out-women school." I've only known her two days, but already I see vintage Cathy.

An hour later I know he is not going to show up.

The journey to the Lake Palace for cocktail hour with Cathy is on a slow motorboat that takes us into the middle of the lake. The late afternoon sun is turning everything a soft gold: the shimmering surface of the water, the ghats of ochre-colored stone, the honey-hued dwellings perched on the hills, the amber-skinned people immersed up to their knees or waists, bathing or playing or doing laundry.

I have to say this for Cathy. She is making an effort not to say "I told you so." In fact, she's made a minimal nod to local standards by covering her long limbs with white pants and a blouse. She actually looks rather elegant.

I'm trying not to show my disappointment. I don't know what to think. This young artist seemed so sincere, so ebullient, so willing to be my guide. I feel foolish, naïve, taken in. I thought of what Jason would say in these circumstances: Something like "There are many guides along your path, but it is still *your* path." Had he actually said it? What did that mean any-way? What did any of it mean? My eyes blur from the effort of trying to figure it out.

Then I have another thought. Maybe something happened to the young painter. "Maybe something happened to him," I mumble.

Cathy shakes her head. "You really just don't get it, do you?"

"What don't I get?" She makes me feel like a child.

"Oh, Indian men," she says with a dismissive flap of her hand. We are just pulling up to the portage of the very grand hotel. Several well-built attendants in dazzling regalia, crowned by sparkling turbans, stand at attention as we disem-bark. From far way, the Lake Palace is ethereal, a floating flower. Close up, it is the embodiment of oriental luxury. Once it was the summer palace of a maharajah, built on this tiny is-land out of pure white marble. At some point, when he could no longer afford it, it was turned into a hotel, and now the fab-ulously expensive rooms are inhabited by affluent tourists. We are seated at a table in the courtyard, surrounded by carved mar-ble facades and tapestries of overdressed elephants and warriors.

"For the price of a gin and tonic, we can pretend we're filthy rich," Cathy says when we order our drinks. We are surrounded by what look like wealthy people—Westerners with designer handbags and sunglasses, beautifully dressed Indian women loaded with gold jewelry. As we wait for our drinks, we try to determine who is really rich versus who is just dressing the part. I find my mood starting to lift. Our drinks arrive, long tall glasses dripping with moisture. The gin goes down like a cool waterfall, further easing my pain.

"So do you still want to tell your story?"

She responds by taking off her sunglasses. "Look into my eyes," she says, leaning toward me and batting her eyelashes. "Notice anything?" I do. I see that her irises are a rich brown, in contrast with her blond hair and pale skin.

"Dark eyes?"

"I have huge brown eyes because I am . . . ." She pauses for dramatic effect. "I am Indian." I try to take in this amazing information. "That is one-quarter of my genes are of Indian origin."

"So is it your mom's side? Or your dad's?"

"My grandma came here from England. That is, she trailed along meekly after her husband."

"Your grandfather."

"Well, actually no. That's part of the story. Anyway, they both came here in those days when the sun never set on the British Empire and all that *rawt*," she says, affecting a British accent.

"Let's see, the sun actually did set in, what was it, 1948?"

"You've got it. Anyway, Grandma Rose came with husband Hector. She was one of those porcelain-skinned babes with big boobs and big blond '40s hair. Hector had a job ordering Indians around. Rose spent her time going to lawn parties until she got very bored. Anyway, long story short, Rose became interested in spiritual matters and ended up having an affair with an Indian man—a medical doctor and a follower of Krishnamurti. A fatal attraction, you might say."

By now I'm no longer hearing her words, but imagining the story she's telling. I see Rose's pale face flush with excitement as she makes an excuse to her husband and flees the house—with its tea-at-five and fresh-linen-every-day propriety—to meet her lover in the garden where the great Krishnamurti holds forth. His enormous black eyes shine in his thin face as he speaks, ever so thoughtfully. The two of them are rapt at his feet. But they're even more enthralled with each other. What was it Krishnamurti used to preach? Something like: Understanding yourself only takes place in a relationship, in watching yourself in relationship to people, ideas, to the earth, the world around you and the world inside of you—something like that. I remember his famous quote, oft repeated by Jason. "'Relationship is the mirror in which the self is revealed,'" I say out loud. I had always loved that idea, although I hoped it was not my true self that was revealed in my relationship with Peter. Surely not.

"Huh?" Cathy says. She flicks her long fingers at a lone fly circling her drink. "I would think this ritzy place was a no-fly zone." She grins and shrugs. "Sorry. Can't help it. What were you saying?"

"Oh nothing. Just citing the spiritual master." I repeat the quote.

"Now that's interesting. I'll have to think about that. But, you know, Rose wasn't the only English babe fooling around with a very *dawshing* native. The fatal part was when Hector was sent back to England. Rose refused to go with him. She couldn't bear to leave her lover. So it all came out kind of horribly, and Hector divorced her. Her Indian lover, you see, was from a pretty wealthy family, and he pretty much promised to marry her and take care of her. And he was kind of pretty too. My mom showed me photos of him."

As Cathy speaks, I picture him: big, half-closed eyes, sleek hair, a cruel mouth. "It sounds like a novel."

"Oh, it gets worse. They had a kid a year or so later. Hello, mother! It was uncool enough to be a biracial couple, but to have a biracial child. Oh my God! She was rejected by the Anglos who stayed on here and totally rejected by the Indians. She was a little girl named Jasmine, my mother, and she couldn't even get into a school. She told me she remembered her father being kind to her when she was small. And I guess he supported them to an extent. But the pressure from his family was too much. Eventually, my grandmother's wonderful, oh-so-spiritual Indian lover married an Indian woman with a big dowry. He started treating Rose like a concubine—you know, visiting her once in a while when he was in the mood.

"So Rose homeschooled my mom in proper English subjects until she was a teenager, and then she had the sense to send her back to England while she stayed on in this half-life. My mom lived with relatives in London, went to school, and started to have sort of a normal existence. By that time it was the swinging '60s. She was so gorgeous. Instead of blond hair and dark eyes like me, she had that smooth tawny skin and pale green eyes. Anyway, she fell in love with a big, tall, blond American guy who came over to do the British music scene, and they moved to Chicago. Actually a pretty cool guy, my dad. And then there was me, la de da! So I guess in some ways it was a happy ending. Except my mom died a few years ago—cancer. You'd think that would be enough to make me quit smoking."

Cathy lights up another cigarette and takes another swig of her drink.

"So what happened to your Grandma Rose?"

"That's the sad-ending part." She lets out a ragged breath. I can see tears starting to form at the corners of her very brown eyes. "My mom sent my grandma letters and begged her to come to England. No. Poor old Rose was so addicted to her lover boy that she stayed on and on. He kept treating her like a dirt bag, until, without even her child now, she finally walked into the Ganges or something. Nobody's very clear on that point. So that's the *Enquirer* story in five hundred words or more." She wipes the tears away and puts her sunglasses back on.

I don't know what to say to such an unexpected universe inside Cathy's to-hell-with-everything persona. "So it was your mother who taught you Hindi. She remembered it from her childhood here."

"Yeah. She learned it playing in the street with other children."

"So let me see if I've got this right. This Indian spiritual romance guy is your grandfather."

"You've got it."

"And you're here to reconnect with your roots?"

"Yeah, kind of. My mom was bitter about the whole thing, especially after Grandma Rose disappeared. But somehow she remembered her early childhood days here as magically free, the days before she was shipped off to school in England. When she died, I decided I'd try to chase her memories. But I'm not feeling the magic, as is probably obvious. I'm also here for another reason."

"OK. What's that?"

"To get even." She bites her lip, then forces a smile. "I hate my bastard grandfather, and I'm going to track him down. And take him down, if I can."

"I don't blame you." The whole grand tale of treachery fuels my resentment contained in my small story of the painter not showing up. The waiter is back; my first drink has disappeared in listening to Cathy. Another gin and tonic seems exactly the right way to spend the rest of the afternoon.

"You know Elena, I hate him, but I feel also Rose should have stuck up for herself. You know that old model of being female—where you give up everything for your great love. Ain't going to happen to me."

"Me either. Let's drink to that."

"Men are all different, but they're all alike in their selfishness."

"Except for Gandhi."

"Oh, I've heard stories about him too."

I frown, trying to imagine the tiny saint as a seducer.

"But, India, yeah, it's a love-hate thing. Hey, do you want to reconsider going to Delhi with me in a few days? As I said before, we could stay in a gorgeous place with a view and my Aussie boyfriend—for free."

"I don't know. I'll think about it." I take a deep draught of my fresh drink and then rub one of the ice cubes over my lips. I love watching all these civilized people surrounding us, listening to their murmured conversations, possibly about very uncivilized events like those in Cathy's ancestry.

"Better than sitting around here, waiting for Lover Boy."

"He's not Lover Boy. He's an interesting person who was going to help me find the maker of my lost painting. Still, you're right. He's a flake."

"OK. Whatever. Anyway, I think my grandfather, the old seducer, might be hanging out near Delhi. According to my sources."

"He'd be how old?"

"About eighty. Probably still a manipulator. The typical Indian man, professing great wisdom but thinking only of himself. That's why I get pissed," she said. "They're my people in a way, so I guess I can do that."

"So what are you going to do if you find him?"

"I haven't decided yet. At the very least, I want to know what the hell happened to my grandma." A big toothy smile appears under her sunglasses. "I don't know what I'm going to do. But it's not going to be pretty."

We clink glasses. By now I'm drunk enough that everything seems beautiful and tragic and funny at the same time. And going with Cathy to Delhi seems like a good idea.

On the boat ride back, I watch the women on the faraway shore slap their laundry. There is a splash of color, and a split second later I hear the *thwack*. I have always loved the idea that sound moves more slowly than light, that I can see something far away before I can hear it, as if the two phenomena were uncoupled at the moment they escape from the perpetrator, two spirits from the same body, one fast and one slow.

CHAPTER FOUR

A Visit to the Temples

The streets are empty and eerily quiet as I set out for the train station to buy tickets for Delhi. Everything seems to stand out against the emptiness, like brushstrokes on a blank canvas. The scent of charcoal and spice drifts from a window. A hollow tin voice from a loudspeaker somewhere calls the faithful to prayer. A black dog slinks around a corner and disappears into the alleyway. I have mixed feelings about going to Delhi with Cathy. I've spent the last couple of days wandering the streets, immersing myself in the sights and sounds of this exquisite city, breathing in the scent of frangipani trees, imagining myself as not just an onlooker, but an inhabitant. Yet, I also want to keep moving and, outrageous as she is, I enjoy Cathy's company.

As I round a corner, I hear a voice call "Hellooo." Then, like a magician stepping out of the shadows, the dark-haired painter appears beside me. Far from being apologetic for not showing up, he's smiling as if he has done something wonderful and the world is applauding him. "Good morning, Miss Elena. Did you sleep well?" I'm a bit taken aback at this greeting, which seems at once old-fashioned and intimate in its allusion to beds and dreams and darkness, and inappropriate given the circumstances.

"Good morning," I say, with as much ice in my voice as I can muster. Just seeing him rekindles my frustration with the whole ridiculous circus. I pull my hat more closely around my eyes and keep walking.

He laughs as if I'm clowning and keeps pace with me. My frigid response doesn't seem to deter him one bit. "Do you remember me? My name is Sahil. I am the artist."

I don't reply.

"Why are you angry, Miss Elena?" I glance at him. He's wearing fresh clothes, a white shirt, pressed jeans, shined leather shoes. In the glare of daylight he seems less intriguing.

"I am not angry."

"Why do you not talk with me?" I wonder if he is genuinely puzzled.

"Why are you so flaky?"

"What is this word *flaky*?"

"Actually," and I stop and face him with what I hope is a serious expression, "*flaky* in my country means unreliable, undependable." He smiles and cocks his head as I struggle for the right words. "It means someone who . . . doesn't do what they say. Like showing up on time."

"Yes, I am on time. I come for you. You are not at hotel."

"What do you mean 'I am not at hotel'?"

"I ring the bell, I ask the hotel man. He says to me you are missing."

"What man?"

"The man who has skin with holes."

Ah, the manager with his pockmarked face. "But I was not missing. I was there. Ready to go on our expedition." I sigh and resume walking. We're now in a busier, noisier part of town, bustling with the color and motion of cars and cows and rickshaws and people.

"Now I understand." He sounds angry. "Your hotel man does not like me. So he says to me you are missing."

"Really?" I think about this as I move out of the way of a bicycle rickshaw carrying the English boys I recognize from my hotel. They wave at me. Is it possible that Sahil showed up at the front gate and they sent him away without letting me know? How strange. Why?

"I come to tell you that I cannot go with you because my grandmother is very sick. I need to go to my grandmother's village with my mother."

I turn and look into his eyes. There is a look of worry there that seems genuine. "OK," I say. "I'm sorry for your grandmother. Is she all right?"

"She is not so strong. She wants me to stay there in village, but I cannot. I must work."

By now we have reached a busier part of town. Among the moving throng, three old men with white brush-broom mustaches and wire-rimmed spectacles are engaged in animated conversation. Sahil stops momentarily to chat with them and then catches up with me again.

"Where do you go today?"

"Actually, I'm going to the train station."

"If you like, I can go with you."

"No thank you."

"I can help you get a ticket fast. Then I can take you today to find the master painter. Now I am free."

"No, it was possible before but not now. Tonight I must leave on the train for Delhi with my friend."

"What time is your train?" he asks me.

"I think there's a train at ten o'clock in the evening. I don't have the ticket yet."

"This is not a problem. The bus to the town of master painter is twenty minutes. Also this is the place of very old temples. We have one or two hours. We find a very beautiful painting for you to take on your journey to Delhi. We come back here by five o'clock. Before the time on the town clock. See, here it is always six-thirty." He gestures up to a huge clock face on a tower where the hands are indeed stuck at six-thirty. The clock looks as if it should be in England instead of India.

A thought occurs to me. Why does he want to take me to this town anyway? Does he see himself as my guide? If I accept his offer, should I pay him? I'm in a country where I don't really know the rules. "Don't you have things to do?" I ask him. "Your job. Your family."

"My family is my mother only. I do not work today."

The train station looms in front of us, crowded with people who seem to be more or less living there, squatting together in little family groups with ragged children running everywhere. Food vendors hawk chapatis and sweets and drinks from their mobile stands.

"Miss Elena, do you like one cold lassi?"

I would, but I refuse. "No, really. I must get my ticket."

"OK." Sahil's attention is diverted by a middle-aged man in a white tunic standing by one of the taxis who is waving at him.

"Excuse me for a moment, Miss Elena. I must go see my friend."

I smile and shrug. "That's fine. Nice seeing you."

Inside, ticket buyers are waiting their turns in a chaotic queue. My first task is to find the end of the line, which is a little vague, and then plant myself in it, making sure I inch forward. Twenty minutes later, I've made no progress at all. There seem to be endless interruptions at the front of the line, where people crowd in and shout at the clerks behind the partition. Rather than telling them to wait their turn, the perpetually nodding clerks seem to respond to the loudest and most aggressive demands.

When Sahil appears again, he tells me it was important to talk to his taxi-driving friend who has many family troubles. He repeats his offer to help me buy my ticket. "No thanks," I say. I really do want to do this ticket-buying thing on my own.

"Miss Elena," he says, "see that old man over here?" He nods at an elderly man sitting in one of the alcoves, a vacant stare on his face. "He comes here a long time ago to buy ticket to see his wife in Delhi. He waits and waits in the queue. She waits and waits for him and he does not come. Then she dies. Now he is very sad, you see, and sits here all day."

I shake my head at the ridiculousness of it. "You are making this up."

He holds up his hand in a gesture of scout's honor. "This is India." I look again at the hopelessly stalled queue.

"OK, I need two tickets to Delhi tonight, first class. How much?"

"Do not worry." He's gone in a flash. A minute later I see him behind the glass partition, chatting with one of the harried clerks, who now is emitting a series of chuckles. In what seems like seconds, Sahil appears at my side. "Two tickets to Delhi, ten p.m. train, best class," he says, and names the price, which seems very reasonable to me. I give him the rupees, he reappears with the tickets, and it's done. I expect angry stares from the people ahead of me in the queue, but no one seems to mind or even notice.

Sahil breaks into a grin as I put the tickets away. "You see. You save much time. And now *chalo*, let's go. We use this extra time to take the fast bus to the beautiful town of the temples."

I'm a little dazzled by how easily he's maneuvered through the maze of train ticketing. But I still have my doubts that going to a village for the afternoon would be a wise choice.

"You say you believe the master painter might be in this village?"

"Yes, Miss Elena, I believe this."

Who is this master painter? I would love to meet him. If he were there, I could not only find something close to the painting I lost, but maybe others of equal beauty. But then there's Sahil. I don't like the way he appears and disappears. It's disconcerting. On the other hand, he's part of this amazing culture that I want to get to know. There are the two voices inside of me again, one saying "be careful" and the other "why not"? They always seem to be vying for top place. The "why not" is now whispering in my ear, very seductively.

"I have to be back by five o'clock."

"Before five o'clock."

Minutes later, across the street from the train station, Sahil finds the right blue bus in a herd of dilapidated busses, and soon we're swerving down the road into the countryside. There are a few other passengers—a woman with a large bundle of rice and a small bundle of child, some shy young women who peek out from behind their veils, several old men with bare sagging chests in lungis. Sahil finds a seat for me as the bus starts up. But instead of sitting next to me, he walks up and down the aisle, conversing amiably with his fellow passengers. He's speaking in Hindi, so I can't follow, but whatever he's saying seems to bring guffaws of hilarity.

We rattle past huts and oxen and barely miss whole families of orange-wrapped pilgrims walking by the side of the road. Finally, he sits down next to me. "Miss Elena," he says, "you are from a famous place called America. But when I first see you, I think you are French."

"Why did you think so?" I ask. Do I look mysterious? Sexy? Do I want to?

"Because American people are happy all the time. Talk loud. Laugh loud. You are more … more thinking, like French people. You are more, what is the word . . . serious."

Well, it's not exactly a compliment, but I decide to make the best of it. "Very serious." I frown and turn down the corners of my mouth.

He laughs. "But today you are very happy. We find the master painter. I like his painting very much."

"How about you?" I ask. "Are you serious? When I first saw you in your shop, you seemed quite serious."

"Yes, *moi aussi*. Serious. I am a serious painter." Where does he get his French phrases, I wonder. He turns toward me and puts on a long-faced expression, just briefly. "Since I am sixteen I study to paint. This is true. For ten years I work to become a good painter. It is very difficult. I go to Varanasi to study. The place they call Benares. My first teacher is the master painter we go to find today. "

"The holy city where they burn the dead by the Ganges. I would love to go there."

"Yes. That is the place. Many Western people like to go to this city. But I do not like it. My friends do not like it. I do not like the dead people. It has a smell. But I stay. I paint very hard. But now you see, I cannot be famous. Because in Rajasthan they don't care about the painter. Only the shop owner can make money."

"Then it's like America. There too, it's difficult to be an artist."

"I think you are an artist too," he says. "I see this in your eyes, sometime serious, sometime happy. I think there are many things you want to say."

"Well, I don't know if I am an artist. I'd like to be. But instead of paint, I use words."

"Ah, yes, words are good. Like paints. Blue words. Red words. Black words. Gold words. So many colors of words."

"But lately, I haven't been able to . . ."

He cuts me off. "I think you are like Saraswati."

"Oh, yes, Saraswati. The goddess of the arts." I think of the moment this all began, when Jason's statue of this very goddess fell off the shelf and broke.

"I like this Saraswati. She has many colors inside as well. Like you."

"I wish that were true," I say. At first, I feel myself being charmed by him, being pulled along by that idea. Then I pull back. It feels like false flattery, like being told you are beautiful on a day you know you look awful. In spite of my incantations, Saraswati has not made an appearance. Those goddesses inside of me, how can I wake them up? If I were really like Saraswati, I could just channel all the colors in the exploding universe instead of facing my blank sheet of notebook paper.

Sahil changes the subject. "I would not like to go to America," he says. "Paris. Maybe. America, no. My friend goes to America and says, good for making money. But not good for the life." In the middle of nowhere, in a countryside of dry grass and brown hills, the bus heaves several times and comes to a jerking halt.

The town is not at all promising. It is not a town at all, in fact, but a nearly deserted dirt street lined with hole-in-the-wall shops hovering over knee-high cement sidewalks. The few people here, mostly shopkeepers hiding behind their wares, are barely moving. A child sits on one of the sidewalks, humming to herself and dangling her feet over the edge. A white-haired woman, perhaps her grandmother, dressed in a bright yellow sari with a flower tucked behind one ear, is gracefully lying on her side. She looks like a sleeping bodhisattva.

The breeze from the open window in the bus cooled me off on the trip here, but now I'm starting to feel the heat seep under my skin. Sahil buys a Fanta in a milky glass bottle for me. It's delicious, an icy orange explosion in my mouth.

"I talk to these shop people to find the master painter," he says. As I sip and wait under the shade of a metal overhang, I watch him chatting in Hindi with the shopkeepers. I like watching the way he moves. He looks so effortlessly graceful in his white shirt with rolled-up sleeves. Even with his shiny leather dress shoes, a little incongruous with his blue jeans, he somehow looks cool. I wonder how old he is, somewhere between twenty-five and thirty, I'm guessing. Too young for me. He gestures in the air, his lean arms and long fingers flashing, hypnotizing to watch. In response, the shopkeepers bob their heads vehemently.

Is he really describing this master painter? He could be talking about cricket scores for all I know. After some time of back and forth gesturing and bobbing, Sahil shrugs. He reports back to me in a solemn voice. "The master painter is not here now. Business maybe. Family maybe. But is possible he is here later today."

I am disappointed, but somehow not surprised. There is the feeling of wild goose chase about this entire expedition. I feel alternately charmed and bamboozled by this mercurial young man. "Possible? Not possible. So what do we do now?" I'm not sure I'm successful at keeping the annoyance out of my voice. I'm not sure I want to.

He cocks his head and looks puzzled, as if I'm being purposefully difficult, which maybe I am by Indian standards. "Miss Elena. We are here. We see the master painter later, the temple now, very beautiful. Not very far."

"I suppose as long as I'm here I might as well see the temples," I say with a sigh. I want somehow to convey to him that he promised one thing and didn't deliver. Sahil takes our empty Fanta bottles and returns them to the shop, and then leads the way down a path away from the dusty street.

Outside of the one-street town, we cross a sparse landscape, fields of stubbed grass littered here and there with crumpled plastic bottles. Sahil is ahead of me. I have to hurry to keep up with him, brushing away buzzing insects as I go, heading for a green patch on the horizon.

At the field's edge, we follow a path that takes us into a woodland of broad-leafed trees. The light changes suddenly and dramatically. We've entered a quiet world of dappled sunlight, of birdsong, of the cool smell of smooth-barked trees. Our footsteps are nearly silent on the soft floor of fallen vegetation. I feel myself relaxing, as if time itself is slowing. Sahil has wandered ahead and I'm alone. After a while, I come to a shallow stream. Clear water ripples down the streambed; moss creeps over the stone wall that follows the opposite bank.

I round a bend and come upon a woman sitting back on her haunches on a flat rock in the middle of the stream. Her brown legs emerge from a scarlet sari, startling in the midst of the green, like a bright tongue or a flower. The sari wraps around her head and hangs over one eye. As she wrings a rope of cloth, the muscles of her arms flex. She looks up to see me watching and smiles. Her teeth show white, and her face is beautiful in the light. Not beautiful in the way we think of in America— TV-beautiful—but beautiful with a spirit that says she loves being in the world, in this place.

I want to linger a while, to somehow cross the barrier of my station as a traveler just passing through. I want to get to know this woman. We would not have to talk. I could simply sit by the stream and wash clothes with her. I try to imagine her life. She would go home to her husband and children and cook chapatis near a fire outside her hut. Her children would be playing and she would be humming. And then the stars would come out and she would go inside and sleep on a mat on the floor next to her husband. Her eyes would close and the warm Indian night would pass. She would wake up to another day very much like this one. It's a kind of happiness, I think, so different from America, where happiness is something always in the distance that can be reached only by accomplishing a long list of goals for self-improvement, where we are always chasing something, the next thing, without even knowing why.

"I think she is very happy," I say when I catch up with Sahil.

"Yes, she is happy. She enjoys her life." He says it with such conviction that I feel he understands her, that the inhabitants of this corner of the world have a shared knowledge that is just beyond my grasp.

We emerge from the woods into pastures of hip-high grass. A family of women and children are moving through it, cutting the grass as they go, brightly colored fish in a sea of green. I can now see the temples in the distance, three of them, like pale ships on the horizon.

"Look," says Sahil, gesturing toward a small nearby tree. "This place has a special bird." On the tree's spindly branches sit a pair of blue birds with long, brilliant red tail feathers. They look like elegant parrots. "When I was a small child, I come here and try to catch these birds. But they are too fast for me."

I smile at this little story. His childhood must be very close to him. All its memories. My own childhood seems almost like another dimension. A demure little girl in a smocked coat and rubber boots who, even then, had the conflicting urges of wanderlust and trepidation. My mother loved to tell the tale of the time when I was four and I announced I was leaving on a trip, and then packed my cardboard suitcase with my toy tea set. My parents, highly amused, watched from the picture window as I marched down the street as if I knew exactly where I was going, until I got to the first corner at the end of the block. There, my confidence wavered. I could not get the courage to cross the street. Eventually I turned around and came home to where my parents were waiting for me. So far away, that childhood, or was it? I had almost done the same thing this trip, almost gone back before I started, but somehow I had gathered my courage. And now, like Alice, I was on the other side of the looking glass. But I was still me, with all my anxieties, pulling them along wherever I went.

Sahil calls my attention to birds again. They are on the ground now, pecking around for something to eat, heads down, red tail feathers moving from side to side. "We call these birds the tuk-tuk. Because, you see, they move their tails just so. Tuk, tuk, tuk, tuk." He makes a motion with his hand, back and forth. "They like to move their tails very much."

Is he trying to be racy, to get a reaction from me? I roll my eyes, although I'm not sure if he sees it, or even if he did, whether he would know what it means.

"Yes, they're pretty birds," I say blandly, to take the conversation in a different direction. "Their colors are beautiful. And they're free. Where I come from, we like to keep pretty birds in cages."

"Very sad." As we walk, every so often he stoops over and picks up what look like pebbles. He opens his palm and shows them to me. I see they are not stones at all, but large round seeds. "Look," he says. He turns one over. It's black on one side, white on the other. "Very good karma, for me and for you. Here, take one."

I open my hand. He turns to face me, so the sun is behind him, turning his hair into a dark halo. He gently presses a seed into my palm. His fingertips linger on my skin for just a few seconds, but in those seconds the seed sprouts filaments of electricity that shoot up through my arm. I stare at my hand as if it has a life of its own. I know I should close it and pull away. But I don't. Instead, I watch his burnished brown hand on my paler one, as if my hand belonged to someone else.

"Magic seed," he says.

I raise my eyes to his. He's gazing at me as if I were some kind of amazing creature. And I'm gazing back. This is ridiculous and inappropriate, I tell myself. I barely know him. He's my guide or something, not my date. Not to mention he's way too young. "You keep it," I say, and hand it back to him. The whole exchange has lasted only seconds. His eyes have already moved away from mine to something behind me in the distance.

He calls out "hello, my friend." From nowhere, a bicycle appears, swerving down the narrow path through the fields. The rider nods at Sahil and weaves past us. Sahil shouts something, and the bicycle wobbles to a stop. "Come on," he says, and runs ahead as I follow. The cyclist, a rather rotund middle-aged man with a carefully wound turban perched on his head, appears to be amused. Sahil hops on the back and motions for me to sit behind him, on a tiny section of the back fender.

"I don't think so." I haven't been on a bicycle since I was twelve.

"You are in a hurry to catch your train tonight. We go to the temple fast."

"No, you go. I'll walk."

"Don't be afraid. My friend here goes very slow."

The temples do look a long way to walk in the heat. Reluctantly, I squeeze on the back, side-saddle, holding my feet primly off the ground, with one hand on Sahil's shoulder, balancing as best I can. We careen unsteadily down the road. From my perch it feels as if we'll all go over at any second. Yet in almost no time at all, we reach the temples and hop off. Nothing to it. The cyclist smiles and nods at Sahil as if to thank him for hitching a ride on his bicycle. "You have so many friends," I say to him.

"Yes, he is my new friend. Before now I don't know him." I see again that this dark-eyed young man who seemed so serious when I first encountered him has a kind of charm which he can work on everybody—women and men, young and old. I resolve again he won't work it on me.

"Come, I show the temples to you. Very beautiful." He takes long leaps up the stone stairs to the first temple. He holds out his hand to me, but I shake my head and climb the stairs on my own. From the raised platform I can see the expanse of lush fields. In their midst is a tiny lotus-choked pond. Except for the women and children cutting grass in the fields, we are alone. The bustling world of the city and the busy universe of time, even Indian time, seems far away.

The temples are lovely—pale, intricate, ancient ruins. The soft stone walls are covered with exquisite images of long-thighed, full-breasted goddesses and narrow-waisted, broad-shouldered gods, all slowly eroding in the afternoon sun. Sahil takes me on a tour, pointing out the various deities that have been given eternal lives in the stone carvings. "What is your idea?" he asks.

"My idea?"

"Of our temples. Very old, maybe one thousand years old. Do you like them?"

"Yes. I like. They're wonderful. Also interesting. In the West, young women often don't wear very many clothes at all, but we cover up our goddesses—the saints, the Virgin Mary. Here in India it's the opposite. The goddesses are nearly naked, but the women are covered up."

He frowns as if he's thinking this over. "Yes. You are correct. Indian women. They are beautiful, but they are always covered up . . . and afraid."

"What do you mean, afraid?"

"Of parents. Of what people are thinking."

"It sounds like it could be a description of many American women too," I say.

"You, are you afraid?"

"No, of course not," I say, although it feels like a lie. "What I meant is that people in general try to be conventional . . . do what others expect of them."

"Yes, everywhere this is true." He turns and walks away from me, beckoning me to follow him. "I show you very special statues." On the back side of the temple, in a shadowy area hidden among the other carvings, are several erotic images of men and women who are standing on their heads and in other impossible tantric positions and will be doing so into eternity. He looks at me again with that disarmingly direct gaze. Suddenly I feel very embarrassed and uncomfortable. Suddenly I just want to be alone.

"Excuse me, Sahil. I think I'll explore by myself for a while," I say. I try to put just the right tone of archness in my voice, something that conveys dismissal, but graciously.

He reacts with an innocent smile, a very warm, sincere smile. "I am sorry if I offend you, Miss Elena. Many people come here and do not see this. Very important historical statues. Please enjoy yourself in the temples. I wait here and talk to the people in the fields."

One by one, I go through the temples, weaving my way in and out of the sunlight of the outer walls and the shadows of the inner rooms, amazed at the imagination of the sculptors as much as the intricacy of their craft. At the last temple, the largest, I find myself in an outer chamber carved with a congregation of gods, Vishnu maybe, and dancing Shiva.

There, just out of my reach, is a carved relief that may be Saraswati, two of her four arms embracing a lute. She's lush and lovely. Maybe the sculptors of these carvings gave life to Saraswati here first so she could bless their creative journey. I see another opening, leading to an inner chamber. I hesitate for just a moment, then I step into the darkness. It's so still, no sound, no light, a faint musty smell of ancient rock. Whatever deities are here have been hiding in the dark for at least a thousand years.

I reach out and touch the surface. It feels rough, almost alive. I try to envision what my hands are telling me. The ripples of stone are long hair. The round swell is a breast, another swell, another breast. My fingers slip to the side in search of another figure, and there is a long thigh, a waist with a garment around it, the expanse of what must be a god's chest, and above that, the precise waves and indentations that say lips, nose and eyes. And so many arms. Why so many arms? Sensuality frozen in stone. The safe kind. The truth is, I feel more comfortable with these stone images than with a real person, especially a person who makes me uncomfortable. What was that feeling I had when he pressed the seed into my hand? Not one I expected. Certainly not one I wanted. That is not my idea of exploring the culture. Then it occurs to me, a little passing thought, that the reason I'm alone now is not because of Peter's faults or those of any other man, but because I prefer the idea of life, I prefer art, to life itself.

Long ago artists must have spent years here, carving their deities into the stone walls, sleeping in the fields at night. They were part of a communal experience that went on for a lifetime, creating something beautiful that would live forever. I remember hearing about caves where monks spent their entire lives carving the life of the Buddha out of living rock. It took hundreds of years, from one generation to the next. I would like to be part of an experience like that. Maybe that is a better choice than being involved in the chaos and unpredictability of life, the big wave that catches you up and gives you experiences and longings and desires, most of which you can never understand or fulfill, and then casts you down and says, ha, you figure it out. No, I want to experience India from the calm chambers of the temple of my heart.

"Hello, Miss Elena." A faraway voice. Sahil's voice. For a moment I'm torn—should I stay or go—as if I have a choice. After all this is today, a real day, and for one thing I have a train to catch. I touch the stone with my fingertips one last time, turn around and walk out into the waiting sunlight. When I do, I see Sahil chatting with the women and children in the field. He waves me over when he sees me. He looks so happy, so eager to make others happy. Again, I've overanalyzed everything in my typical way. He really is just a sweet, exuberant young man who, after all, has taken me to this amazing place. I don't have to project scenarios of romance that have more to do with my imagination than reality. I am leaving tonight, but today, well, today I can enjoy, without judging him—or myself for that matter.

"Meet my friends," he says to me, and he tells me the name of each of the women. They beam smiles at me. Sahil offers to take our photo. I give him my camera and we line up in a row. A woman next to me wrapped in vivid green holds a basket on her head with one hand. Another tiny woman, a grandmother Sahil tells me, grins and then lifts the edge of a yellow and orange sari scarf over her face. A little girl, her dark hair braided in looped pig tails, can barely get her arms around the bundle of an infant in her arms. The camera clicks. In moments, they float off into the fields again, laughing and chatting.

Sahil nearly sprints over to the platform of the nearest temple, springs up and sits down, dangling his jean-clad legs over the edge. "Do you like to play a game?" he asks. Without waiting for an answer, he takes a pebble from his pocket and scrapes it against the stone floor of the temple platform. A grid of lines appears. He hands me the pebble and pulls out another, along with the seeds he collected on our way.

He holds up one. "This is the magic seed you give back to me. Six seeds all together. Black. White. Yin, yang," he says. He demonstrates by turning them over. He gives me three and throws his three in the air. One seed falls with its black side showing, the other two with white sides showing. "Black means one point, white two. I move five." He takes the pebble and moves it forward along the grid. "Now you."

I sit down, cross-legged, my legs tucked under my long skirt, and play this game, picking up the seeds and throwing them again and again, moving my pebble along the grid. My mood has changed. Sahil feels like a friend now—charming, funny, unthreatening. Perhaps the visit to the dark temple chamber grounded me, helped me to relax into the unfolding of the afternoon. Again I have this feeling that this day is extraordinary to me because it is someone else's ordinary day, and I am stepping into it as if by magic.

"Elena-*ji*," he says. "That means Miss Elena, in Hindi. May I ask you a question? Are you married? Have you been in love?"

Just a short while ago, I would have been annoyed at this question, but now it seems a perfectly natural subject. I think about how to answer. "Married, no. Maybe in love. But a long time ago. Maybe another lifetime." The last thing I want to think about or talk about is Peter. He already belongs to a past life.

"I do not believe in this other lifetime. My father is Moslem. But I am not. I am myself. My friend Vijay's father is Hindu. But he just Vijay. My friends do not care about these things. We are here. We must enjoy the life now."

"Yes, I understand what you mean." I do understand and am beginning to feel it. This day, this *now*, is the forever.

"And what about you?" I ask. "Have you ever been in love?"

A shadow comes over his face. "One time I was in love." He keeps throwing his seeds, moving his stone, but his voice is quieter. "I like this girl very much, and every day when I pass by her house, she comes out to get water. She smiles very nice and I talk to her. Then one day, I do not see her any more. I see her brother. I ask him what happened. She is gone, he tells me. She is now promise to someone else. You cannot see her. You cannot. If you try to see her, I kill you."

"Kill you?"

"Yes. Because she is Hindu. As I tell you, I am not any re-ligion. I am myself only. But my father is Moslem."

"That's sad. But you'll find someone else."

"I do not know. For many years I have been alone."

"But you are very young."

"No, not young. Twenty-seven. Every day is longer for me than most people. So really I am older."

"Maybe you are young on the outside but old on the inside."

"I think this is true."

"Do you like this place?" he asks me as I'm throwing my seeds. Without waiting for me to answer, he turns away from me and stares across the fields. "Many times I come here with my friends. I stay all day. They say, come Sahil, it is time to go back. But I stay and sleep here." He turns toward me.

"*Mera sundara bharata*," he says. "My beautiful India. I teach you to say this if you like."

"That would be difficult for me."

"No. Not difficult. Watch me. He draws out each syllable as if he were singing a childhood song. I try, and he laughs at my efforts. But he shows me again and again until I finally pronounce it right.

"Yes," he says. "Very good. This is your India. Your beautiful India."

"Do you think anyone from outside can ever understand it—India, I mean?"

"To understand is not important. To enjoy is important." He pauses, then tilts his head and looks at me as if seeing me for the first time. "You have very nice eyes. Green eyes."

Now I know he's flirting with me. I'm flattered in a way. But it doesn't mean I have to respond. I remember my promise to myself in the temple. I want to experience India from the calm chambers of the temple of my heart. I turn away and lift my face to the sky. I'm suddenly aware of time, as if it were a dimension of the universe that has been hiding and is now making a sneaky reappearance. I don't know if I've been here minutes or hours, but the sun is lower in the sky, the hills in the distance a deeper violet. The women in the fields are calling to their children as if it's time to go home. "We should go," I say. "We've got to get back. And what about the master painter? Maybe he's returned by now."

"Yes. We must. You must go on the train with your friend. But if you stay here one more day to see a film with me, you like this film very much. I see it three times already."

In some ways he seems like a child. I shake my head. "This was a very beautiful day. I won't forget it. But I can't stay. I have so many places in India I want to see. And I already have a ticket. You helped me get it, remember? My friend is waiting."

"All right. You decide. Chalo. We go to bus, we take fast way through field. How do you call it?"

"Shortcut."

"OK. Shortcut." We gather up the seeds and we start back through the fields. Soon we're up to our knees in grass, breathing in the heady aroma. In the distance, I can see shorn fields, the fruits of the women's work of the day, the grass stacked here and there in hourglass-shaped bundles. Sahil points out the birds again, so many different kinds of birds, and mimics the sounds they make, "cheeerup, cheerup, eeek, eeek, eeek."

"Ah, you have great talent, Sahil," I say. I shake my head, but I can't help but laugh. Gradually I become aware of a different sound, a mixture of squealing and bleating. As if from nowhere, the children from the fields appear, calling out in twittering voices as they brandish twigs to push along a small flock of mildly protesting black-faced sheep. Before I know it, I'm surrounded by woolly animals and half a dozen ragged, happy children. The children look up at me with their big dark eyes, laugh at me as if I'm a very comical person and tug at my skirt. A little boy presses a bunch of wild flowers into my hand. A child, a curly headed little girl, wants me to pet her lamb. When I do, she picks it up and hands it to me. I hold it awkwardly, its legs dangling. The lamb bleats and licks my hand. This moment is so perfect, it seems as if nothing bad could ever happen in this gentle world. I want it to last forever, but I know it can't. At least I must have a photo to remember it.

I look around for Sahil. He's nowhere to be seen. He's not ahead of me or behind me. I call out to him, with no answer. I ask the children, as best I can, if they know where he is, saying "friend" over and over again. I wish I knew the Hindi word for friend. They look at me with startled eyes and laugh again. I begin to feel nervous. I try to push my way through the sheep. Instead, we—the children, the flock and me—are moving like a cloud, ever so slowly through the field.

We reach a path and follow it as it wraps around a small hill and then splits, one fork leading to the woods, the other merging in the distance with the main road. And there I can see a late-model van, black and shiny, stopped in the road, with someone standing near it. The children jump up and down and point to it. Maybe Sahil has found us a ride. With a sigh, I put the lamb back in the little girl's arms, wave goodbye, disentangle myself from the throng and move toward the road.

As soon as I reach the van, I know that something has happened. Something that is not good. Everything is in chaos. Sahil is sprawled on the ground, holding his right foot and yelping in pain. His polished black shoe, which had looked so out of place with his jeans, is a few feet away, completely demolished. A fat, well-dressed man has one hand on his vehicle's roof, stroking it. With the other hand he is pointing at Sahil, and yelling.

Sahil is yelling back. He doesn't seem to be able to get up. "What happened?" I ask, as I help him stand.

"This man breaks my foot. I walk down the road, and he runs over me with his big car and breaks my foot and my new shoe." His face is winced in pain.

The fat man is yelling in Hindi, gesturing wildly as he pries open the doors to the back of the van. Six women are there— big, glowering, matronly women—lined up on facing benches,

all dressed in great swaths of dark fabrics. They are all muttering.

"We go to the hospital. You ride here with the women. I go
in front," he says as he hops and limps toward the van. The fat
man gestures at me to get in. The women are all scowling at
me, their heads wrapped tightly in black scarves that make their
faces stand out like dimpled moons.

"Sahil, is this a good idea? Maybe you should just get this
man's insurance information and we can take a taxi."

"No taxi here," he says, shaking his head. The fat man hus-
tles me forward like one of the sheep. I can't think of a
reasonable alternative so I step into the back of the van and try
to squeeze in by one of the women. She doesn't move an inch
to accommodate me. Six pairs of hostile eyes glare at me. The
fat man closes the back doors, forcing me into the warm flesh
next to me. We start moving. The woman across from me
reaches out and gives me quick little jabs on my shoulder with
her fingers. The woman next to me shoves her hip into mine. I
think of pushing back, but I restrain myself. A headline runs
through my mind: "American Woman Suffocated by Huffy
Harem." I imagine them being interviewed. "She was a no-
good foreign whore, a bad loose woman, she got what was coming to her," they would say.

How amazing that, in the space of ten minutes, the day has
turned from an idyll into a nightmare. Just when I think I can't
stand it any longer, the vehicle stops, the doors open, and the
women, no longer holding back, take their hands out of the
folds of their garments and shove me out in unison.

When I regain my balance, I see we are not at a hospital. In
fact, we are back in the little one-street town where we started
earlier. Sahil hops into a hole-in-the-wall shop followed by the

fat driver. A young policeman in a gray uniform is now on the scene. I just stand on the sidewalk and watch. They shout at each other for perhaps ten minutes. The policeman nods as he listens. The shopkeeper delivers cool drinks to everyone and the shouting goes on a bit more. Sahil shakes his shoe pathetically. The upper leather is now detached and the sole flaps up and down, like a reptile trying to talk. Finally, the fat man takes some money out of his wallet and hands it to the policeman, who keeps some and gives the rest to Sahil. With that, Sahil gets up, carrying his shoe, and hops toward me.

I offer him my shoulder. He puts his weight on me. "You do not mind?" he asks. "I am sorry. This day is not good for you.

"You should go to the hospital," I say as we hobble together down the street.

"We go back to Udaipur. There is a free hospital."

"Free! That man was a rich man. Rich enough to have six wives, or cousins or sisters or whatever. He must have insurance."

He laughs. "You do not understand India," he says. "This rich man has friends who are police. We wait here for bus." Sahil leans against a tree.

"How much did he give you?" He pulls the notes out of his pocket and shows me. "That's, what, twenty dollars?"

"Half for police. Half for me."

"I can't believe this."

"It's OK. I am strong." He doesn't look strong at all. He looks forlorn, sad, and maybe badly injured. When the bus comes, he grabs my shoulder tightly as he heaves himself up.

We sit near the front of the nearly empty bus. "I go for X-ray tomorrow, and when I come back, you go to this film with me. Stay one or two days more."

"I just don't know. I am so sorry this happened. But I have a ticket. My friend is waiting."

"Do not worry about your friend. She waits for you in Delhi. Do not worry about your ticket. I talk to the man at the train station. You do not lose your money." He winces in pain and grabs his foot. He is still holding his shoe.

"I don't care about the money." I look at Sahil, and he looks so pathetic, my heart goes out to him.

"I'll stay." As soon as I say that, it feels right. Somehow, in my anger at this stupid system of road hogs and payoffs and bullying that I've seen in the last hour, I feel a bond with him. When he leaned on me, when I supported his weight, I felt a simpatico that united us against the bad guys. And I think of what my train ticket had cost, about twice as much as he got for what might be a broken foot.

"Ah, I am happy you stay. Even if my foot is broken, I am happy." I realize that in the confusion our search for the master painter has been forgotten, but now does not seem like a good time to bring it up.

I find Cathy in the courtyard under a string of yellow light bulbs around which tiny bugs are circling like worshippers around their guru. She's entertaining a small circle of hotel guests with her story of her victory over the shopkeeper. As she talks, she makes great sweeps with her cigarette. When she does the shopkeeper part, she hunches her head down between her shoulders and shakes her fist.

I signal to get her attention. "Cathy," I whisper, "I've got to talk to you."

She keeps her head hunched down and continues with her performance. "I can't come with you tonight," I say.

Her head pops back to its normal, long-necked, hair-swinging position. I pull her ticket out of my bag and hand it to her. "Here's the ticket for Delhi I promised."

"What's up?"

"Actually, I've got to stay for a few days." I pause.

She looks at me suspiciously. "Right. It wouldn't have anything to do with that kid from town?"

"He's not a kid, he's a young man. Twenty . . ."

She cuts me off. "I meant a kid from *your* perspective," she says, unnecessarily drawing out the "your."

"Thanks, Cathy. In any case, how old he is has nothing to do with it." Oh what the hell, I think. I tell her, more or less, what happened—about the afternoon, about the trip to the temples, about Sahil getting his foot run over.

"Wow," she says, rolling her eyes. "I've heard of plays for sympathy, but this takes the prize."

It takes me a moment to absorb what she's saying. "What? Are you kidding?" I'm incredulous. "You're telling me that he staged the entire operation? That he purposely put his foot under the wheel of a car? I can't believe you're saying that."

"I didn't say anything. You said it."

Anger wells up and curls itself into a hard knot inside of me. "You know what. You're the most cynical woman I've ever met in my life."

"Yeah, OK, I apologize. You're right. I'm a shriveled-up cynic. It comes from working all those years at the *Enquirer*." She sighs. "Hey, I'll give you my email." She grabs a pencil at the desk and scribbles it down for me on a scrap of paper.

"I think you owe me an apology."

"Look, I *am* sorry. I don't know what's the matter with me."
She bites her lip. "Maybe I'm pissed because you're cancelling
at the last minute. I hoped we'd be friends. I was really looking
forward to doing Delhi with you."

She puts out her arms for a hug and I respond with my own
arms. "I haven't told the story I told you to anyone in a long
time. You listened. You cared." She feels so tall, so strong, so
substantial, so blond. Yet I know she's hurting inside.

"I'll be in Delhi for a while. Sincerely, I hope it works out
for you."

"I just hope you can find a way to open your heart. For your
own sake." Then I realize this sounds holier-than-thou. "Forget
I said that. Just good luck on your search for your grandfather."

"And good luck on your search for . . . whatever."

"The lost painting."

"Oh, right."

I can't sleep at all. As I lie awake looking at the stars through
the glassless opening that is my window, I remember the times
Sahil and I touched, just two. The first, when he pressed the
seed into my palm. The second, when he leaned his weight
against my shoulder as we hobbled to the bus. The first sent
filaments of electricity through me. But it is the second touch
that is keeping me here.

CHAPTER FIVE

A Dinner and Movie Date

The restaurant where I am to meet Sahil is just off the main square. There he is, standing on the street, hair combed back like a hipster, a lock falling forward over his forehead. His foot is bandaged and he's on crutches. He waves one of them when he sees me. Standing next to him is a short boy with light brown hair. He looks about twelve.

"They give me this at the hospital," Sahil tells me, jiggling the crutch. Then he points it at his companion. "This is my friend Vijay. His birthday is today. He is twenty."

"Hello," I say. He nods and we all stand there for a moment.

"Vijay understands English, but he does not speak."

When Vijay tags along as we enter the restaurant, it becomes apparent that he is part of the evening. The room is dim; a dozen tables with red tablecloths stand empty. No waiter appears to seat us, so Sahil leads the way to a round table in the center of the room and we all sit down, a little awkwardly. The magic of the previous afternoon has disappeared. I feel like a chaperone. I have a sinking feeling that staying here was the wrong decision after all.

"How is your foot?" I ask Sahil to break the silence.

He reaches into a satchel and fishes out something black and rectangular—an X-ray. He holds it up to the light, the smoky film burned away to reveal a picture of the bones of his foot. "You see," he says, pointing to the big toe. "Hairline fracture." I can see the dark thread of a break that runs across the bone.

"It looks bad. Does it hurt?"

"Yes, but it is a small hurt. The doctor says I am very lucky I do not break my bones worse than this. Maybe six days— maybe six weeks for healing. But I am OK."

Vijay repeats "OK."

"I am happy you stay," Sahil says to me.

"I am too," I say, although I don't know if I'm being sincere or not.

We leave the X-ray on the table, a kind of centerpiece, all through dinner. It looks like an ancient map of a strangely shaped archipelago, little islands of bone that connect to each other in a black sea.

"Do you want a wine? I know Americans like wine very much with their dinners." When I nod, Sahil signals to the waiter, and soon a sweating green bottle appears. Sahil elaborately pours some for each of us. The wine is cold and a little too sweet, but after a few swallows the room seems less gloomy. Dishes start appearing, a *thali* dinner consisting of many small plates, fragrant vegetable paneer, chicken smothered in ginger sauce and heaps of rice. Sahil looks over at me anxiously, asking if I like each dish.

"Are you a painter as well, Vijay?" I ask Sahil's friend.

Vijay just looks at me. "He does not speak English," Sahil says.

"Sorry, I forgot." Vijay smiles and eats, scooping up the rice and the sauce with his fingers even though this is a knife and

fork restaurant. Suddenly, he stops eating, and points to a painting on the wall. It is large and vividly colored with reds and
yellows, a picture of a group of men in traditional Indian finery
at a table heaped with succulent looking dishes—the kind of
picture that a restaurant manager would put on the wall to encourage people to eat as much as possible.

Then Vijay points to Sahil, and murmurs something in
Hindi.

"Interpret for me," I say to Sahil.

"He says 'this is my painting.'"

"His painting?"

"No, my painting." Sahil touches his own white-shirted
chest with his finger.

"You did that?" I look at it again. It's well done, but a bit
commercial. "It's impressive."

Sahil sighs. "Yes, the shop owner asks me to help him on
this painting, but then he leaves me to finish. So I work very
hard and then he comes and signs." He makes a writing gesture
in the air.

"That's terrible."

"Yes, this is the way in India." He raises one eyebrow, gives
me a half smile and shrugs in a what-can-you-do gesture. I'm
beginning to see that maybe acceptance is a way of survival
here. I think of my own job, and how many times I had slaved
over a project only to have my boss take credit, with little or no
acknowledgement. "Maybe this is the way of the world, sad to
say."

"I do not care, because this painting is not for the soul, you
know. It is only for the business. So in a way it is my painting,
but in a way it is not my painting."

"Yes, I understand."

"Ah," says Sahil, "I hope you stay to see my true paintings. But let us not talk of business things. This is a happy night. Chalo, we go to the movies." I'm not sure what the protocol is but when I take out my purse to offer to contribute to the bill, he waves his hand in dismissal. When he hands over his money to the waiter, I wonder if that is the same money he collected from the accident.

On the way to the movie theater, Sahil theatrically swings his crutches while he nods and smiles at people, many of whom nod and smile back. It's dark now, and people are everywhere, mostly young people, young men walking and holding hands and young women with their arms around each other.

Sahil already has tickets. We follow a queue into the back door of the theatre and then up a staircase littered with wrappers, papers and cigarette stubs. Sahil swings his leg wide at each step, supporting his weight on Vijay. "Are you sure this is a good idea when you've just been injured?" I ask him.

"No worries," he says and flicks his hand in a dismissive gesture. We emerge at a high balcony. Sahil winces and hops his way down a row of seats with cracked vinyl covers. We squeeze in, Sahil between me and Vijay. The seats are narrow and uncomfortable, but every one of them, both in the balcony and on the main floor, seems to be taken.

The crowd is restless, even jubilant, the chattering of a thousand voices fills the room. Vijay giggles every so often. I notice that there are very few couples. The crowd is mostly made up of groups of young men and young women who give each other sly stares. Then it hits me. Of course, Indian men and women do not date, except perhaps a very elite Westernized crowd in the big urban cities like Delhi. I know that. So Sahil brought along Vijay as a kind of chaperone to make me feel comfortable, and maybe to make himself comfortable too, to avoid the stares of the people he knows. And it worked. Even though there are some idle glances in my direction, mostly people are absorbed in their own excitement and conversations. When I think about it, Sahil is taking me on an American style "dinner and a movie" date. I'm touched by his gesture.

"I see this film four times," he says. "I tell you the story so you understand because you do not speak Hindi. I like this story because the hero is very brave. He tells his father that he cannot do what his father says. I too am like this. My father tells me I must do what he says and work for his business."

"What is his business?" I ask.

"He is a very rich man. He makes guns. He has a gun factory."

I don't quite know what to do with this information. It seems incongruous in this country where ancient daggers on display behind glass in shops seem to be the latest thing. Then the screen lights up, the theater goes dark, the crowd goes silent. I don't need sub-titles to understand what is going on, although every once in a while, Sahil leans over and whispers a comment in my ear.

The plot is simple. An older man, who has fallen on hard times, goes with his beautiful daughter to stay in his wealthy friend's house. The wealthy man's son, a beefy and handsome sort, is attracted to the beautiful girl and a friendship forms. This is symbolized by the baseball hat he gives her, which she tries on as they burst into song together. When the girl and her father must leave to go back to their own house, the young people know it is love. This is portrayed by a white dove carrying a message from the boy to the girl. The scene ends with a giant close-up of the bird's bloodshot eye, held for a very long time.

After a dancing scene on the rooftop, where she kisses a glass door, and he kisses the lipstick mark she leaves, the boy decides to marry the girl. Because she is from a poor family, his father disapproves vehemently, and when the boy insists, disowns him. With no inheritance, the boy must go to work with a pick axe on a rock pile. But the girl is now by his side, handing him heavy rocks. They are both singing. It's a moving scene in spite of the schmaltz, in the Gandhian spirit of the glorification of simple work. In the end, of course, the boy's father recognizes the error of his ways and everyone is reconciled and lives happily ever after. The parents have learned a lesson in tolerance from their children.

Through it all is the crescendo of violins and the ticky rhythm that is Indian pop music. At one point, an over-excited fan gets up on his chair and starts jumping up and down. The entire bank of chairs starts to shake. I look at Sahil. He's staring straight ahead, and so is everyone else. I'm the only one that even notices.

When the lights come on we are again swept up with the crowd down the narrow stairwell and back into the street. "Do you like this movie?" Sahil asks me, as the three of us climb into a tuk-tuk taxi. Vijay sits beside us, very quiet and serious. I imagine he is thinking over the implications of the film.

"I liked it very much," I say, and it's true. I love the innocence, the charm, the exuberance. It is so different from the cynicism, the jaded sophistication of the West. I've experienced something through someone else's eyes, Sahil's eyes, and the eyes of everyone in the audience.

"I think someday my father can see he is wrong," Sahil says, "the same as the father in the film."

Sahil says something to the taxi driver, and suddenly the film music pours into the warm night, accompanying us as we wind our way to the quiet, steep streets that lead up to my guesthouse. As the top of a curve, Sahil calls to the driver to stop. The lake appears beneath us, the ghostly white palace floating on its surface, the dark shapes of hills looming in the background. "Look," he says and gestures toward the hill. I can barely see a fortress shaped building etched against the deep night sky.

"I think I see a castle," I say.

"This is the Monsoon Palace. Long ago the maharaja and maharani go away from the city to this place when the rains come."

"To get away from the floods?"

"They go to enjoy the wind and the rain. To be close to it. Tomorrow I take you there. We have a picnic as you say in English, and pretend it is the monsoon. If you want to go."

"Yes," I say. "I will go." It will be another perfect day, I think, like the day we had at the temple yesterday. But I wonder if he will bring Vijay along, who now seems to have dozed off.

He murmurs to the driver and we turn a corner and stop in front of my hotel's wooden gate. "You must meet me at the tunnel and we go together."

"Why don't you come here to get me?"

"No, I cannot come here to meet you."

"Why not?"

"You know why. This hotel is only for tourists—for you."

"I cannot believe that."

"Yes, this is true."

Something angry flashes inside of me. "I don't care. It's all right. Come here tomorrow morning, at eleven o'clock. Come inside and ask for me."

He shrugs. "You see."

Before I get out, he presses something into my palm, secretly. It's just a touch, and yet that spot feels like the flaring center of its own tiny universe.

"Friends," he says. "Like the film."

"Yes, friends," I say. In the dark, I can see only his smile and his white shirt.

Back in my room, I turn on the light to see what Sahil gave me. It looks like one of the seeds we used to play our game with yesterday. Black on one side. I turn it over. On the white side, there is a tiny ink drawing of a woman with long hair playing a lute. Saraswati.

CHAPTER SIX

The Monsoon Palace

When I wake up the next morning to the smells and sounds of the lake coming in through my window, I think back over the evening, how awkward and silly it all was. Then I think of the little things Sahil did, not just arranging "the dinner and movie" date, but explaining the film to me, and especially pressing the seed with the drawing of Saraswati into my hand. I pick it up again. She's sitting on wavy lines meant to be a river, with other wavier lines for her hair. It's beautiful that he did this little art work for me, but a little scary. On the other hand, isn't that what I keep telling myself I'm here for, to get beyond being scared of everything? I have an insight, a small one: There are two kinds of people in the world, those like Cathy, who push their way through life, full of chutzpah and bravado, willing to tackle whatever comes their way. Then there are those like me, who feel themselves pulled, like the sea pulls the river. All I have to decide is whether to resist the pull or let myself go with it.

What does Sahil want? I don't know. What do I want? I don't know that either. But I feel the bitterness that followed my breakup with Peter gradually seeping out of me. I want to be free of desire, because I know its traps. I want to stay in the peaceful watching place I felt in the temple. And yet with all my heart I also want to go up to that dark palace on the hill with Sahil, the palace of the monsoons, and feel the wind and the rain on my skin.

I'm sitting in the courtyard waiting for Sahil when the manager approaches me, black eyes simmering in his pockmarked face. "Someone comes for you," he says, not looking at me. "He must wait outside."

"Why must he wait outside?" I use my best California "peace and love" tone of voice. I'm determined to stand up to this bully without spoiling my exuberant mood. It's a gorgeous day, warm, pale blue sky, with the hint of a breeze that scatters leaf shadows across the stone floor.

"This hotel is for tourists. Only for tourists. He is no good."

"What do you mean by that remark?"

"Many Indian men no good."

Maybe including you, I think, as I grab my daypack. Sahil is outside the gate. Today, thankfully, there is no sidekick. He's leaning against the wall, crutches dangling, His white shirt is immaculately ironed, even his blue jeans look pressed. He's wearing black athletic shoes, one of them loose to accommodate the elastic wrap. He looks so vulnerable that I feel a little bad putting him through all this. I could have met him away from the hotel like he suggested, but no, I had to prove a point. "You see, I tell you," he says.

"Oh, who cares about him? He's a bigot." I shrug, to make light of it.

"What is this word, *bigot*?"

I think for a moment about how to communicate this concept—by talking about the treatment of blacks in America,

Cathy's bi-racial mother, any of a million examples of prejudice and intolerance. But in this case, the bigot was trashing someone of his own race. I saw the complexities. "A bigot is someone who thinks they are bigger than everyone else, even though inside they are very small," I say finally.

He frowns as if thinking it over. "This is a good word. I remember this word. Bigot."

"Anyway, I'm sorry you had to go through that. And how is your foot?"

"OK for our picnic at the Monsoon Palace," he says, and pats a leather satchel radiating rice and curry smells that's slung from his shoulder. We make our way down the street to a shop where he buys cold sodas that he adds to the satchel.

Not far away is a stand of tuk-tuk taxis. Sahil goes directly to the driver, and greets him. It's the same man he spoke to in the train station a few days ago. "Elena, this is my friend Amar. He takes us up the high mountain."

"Namaste," I say. He nods without smiling, and yet there is something quietly gracious in his manner. Amar is a handsome man, a few years past forty I'm guessing. Why are his eyes so sad, I wonder. He extends his hand to offer us seats in yet another vehicle that resembles a dilapidated golf cart, and we're off, winding through the urban parade of people and animals and machines at a pace that takes my breath away. "He is a good driver, no, my friend Amar. He is a good man, his wife is a nurse at the hospital. She helps me with my foot. I am good as new very soon." Amar turns around and smiles, as if hearing about her gives him pleasure.

With Sahil alongside of me, the swirl of colors and motion and smells starts to fragment into individuals with quirks and back stories and motives, like characters in a play. He points to an elderly man weaving along on a broken down bicycle. "He is a rich man until he gives all his money to his daughter to buy her a husband. Now, the husband does not give money even for a new bicycle." When we pass a band of gypsies, the tiny mirrors in their skirts and the gold teeth in their smiles catching the sun, Sahil tells me this is the land where gypsies began, where they played their music all night until the maharajahs were jealous "because, you see, the gypsies are poor and also happy, and the maharajah is rich but not happy, so he is jealous and tries to drive gypsies away." I am lulled, almost hypnotized, by the rhythm of his voice. I love the way he sees the world. But he belongs to this land, to this vision. And I don't. I am just an enchanted traveler.

Ahead of us, the road twists its way up the barren hill. Long ago maharajahs must have come here in ornate covered pallets carried by servants. As we climb, the switchbacks get sharper and our flimsy vehicle swerves with every curve. We sway with it, sliding back and forth. I self-consciously try not to bump against Sahil. And yet, here we go, around a hairpin, and my hand reaches out to brace myself and somehow ends up on his jean-covered thigh. I quickly withdraw it, but as we sway back on the next curve, he reaches out with his own two hands and holds mine, just briefly, as if my hand were a very special and lovely thing. "Don't worry, Elena," he says. "We are safe in this mountain place." As he puts his hands back in his lap, I notice his wrist bones extending from the ironed cuffs of his white shirt, strong, yet delicate too.

With two curves in the road to go, the engine makes a popping sound and stops. Amar gets out, Sahil follows, they look under the hood and shake their heads. "Sorry," says Sahil, "we must walk. Amar waits for us here." I offer to carry his bulky satchel for him, but he refuses, pressing it tightly under his arm as he moves up the road on his crutches with an agile thump and glide rhythm, urging me to keep up with him. The climb is exhausting, and without the breeze from the motion of the tuk-tuk to cool us, I feel the heat of the sun on my skin through my gauzy dress. A trickle of sweat glides down between my shoulder blades. It takes two or three switchbacks of trudging before we arrive at the lonely palace at the top of the hill.

The palace is fortress-like, a sprawling monument of terraces, staircases and massive walls of stone. Sahil stashes the picnic satchel in the shade of a tree, and we wander around, moving from terrace to terrace, vista to vista. The plateau spreads out below us. From this distance, all appears still: the sunburnt land in meditation, the lake—two interconnected lakes I see now—a pair of sapphire eyes staring back at us.

With a quick movement, Sahil scrambles on top of a low wall. He holds his crutches in one hand, balancing his weight on his good foot. Then he holds out his free hand to me. I let him pull me up. I catch my breath when I see I am looking over a sheer drop of at least a hundred feet. "Don't be afraid," he says. The wall is several feet wide, just enough for a maharajah's sentries to patrol. My pulse is pounding in my ears. When Sahil looks over his shoulder at me, I smile and shrug. I feel tingling, alive, exhilarated. I can't believe I'm here, in this place, with this man.

He waves his crutches as if they were the extra arms of a deity, then hops down and again holds out his hand for me. "I have a plan," he says. "We must go inside." He pounds on a massive door with the tip of his crutch. I pound with my fist, caught up in the moment. We make our way around the palace, pound on door after door, but they all look as if they've been bolted for centuries.

"What is the monsoon like when it comes?" I ask him, out of breath. We are at the highest point in the complex now. He stops for a second, leans against the wall and looks out at panorama below us as if he is trying to remember. I move closer to him, so we are shoulder to shoulder. "Very beautiful. Many families have picnics at monsoon. They sit on the roof and are happy for the gift of rain."

He gestures out toward the horizon with his crutch. "This is my India," he says, melodramatically. And then, in my imagination, the empty blue expanse fills with great cauldrons of clouds that rumble and spill down cool sweeps of rain on us. The sky is a giant breathing creature, the palace walls a play of light and dark. I can feel the whip of the wind in my hair and hear the rattle of the bolted doors. The monsoon has begun.

"I feel like it's four hundred years ago and I am seeing the monsoon in front of me," I say.

"Maybe I am maharajah and you are maharani."

"We've come here with our camels and horses and servants so we can watch the rain from our windows inside the palace. But wait, we're locked out. We're in exile."

"Exile? What is exile?"

"Sahil," I say and sigh, "you're ruining the mood. Let's see, exile, we have been sent away because we have done something wrong. We're . . ." illicit lovers, I almost say, but catch myself.

He gives me a wild flash of a smile, and moves closer to me. It's almost as if I see water running down his face, dripping from his eyelashes, plastering his hair to his head. My own dress is soaked and clings to my skin. I want to reach out and push the wet hair off his forehead.

Just then, at the edge of my vision, a party of people, real people with tourist clothes and binoculars which they are directing our way, appears on the scene. Abruptly, the imaginary clouds give a few last coughs before they withdraw and disappear. "The monsoon is over," I say. A good thing, I think, as I'm getting a bit too carried away.

Sahil raises one eyebrow and gives me a half smile. "It is good the rain is stopped. Our picnic is in the sun."

We find our way back to the picnic satchel and a grassy spot with a view through the trees. Sahil puts his crutches behind him, spreads out the provisions between us, a series of tins that he lines up in a row. When he pries off the lids, little culinary wonders are revealed, scented with fragrant spices that traders hundreds of years ago traveled thousands of miles to obtain. Food from a very old civilization. "Today we eat Indian style," he says. He scoops up a bite-sized morsel of rice with his fingers, then dips it in sauce, from where it takes a precarious journey from the plate to his mouth. And yet the fluid way he uses his fingers makes it look natural and elegant. "Do like I do," he says.

I try. At first it's awkward, and a few rice bits don't make it. Sahil is amused by my efforts. But then I get into the rhythm, scoop, dip, into the mouth, lick the fingers a bit. It's an entire new sensual experience. This is the kind of food that *should* be eaten with hands, I think. After all, it comes from a long chain of hands that planted it, sowed it, threshed it, prepared it and spiced it. When I really think about it, knives and forks are a bit clunky. They're manufactured tools meant for Western food that is grown in mega-farms and processed by huge machines and broken down in food factories and packaged in plastic—a chain not of hands but of machines.

"It tastes better this way," I say. "Better than any food I've tasted in India."

"This food is from my mother. She likes to cook for me."

"Oh. Your mother." Now I understand why his clothes are so pressed, his mother probably does his laundry for him as well. I feel a little strange eating the food she prepared. I'm sure she would be shocked if she knew he was sharing it with an American woman, that is, knowing that women marry and have children in their teens, probably not that much younger than she is. But I suppose I am getting used to feeling strange.

"Do you live at home?" I can't help but ask even though I'm afraid of the answer.

"I have a place, a studio. I paint there. Sometimes I sleep there." I'm relieved to hear it. He sighs. "I love my mother very much. My father is very busy in his business, because he cares too much about money. My sister lives far away with her husband. My grandmother lives in her village. So my mother is lonely in her small house by the lake. Sometimes I go to visit her and she cooks very nice for me."

Well, at least he doesn't actually live at home. And I like that he cares so much about his mother, about his family. My fingers now feel sticky. Sahil hands me a plastic bottle of water and a napkin. He, or maybe his mother, has thought of everything.

"We are at the Monsoon Palace, so I tell you a monsoon story about my mother. When I am a small child, I am very bad. I always do things she tells me not to. One day, after much rain, the water is very high. My mother walks on the bridge and sees her friend. She tells me to stay close when she talks to her friend. But I do not. I see a swimming bird and jump from the bridge to get him, and I go under the water. But my mother does not swim."

He pauses, and takes a final swipe of the curry, then opens a soda for himself and one for me. It's warm now but I like the sweetness.

"So what happened?"

"She takes off her sari right there." He makes a twirling motion with his hand. "She throws it to me and I catch it and she pulls me in. So I am saved. Even though she is naked in her underwear in front of many people walking on the bridge."

"Well, I wouldn't think that would count for very much compared to saving her son."

"You do not understand India," he says, but with a wry smile.

I too have a memory of almost drowning. I tell Sahil the story of when I was six years old, standing with my brother on a dock by the swirling river that ran beside our house in the mountains. I don't know if he fell or jumped, but suddenly he was in the river. I jumped in after him. I can see it now as if it happened yesterday—the cold green of the water as I went down, the realization that my short life was nearly over, and my calmness about it all because I had not yet learned to fear death. We were wearing life jackets, so we popped back up. And both my parents jumped in after us. "Afterwards they told the story many times of how I had jumped in to save my brother," I tell Sahil, "but I knew I was not being brave. It was really some mysterious pull that I was following."

"Ah," he says, when I've finished, "I understand you. I too feel that. We are alike. Yes, we both almost drowned when we are children. But we are both saved from drowning."

That thought gives me shivers. At one point both of our lives could have taken a path to oblivion, and then someone or something reached out for us.

The shade from the fortress above us has shifted so we are no longer in the sun. Our legs are dangling over the edge of the terrace. I look at him and notice that the shadows under his eyes are blue, the shadows of experience, and yet his smile when he turns toward me is so innocent, so open. The childhood stories we have told make me feel closer to him, almost as if we are still children and the differences in our cultures or age don't matter. The world where that matters is far below us, and no longer watching.

We are nearly finished with our picnic. The bugs are coming out to nip our ankles and arms and a few brown birds are hopping around, looking for a meal. We put our tins back into the satchel, which stays between us. We watch the bravest of the birds come up to nibble at the grains of rice. I think it will be too spicy for them, but they gobble it up nevertheless. Again, I have the feeling that I had that day at the temples—this is a moment that could last a hundred years. "You know in America, they have a saying, live each day as if it the last day of your life. But I don't agree with that. I think you should live every day as if it's the first day of your life and everything is new, and you have a very long time to . . . I don't know, breathe it in."

"Because if it is the last day, then everyone gets drunk, even Hindu, who do not believe in drink." It's not really that funny and yet I start laughing and he does too, and then we can't stop laughing. We laugh until it feels like we are laughing with the bugs and the birds and the ghosts of exiled lovers and the almost-drowned children in our memories.

"Elena," he says abruptly, "I tell you a lie."

"About almost drowning?"

"No, that is true. I do not lie about that important thing. But when I say you do not understand India. It is not true. A lady gives my mother a cloth to cover her. People are very kind. They are happy I am saved. They kiss me." He moves the picnic satchel so it's no longer between us.

"I would like you to kiss me." He leans over and very deliberately puts his mouth on mine. It shocks me a little. I know in India kissing is not allowed in public, although I'm not sure what the penalty is. Maybe jail. Maybe just horrified looks. But of course no one is watching at the moment, so I guess there is no public. He is kissing me and I can't seem to shut my eyes. I simply stare at his face, his closed eyes, now so close to mine, and all the easy familiarity I was feeling with him a moment ago disappears instantly. It's startling in a physical way. He is suddenly a complete stranger. The perfect mouth which had seemed so beautiful when it opened over his teeth in a smile is now like some tide pool creature, opening and closing for its prey. I pull away.

"I just want to be friends," I say, even though it feels like a lie.

He is not at all discouraged. He just keeps talking, murmuring in a low, rhythmic voice. "Yes, you are my friend. We can be friends if you want but this is better, this is much better."

And then, my inner eye, the same eye that watched myself drowning with calmness when I was a child, is now watching myself being kissed by this beautiful young man, and at some indefinable moment his mouth is no longer strange and I kiss him back. The same feeling as when he pressed the seeds into my palm is now flowing everywhere. He runs his fingers down my bare inner arm.

When the kiss is over, he looks into my eyes. "That is very nice, Elena. I like to kiss you. I like to say your name."

Over his shoulder, I can see the tourists with binoculars ascending from the lower terrace. "Here they come," I say, pulling myself away. "Shall we go back?" I ask, with as much nonchalance as I can muster, as if nothing at all had happened.

"Why do you hurry?" he asks, "We are not in the last day of our lives, remember?" Still, he picks up the satchel.

"Look, I'm just a bit nervous. No one has kissed me for a long time." I begin walking down the road in the direction of our taxi. Sahil catches up with me, then moves ahead of me, stops and puts his crutch out just enough to stop me.

"I am sorry," he says. He looks into my eyes as if he is trying to understand me. The truth is, I don't understand myself. "No, I am not sorry, but I am sorry when you are angry."

"I'm not angry." Actually, I feel exhilarated, as if a thousand insects with cool downy wings had brushed against my skin. And yet . . . it's strange but I want to be alone. I want to go back down the mountain and lie on my bed in my cool room, line up my thoughts and feelings like precious objects and mull them over. I want to think about how that kiss felt, and about how he smelled, like the earth after rain, plus a whiff of something lemony like a citrus aftershave, and of how cool his touch was as he ran his fingers down my arm. And yet, now he's here in the flesh and I don't quite know how to deal with that.

I force myself into the present. "Do you think the taxi driver will be waiting for us? We've been gone a long time."

"Don't worry. He is there. He is my friend. Plus he needs money for his two wives."

"Two wives?" The sun is lower now, and the shadows of afternoon are stretching across the land below us. I am struck by his comment. India is many things, but always unpredictable. "Your friend has two wives?"

"Yes, it is true. He has two wives and I have none."

"Isn't having two wives against the law?'

"Yes. The first wife is official wife, the second wife is for love. She works in the hospital. She is a nurse. She helps me with my foot. I tell you this before. She is very nice. Very calm."

"What does the first wife think about all this?"

"She is a bad woman. Crazy. I don't like this woman."

"Why?" I ask, but by now we have reached Amar, the taxi driver with two wives. He's waiting patiently, sitting on the hood of his vehicle, running a hand through his head of greying hair as if only a moment has passed. He looks like an intelligent man, a thoughtful man. A troubled man. And yet, when he sees Sahil, he breaks out into a smile. The Sahil effect, as I am starting to think of it.

CHAPTER SEVEN

Email

"It was a beautiful picnic," I tell Sahil when we part, half a block away from the guesthouse. "But I need my space for a while."

"Space? Like the stars?" He cocks his head and looks at me as if he doesn't understand. How can I explain?

"No. Not like the stars. I need some time alone. To think."

He nods, but I don't think he really understands. "Later I see you. Maybe we walk under the Rajasthan night sky."

"Maybe."

"OK. I come later."

"Well, maybe I'll be up for a walk in the evening, maybe not." I don't want to make any commitments.

"OK." He shakes his head. He's disappointed I know. Maybe it's a cultural difference, this need for personal space.

I'm grateful that my cool room is waiting. But before I have a chance to put my key in the lock, I hear the tinny sound of a Madonna CD coming from cheap speakers inside. Strange. What's going on? I rap on the door. It opens a crack and a wan male head, hair pulled back in a ponytail, peers through. "What's up?"

"Uhmm, this is my room."

"No, it's my room, dude." I can see a guy's clothes draped around the chairs and the bed.

"Can't be. I've been here for a week."

He shrugs. "Dunno. All I know is I paid."

I stomp off to the manager's office, a tiny room behind a counter just off the courtyard. He's at his desk, head down over a grubby ledger. I am amazed to see my suitcase propped against the wall, one forlorn sleeve of a violet T-shirt sticking out of it. This morning, that T-shirt and all my other things had been neatly stacked in that same room now occupied by someone else.

"Someone is in my room."

"Your room finished," he says. "No more rooms. All full." Without looking at me, he lifts his chin several times in quick succession, as if he's trying to shake a fly off his face.

"Excuse me, I have a room here. You cannot give my room away. You cannot just take my things and do what you want with them. That's against the law."

"You no pay. Today one week rent due." He glances at me with his reptile's gaze, the corners of his thin lips turned up.

"What? Yes, today it is due. And I was going to pay it."

"Too late. No more rooms."

"That is not the reason. You know that is not the reason."

He shrugs and peers at his ledger again. "You owe rupees, madam."

"For what?"

"For too many *toastbutterjams*." I really want to go in there and tear up his ledger. I really want to kick him.

"Belongings packed up and ready to go." He puts my suitcase by the counter. The guests in the shadows bend their heads over their game, pretending not to hear.

"And who pray tell went into my room and packed up my belongings?"

"One of our boys, madam."

"How do I know that all my things are here?"

He wobbles his head in that irritating way, like a light bulb loose in its socket.

"What does that mean?" I imitate his gesture in a mock sarcastic way and roll my eyes. "Does it mean yes, no, or I'm an idiot and don't have a clue." I can't help myself. Adrenaline is shooting through me like hot tea.

The three or four guests in the courtyard look up expectantly from the board game they are playing. If they want drama, I'll give them drama. I lean over, hoist up my suitcase onto the counter, open it up and proceed to take out my worldly possessions one by one. Four T-shirts, three skirts, two Indian style tunics, two dresses, various items of underwear. A cup and strainer for tea. Three long scarves. Sandals. My writing notebooks. My still empty writing notebooks. So sad. My copy of E.M. Forster's *A Passage to India* (in which a young Indian man is accused of molesting the pure white English heroine, or is it simply a figment of her repressed imagination?), my five hundred years of Indian poetry book, my see-through plastic cosmetic bag with all my American products from hair conditioner to sunscreen to tampons.

It feels like a violation, knowing that some stranger actually picked up these things. The pile is getting larger. My manila envelope with my papers. My guidebooks. And my slightly lopsided copper cow from the ashram that I had used to do my water blessing ceremony just a few short days ago. I open the satin covered box that is my jewelry case and look over its meager contents, a garnet pendant, a silver chain, and the most recent addition, the painted seed Sahil had given me. I put the case on top of the pile. It all seems to be here. I want to call out, falsely, "My diamond ring, where is my diamond ring," but I know that whatever boy had packed my things would be in trouble for doing what he had been ordered to do. I don't want to be like the overwrought heroine in *Passage*. I want to be sensible. I want to keep my head. I fail miserably.

Two new guests arrive, a young couple. They gaze with puzzled expressions at the pile on the counter. "You will love this place," I tell them. "Fabulous service, including gratuitous clothes management."

The manager mumbles. "Not necessary to pay rupees, madam. On the house."

"Oh thank you ever so much," I say and stuff my things back in my suitcase, roll it out the door on its barely functional wheels. I hate this country. I hate its stupid venal petty people, and its absolute disregard for anyone's personal belongings and space, and especially I hate the hypocritical morality, where they presume to tell people what they can and can't do.

I pull my suitcase with the wobbling wheels through the cobbled streets. It makes a thumping sound and every third step or so gets stuck and I have to give it an extra yank. My guidebook, with its recommended hotels and cheap guesthouses is at the bottom of the pile, and I don't want to sit in the middle of the street to take it out. I'm on my own, with no idea of what my next step is. I am now aware of what poor independent travel skills I have. All my earlier travels were prearranged, prepackaged. I didn't really have to think about much at all.

Now that Cathy's gone, I don't know anybody except for Sahil, and I have no idea how to get a hold of him.

I feel as if I'm in a trance, as if I am reliving the exile I fantasized on the ramparts of the Monsoon Palace, only in a much more banal way. I'm not a princess or a maharani who's been shut out of her castle. I'm an angry, homeless woman aimlessly wandering through the streets, dragging her pathetic bundle of worldly goods behind her. My feet ache. My hair is wet from sweat and flopping in my eyes. My face is burning from the sun and I have no idea where my hat is. I can feel the cobblestones transmitting their shape up to me one by one through the handle of my suitcase into my arm all the way to my teeth.

Children gather round a flavored ice vendor and cover their faces with their hands, then open their fingers to point at me, probably because I'm scowling like a witch. I pass my favorite trio of old men in white, their mustaches pomaded to extravagant perfection like the perfect horns of a bull, orange turbans and polished spectacles, bemused expressions on their faces. I want to stick out my tongue at them. And the child with the beautiful face who walks on all fours like a crab that tears at my heart. He extends his hand and I give him some coins and try to keep from crying. And yet even he exudes some kind of inner peace and understanding that eludes me. These are the denizens of deep India, who have always been here, as if this is a garden and they are the native plants that grow here. I'm a mere transient, a bug in the garden really, and my search for transformation and beauty has come back to mock me.

I take a random turn up a side street where at least there is shade. And there, miracle of miracles, is an internet café. I have one thought: If I rush in will I be saved. The café is a rundown mecca for Indians and Westerners alike: red walls with an eight-armed scary god painted in gold, a mishmash of tables, gooey sweets behind a cloudy glass cabinet. But there are three computers, two occupied by earnest-looking young Indian men. A guy at a table near me who has a European accent, German likely, although his speech is slurred, says namaste to me and then recommends a bong lassi, "guaranteed to take you to the moon," he tells me, even though it's quite apparent to me that we're already on some version of it. He'd been going to catch a train three days ago and somehow he just couldn't find his way to the train station. Another lost soul.

I order a chai tea and a half hour online. I take my tea to the computer station, stash my suitcase by my knees and sign on. And there it is, threads from the world I had left behind, a world that's hard for me even to imagine now. Big white rooms. Lawns. Freeways. Strange. I'm disappointed there's nothing from Jason. After all, we did agree to try to meet in Kathmandu eventually. The trouble with him, I remember from that other world we lived in, is once he's caught up in some romance, he gets very spacy. Among the spam, there are two I want to read. One from my mother, and one from Cathy.

I open the one from my mother.

We hope you are having a safe journey dear. It's cold here, the middle of winter on this side of the world. Your dad is shoveling snow, and we're getting ready for a visit from the Clausens. You remember them don't you? Dorothy was about your age. Their daughter will be starting college soon.

How does she do it, and I know it's on purpose, instead of asking about me, showing any interest whatsoever in my journey, she makes me feel like I have absolutely screwed up my life by not finding the right man and raising college-bound children. I continue reading.

I'll bet it's hot there, although we still don't know what you're doing on such a long trip. Travel does broaden one's horizons, but why can't you just see the sights and come home? We hope you can find a good job when you get back as the newspapers are full of talk about the bad economy. Your dad always said don't quit your job till you have another one, but you obviously didn't take that advice.

As to the other, well, you know I'm not surprised about Peter.

What did she mean by that?

But there are lots of nice professional men out there. Time to keep moving, as you know you're not getting any younger. I'm certainly not. My bursitis is acting up again. Well, I have to go to bed now, they finally gave me three days of work at the hospital, which will be a help for our retirement savings. I have to be up early. I don't need to say, write us.

Love,

Your mom (and dad.)

In a way she's right. Maybe I am here because I can't face my problems at home. There was a life I was supposed to be living, the next step in my career, a new, improved relationship, a home, a garden, I had always dreamed of my own patch of earth, belonging. Will it still be waiting? Do I want it to be waiting? I hit the reply button.

Dear Mom (and Dad),

I'm having a wonderful, productive time exploring the culture of this fascinating country. Travel, as you yourself have implied, will make me a more well-rounded person, and much more attractive to both future employers and suitors, if any.

Love, your daughter

I hit send. Then I think of how cold it is there. My old dad would be shoveling snow off the driveway so my mom can get up in the gray dawn, put on her registered nurse's uniform and go to work. I feel somehow ashamed for being here, for pursuing such a chimera. I open Cathy's email. I've saved it for last because I know it will cheer me up.

Yo Elena,

Delhi has been great, Mark (the guy from Australia) has an awesome high-rise pad with a view of the smog, which I don't notice so much as mainly I'm indoors in A/C comfort. I am trying to stay focused and do my work tracking down my grandfather (the Indian doctor who ditched my grandmother you remember that story I told you). He owes big time, though I'm not sure exactly who, as my grandma died a long time ago.

I'm still here for a while if J Depp turns out to be J Dipp. So reply already.

Cathy

I start to compose an answer, when something makes me look over my shoulder. There, beyond the spaced-out German, is Sahil, ambling across the room toward me, on just one crutch now. He's smiling that lovely smile of his, as if nothing in the world can ever be wrong. He shakes his head when he sees me, as if I am the most exasperating person on the face of the earth. I just sit there, gripping the handle of my suitcase. "How did you find me?"

"I come here to see my friend." He gestures to the man behind the glass counter. "Do you leave Udaipur?" he says, looking at my suitcase. "This makes me sad."

"I don't know," I say. "I don't know where I'm going or what I'm doing." I tell him what happened at the hotel.

"Yes, hotel wallah is a bad man. Because he sees me with you. He does not like this."

"In America I could get a lawyer for this."

"Yes, same lawyer as you get for my foot. But he is in America, this lawyer, not here. When he visits, he can fix everything in India."

This makes me laugh. "I'll email him to come right away."

"Do you want to stay or go?"

"I really want to . . . ," I hover for a moment, suspended. "I really want to . . . stay."

"I am happy this is what you want."

"But where? I can't go back to that hotel obviously."

"I take you to a very nice place."

I nod and turn back to the computer to finish my reply to Cathy. *Good luck on your search. More later.*

CHAPTER EIGHT

Exile

Pulling my suitcase, I follow Sahil back to the street that no longer looks like chaos to me, but an order so intricate that it would take me a lifetime to discern it.

"From the window of this place you can see—what do you say—birds with long legs in the water."

"Storks."

"Yes, storks. Very nice birds."

"Very nice birds," I repeat mindlessly. We pass near the water pump. Usually the gang of ragged children are playing there, but now it's quiet. It's late in the day. Everything is hushed and silvery, the old walls and the cobbled streets and the sky. I walk over to the pump and lean on the handle. A gush of water comes out. I splash some on my face, let it run down over my throat and down my arms.

"I feel like an outcast."

"Yes, many people are outcast in this country." He is standing near me, leaning on his crutch, very calm, very patient.

"Maybe I *am* an outcast, an untouchable. How do you say it in India?"

"*Harijan.*"

"Yes, harijan." I know I'm being ridiculously dramatic. Not to mention disingenuous. After all, on some level, I know I can go home, that the real untouchables that live here have lives and burdens they cannot escape. Thinking about that makes me sad again, as if all the sorrows in the world, big and small, were somehow connected in a web of misery. Just then, a threesome of baseball-cap-wearing, backpack-toting tourists—a man and two women—pass us, consulting their guidebooks. They seem far away, from a different world. I feel as if I've crossed some kind of invisible boundary.

"I am a harijan together with you," Sahil says.

"Yes. We will be harijans together," I agree. And I know when I say it that some part of me has always been in love with the idea of totally stepping away from the identity I was born with, leaving it behind as if it were nothing but worn-out clothes.

"Come, before it is dark." And so I follow him as we walk, a long way, around the road by the lake. There are fewer cars here. People walk or ride bicycles or travel in carts pulled by donkeys. We cross an arched stone bridge over an estuary and make way for a turbaned man driving a camel the other way.

"I say I am harijan," Sahil says, "but I must explain something to you. I do not believe in this untouchable. This is a Hindu idea that some people are better than other people. No, for me, all are the same." He stops in the middle of the street and faces me, very close to me, enough so that a trio of women flash piercing glances at us as they walk by.

"I want you to know who I am," he says. But I don't know who he is, not yet. Just in that moment, looking into his eyes is like entering a forest that promises shelter, but also surprises, where I might weave around a fallen tree and find a fox waiting, or a sleeping tiger. A forest that is mysterious and dark and irresistible.

"So if I'm not untouchable," I say, "does that mean I'm touchable?"

He looks puzzled for a moment, as if something has been lost in the translation and he has no idea what I mean. Then it clicks and he laughs. "Yes, very touchable. Very beautiful." He pauses. "Come, we must find this place before dark comes." He runs his fingers up my arm, just briefly, before we continue.

"See there." Sahil gestures with his chin to a sober stone building that rises up directly from the water. Tangled greenery grows on the banks on either side of it. Here, the lake feels subdued, remote, a place away from the hubble-bubble of the town. A place where change happens very slowly. When we reach the hotel, we go around in back, away from the lake. A scrolled iron gate opens onto a garden of untidy flower beds. The roof of a porch shades two matronly women. Their gray hair is pulled back tight on their heads; their knotted hands are busy with embroidery. One has a tiny gold ring in her nose. When they see Sahil, they break into broad grins and clucking sounds of affection.

"These are my aunties," he tells me. "They are not really my aunties, but that's what I call them because from when I am a child they take care of me." He says something to them in Hindi and they shake their heads and answer in high, worried voices. He says something back, and they raise their eyebrows, looking at each other and shaking their heads again, but this time in what seems like acceptance. The auntie who has a gold ring in her nose calls out. From inside, a tall, awkward boy appears. He takes my suitcase and we follow him inside, up a narrow set of stairs and down a dim hallway. "You are my friend," says Sahil, "so they make a good price for you."

The boy opens the door onto the most beautiful room I have ever seen. It's spacious, with high ceilings and a tiled floor, and furnished simply, with a large bed in an alcove, a wardrobe, and a chintz-covered chair and table near the window. The walls are a mysterious shade of aquamarine that makes me feel like I'm underwater in a swimming pool.

"Come," says Sahil, and leads me over to the window. A story beneath me, the murky water laps up against the building. In the distance is the arched stone bridge, and further, on the other side of the lake, the hills of the city proper where we came from. The pale buildings glow in the twilight. One by one, the lights come on, winking, as if the residents are trying to send us messages.

The bath too, I discover, looks out over the lake. "It's lovely. How much?"

"The aunties tell me three hundred dollars."

"For a week? Very expensive!"

"For one month. You must take this room for one month."

I take a deep breath. A real commitment. "All right."

"Come see," says Sahil, after the boy has left. He takes me again to the window and points to the near distance. Standing out against the dark water, a white stork is perched on one leg on a lonely rock. "He is very quiet because he is hunting," says Sahil.

Then he turns to me and pulls me close and kisses me, a long, slow, sensual kiss. A very pleasurable kiss. Abruptly, he pulls away. "I must go. The aunties watch when I leave. Later I will come back. When you see the moon from this window."

After he leaves, I watch the stork for a long time. He is so still, it's hard to believe it's a live creature and not a statue. Then, like the flash of a mirror in the fading light, his narrow head slices into the lake and he comes up with a silvery fish in his beak.

Now that I'm alone, I take off my limp, sweaty dress. I want a shower, although it's not really a shower; it's a nozzle connected to a hose. As the lukewarm water streams over me, I watch the silver skin of the lake's surface. I wonder what's going on beneath that skin. Little fishes and frogs, no doubt, are just living the lives that belong to them. I let the water run over my own skin and wonder what lies beneath it. All those murky things like anger and desire that seem to have lives of their own, like the fishes and frogs.

The nearly full moon comes out early tonight and shows up in my window. Sahil knocks. I let him in, and right there, by the door, he kisses me. Even in the dark, through closed eyes, I can see him. He is beautiful and strange and fascinating. He locks the door and I take his hand and lead him to the bed. "Does your foot hurt you?" I ask him as he drops his crutch by the side of the bed. "You heal me," he says. We shed our clothes and the wind comes in over the water and through the open window to wrap itself around us.

Part of me is curious, merely curious, wanting to see where it will lead, this shocking softness of his mouth on my bare arms and shoulders. I love his touch. It's as if my skin is the night and his hands are lanterns. Everywhere he touches me, I begin to glow. How strange that we are here, in this exact time and place, because of so many accidents—an overnight train moving across India, a girl leaving her handprint in the wet plaster before she walks into a fire, a search for a missing painting, the cracking of a foot bone, my own wandering spirit. All those things that have brought us together now in just this way, just for this. We are drowning, he says. I say it back and we both laugh. I can see his arms at my sides and his lean body over mine, the dark rectangle of the window appearing and disappearing as he moves. Our bodies become a path with only one direction, and we follow each other with abandon, like children on an adventure.

"You are very beautiful," he says afterwards. And when he says it, I feel beautiful. Then, somewhere in the middle of the night, he dresses and lights a cigarette. He will come again tomorrow, but now he must go, he says, and kisses me. I watch the flickering ember of his cigarette tracking his path as he crosses the room. I already miss him.

In the morning, I wake up to the ceiling fan circling slowly over my bed. It's one of those large old fans you see in movies about the tropics. Riding on its blades are a pair of mauve-colored birds, doves maybe. What am I seeing? I shake my head to make sure I'm not dreaming. A bubble of laughter comes up from somewhere inside of me. As I watch, the birds take off from the fan and fly out through the window, over the lake. A few minutes later, they return with twigs in their mouths. They land on the fan, setting it slowly in motion again. When the fan slows down, they flutter over to a high bookshelf and deposit the twigs. They are building a nest. Those crazy birds are building a nest in my room. It's so exciting. Everything is so exciting. I feel like a little girl who is discovering up and down and inside and outside for the first time. All things seem possible if only I watch and listen, if only I open my heart.

I tiptoe to the shelf to look more carefully at the intricate design the birds have made with their twigs, leaves, bits of flotsam and downy stuff they must have pulled off a cattail at the water's edge or maybe someone's laundry pile. I wonder about their view of the world. They don't have to think about their creativity, or do they?

On a shelf below the nest is an old pen, the kind with a coppery pointed tip. A small bottle of ink is there too. A former inhabitant must have left it. I take the pen and ink, along with my blue-lined notebook to the table by the window. I dip the pen into the ink, which is a very dark blue, the color of the lake beneath the surface. I call on Saraswati, the goddess of creativity, the goddess of the river that gathers everything in its eternal flow.

Stick by stick, word by word, I begin to write:

When I fled the ashram and took the overnight train to this shimmering city in the desert state of Rajasthan, India, I was not at all sure why I had come. But I knew the moment I first saw the Rajasthani people, wrapped in the flaming colors of the sunset, looking back at me with their eyes of fire . . .

PART TWO

PARVATI

Parvati is the goddess of love, beauty, and sensuality, the complement to the ascetic, world-denying tradition. And yet, madly in love with Shiva, she believes she can win his heart through a series of austerities, bleaching her body by sitting in the midst of four fires and starving herself by living only on leaves and air.

CHAPTER NINE

The Rooftop Restaurant

The heat is settling in, draping around us like a heavy silk sari. That's why the birds have come into my room to build their nest, to escape the heat, the French couple tells me. They are the only other long-term guests in the hotel, now that the season for travelers in this part of India is drawing to a close.

In the mornings I go to the mostly empty rooftop restaurant that looks out over the lake. There are no glass windows in the room, just a waist-high wall, then pillars supporting a roof. Every day I order an omelet from the gangly boy who shows up with a stained towel over his arm. Yes, I can have an omelet, he tells me, but first he must go out to buy the eggs. There are no guests except for us, the French couple has explained to me, so there is no reason to stock up.

"Can't you buy at least six eggs?" I ask the boy. But he buys only enough for that day. The next day, we go through the same conversation all over again. It's a kind of comedy routine, or maybe it's more than comedy, it's philosophy. I represent the Western view of building capital, preparing for the future. The waiter represents the Indian view of expending only the energy sufficient for the day. It's his country and he wins.

After breakfast I open a notebook and write. I'm going through them, but they're cheap, a few rupees at the local news shop. They have pale blue tissue covers and thin lines that are like the grid on a map of an empty pale sky. In the afternoon, in spite of the heat, I explore, often on my own. I take pictures, sometimes real ones, sometimes in my mind. I go on expeditions with the French couple, Yvette and Robert. We have tea at the Lake Palace Hotel, shop in the markets, or wander through the luscious gardens of the many palaces and mansions of the city. Peacocks wander everywhere, fanning their feathers of a hundred iridescent eyes.

Sahil's foot has healed, so when he's not working, we go on expeditions. I'm still waiting for the discovery of the enigmatic master painter. We've been on several wild goose chases to various villages to find him. Each time it's a different story, told by the locals, translated by Sahil. The master painter is visiting his daughter in another part of India. He has gone to a mountain to meditate. He will return. Be patient. He has taken on a strange allure for me, like a ghost in a family story.

"Tell me more about this master painter," I say to Sahil.

He thinks for a moment, placing his fingers on his forehead. "This master painter is very calm. Very quiet. But also wild. Like a hunter. Not a hunter with guns. But a hunter like a bird or a lion that is hungry and beautiful. He thinks only of his painting. That is how he can discover new things."

When he says this I feel that we are twin souls, connected in our search for beauty and meaning. The master painter is out there waiting for us to discover him. Then an hour later I think I have fallen under the spell of a magician who is concocting stories in a Scheherazade kind of way. I don't push for answers. I like living with questions. I remember my finger tracing on the dusty window of the overnight train: Perhaps the universe began with a question: What will I be?

At night, when the stork flies away from the rock in the lake and is replaced by the turtle, when the air is free from the weight of the sun, when the sky overhead retreats into indigo infinity, then Sahil appears in my room, the swimming pool room, in his black T-shirt and black pants and sneakers. Here is a person who didn't exist for me until a month ago and suddenly he's here every night. I wait for his smooth breath, his dark eyes.

I am used to him now, to his smell that reminds me of water in mountain pools, to the taste of flecks of turpentine on the edges of his fingers. I am accustomed to his lean arms around me, to the heel of his hand that he drags down the center of my back until it reaches the hollow just at the base of the spine, the magnetic pole of the universe of the body, the antipode to the heart. I know how he clears his throat and rolls a cigarette and lights it, and then offers it to me. Sometimes I take a drag, savoring the feel of the smoke inside my body, then I cough and hand it back. I tell him they are bad for him, but he just smiles and shrugs. I watch as he moves out of the room, his cigarette a moving ember in the dark, a graceful pattern that finally fades away.

He has a motorbike, one that works intermittently. One golden afternoon, I take the route that leads me across the arched stone bridge to town. Suddenly, Sahil is beside me, gesturing for me hop onto the back. I shake my head. "Come to India to lose your fears, Miss Elena," he says. He reaches out and swoops me onto the back and we're off, swerving through the town into the hills, the wind in our faces.

This morning, as I drink sweet coffee and wait for my eggs, I am reading Indian poetry, a dog-eared paperback that I found in the tiny English language section of the local bookstore. Here is Janabai, a famous fourteenth century poet, who says, "cymbals in hand . . . I go about; who dares to stop me?" She then writes about defying convention by casting off her sari in crowded marketplace "without a thought."

That's how I feel. I have cast off all those old garments from my past—the fears and the inhibitions of my old life. I have thrown away the typical tourist eyeglasses. I have a lover—a young, beautiful, passionate lover. And best of all, I don't care at all that he doesn't fit into the box of society's conventions. I feel sensual, alive, and braver.

I know Sahil is young, but not too young to have a past. I discover this one morning when he walks into the garden where I am sitting under the umbrella shaped tree with the "aunties," the hotel's landladies. I call them Aunty Peaches and Aunty Cream because they are so sweet and motherly. They are busy embroidering white muslin pillowcases with blue stitches that create a line of tiny prancing peacocks. Sahil chats with them and soon they're chuckling. But when I get up to leave with him, one of them puts a finger in front of my face and wags it. Of course they know what is going on. But I suppose they need the rent I pay, small as it is, so they look the other way. Still, they feel they must express indignation. One says something that I interpret as *rascal*. The other nods vehemently.

Then the boy who fetches my egg every day tells me, "You are nice lady, better than French lady before."

"Ohhh?" I say. Sahil gives the boy an angry look.

"So who is this French woman?" I try to sound casual, a little teasing.

"Only a woman who stays here."

But in the late afternoon, when we are lying on the bed, watching the progress of the birds building their nest on my bookshelf, he tells me. "I was not telling you truth about French girl." He's propped up on a pillow, with his eyes closed as if this is all too much for him, and reaches blindly for the pack of cigarettes at his side.

"I wish you wouldn't smoke," I say. "It bothers the birds."

"You are right," he says and puts it down. "I care very much about this girl. When she goes back to France, she says she comes back. But she does not come back. She sends me a letter to say she marries to someone else. This makes me very sad. Not just sad, very angry. Sometimes I dream I go to see her in France and find her house and she answers the door and I kill her."

"Kill her . . . what are you talking about?" I feel the heat rising to my face.

"I only dream this I tell you. It is not my fault what I dream. I would not hurt anyone. I am not like my father who one time hits my mother." He is agitated and gets up and pulls on his clothes quickly. "I must go. I have a job to paint pictures," he says and moves toward the door.

One of the birds has dropped a twig in the middle of the floor. Sahil sees it, picks it up, then, holding it with two fingers as if it were a precious object, places it on the nest on the bookshelf. He looks at me, his handsome face is serious for once. "I am glad I find you," he says. He kisses me on my shoulder before he goes out and shuts the door behind him.

After he leaves I watch the birds as they make their graceful passage through the window to the fan, setting it in motion each time. Their nest is growing with sticks and leftover bits of cloth and even a shiny string of sequins. They seem to have no clue that the rule for birds is to build their nests outside. They don't seem to understand the boundary concept. That's the trouble with this place. The boundaries are blurry, including my own. What am I doing? This was supposed to be a lighthearted romance, an adventure. It *is* an adventure. And yet I feel I am moving into territory I don't quite understand. Territory maybe I shouldn't be in. I know I should go before it all becomes . . . I don't know, too *complicated.* Where can it lead?

Just for fun, I sometimes try to imagine Sahil in America. Driving down the freeway in an SUV, getting a job, as what? A taxi driver? I think of him with the background of California and he's no longer Sahil, because Sahil is not just himself, he's part of this entire world of motion and music and people called Rajasthan. I think of a story the French couple told me about how a friend of theirs had fallen in love with an Indian man and taken him back to Chicago, but he just couldn't fit in. One cold night he was so miserable he flipped out and jumped out of their condo window and broke both legs.

In any case, Sahil tells me again and again he does not want to go to America. "Many of my friends they want to meet American or European girl and go to live there. But not me. My friend marries an American girl and goes to live in New York City. Then he comes back. Too cold, he says. And too much working." He repeats his adage, "America is good for the work, but Rajasthan is good for the life."

He hates his father, he says, who used to beat him. He is an ungrateful boy, his father told him, because he refuses to work with his father in his gun factory, because he insists on being an artist. But his mother, that's another story. He loves his mother. "I cannot be far away from her," he tells me. When he leaves here sometimes he goes to his studio to work or sleep or visit with his friends, sometimes he goes to his mother's house. His father is off on business someplace, so she lives mostly alone. She lives in a house that overlooks the lake on the next hill over, a house full of flowering plants. He helps her water them as they talk. He is his mother's favorite child, he tells me. She understands that he wants to be an artist. He is like her. When they finish watering the plants she gives him something to eat. Then he goes to sleep on the roof under the stars.

"I will signal you from the roof of my mother's house," he says one night to me when he leaves. It's a warm night, with fireflies flicking over the lake, and the only sound an occasional jingle that might be the bell of a bicycle as it swerves down the frontage road, or the music of a tribal family out walking. On those nights I love sitting in the alcove by the window, writing in my notebook. The doubts fly away and I'm content, enchanted to be in this place.

Every once in a while I glance up and over to the hill beyond, to the place where Sahil told me his mother lives. And then it comes, the faint flash of a light, like a motionless firefly in the distance, like a signal from another planet. My very own personal alien, I think. On and off. On and off. On and off. Three times. I know it's Sahil. I cover the candle on my little table with my notebook and flick it three times, trying to send the same signal back, although probably he can't see it. Later he asks me "Do you know the meaning of this message?" But even though I prod him, he won't tell me. "You must figure it out," he says. I tell him I don't want to, that there are too many puzzles in India. But he won't give in.

He tells me the meaning of his name. Sahil means the shore, but the shore that someone at sea longs for. He is like that, he believes, looking for the distant shore.

There is something enchanting in Sahil, but also something mischievous, unpredictable. I wonder if I am reaching back to my own childhood, or to a child I wanted but never had, or if it's something else—wanting to live in a kind of a dream world. "You will spend your whole life dreaming if you don't watch out," my mother would tell me on days when I'd be locked up in a tree house reading or writing or drawing when my friends were out swimming or at ball games. That's what this feels like, a story book, not like real life.

On this particular morning, I'm writing at my table at the rooftop restaurant. The city outside is already shimmering in the heat. Then, suddenly everything is black, black, black. At first I'm startled. Then I hear Sahil's laugh. He's snuck up behind me and put something over my head.

"Now, tell me what you see."

"I see that you're twelve years old." He takes away the basket, that's what it was, and swings into the chair next to mine.

"No, I am a twenty-seven year old man. Do you not remember last night?"

I cock my head to one side and resist smiling. "It's all a blur."

"Here," he says, and takes my notebook and pen. "You can take a holiday from writing. I write something for you. Whatever you want to say, I say it for you."

"I love this country," I say. That phrase just comes out, without thought, as naturally as breathing.

"That is this," he says. He writes something in my notebook in the extravagant curling letters of Hindi.

"Write in English for me. Please. So later I won't forget what it means."

"Of course, I do this for you." I read it as he writes it. "India is mine."

He glances up at me. "India is mine. You are mine. I am yours. This is the message I send to you with lights." He looks around to make sure we're alone, and then he leans over and kisses me. I pull back from his kiss and look at him. Does he really think of me like that? As precious to him? We are so different. If I could conceive of someone as unlike myself as possible, I would have invented Sahil. He moves quickly, confidently. I move cautiously, as if I were crossing a stream and looking for a good rock for my next step. I have a past, with a few crumbling statues in my back yard, he is near the beginning of his journey. He is outgoing, things pour out of him and over him easily. I take everything in, nurture it, try to make sense of it.

"Tonight, I make you a special dish," he says.

"What kind of dish?"

"A fish dish."

"I didn't know you could cook." He's smiling that show-off smile. I can't quite take in that Sahil can actually cook. He is good at many things—at painting, at making people laugh, at getting things done in a country where the idea of time is a circle, not an arrow. But cooking?

"My mother teaches me to cook. To make very nice curry. We have a party. Tonight. Right here. I cook in the kitchen."

"Here?" I gesture toward the enclosure where the waiter disappears to scramble the eggs for omelets each morning.

"Yes, of course. This is no problem. No one cooks here at night."

"A party. I like that." I smile and touch him on his perfect nose. "What a nice nose you have," I tell him.

"Yes, like my father." He laughs. "It is the only way I am like my father." He frowns and reconsiders. "My father makes guns. And guns make money. I am an artist. And make not so much money."

"We are poor artists together. Poor us." I sigh an exaggerated sigh. I think, yes, we are different, but we are also alike, in a way that I have never felt with anyone else. I reach across the table for his hand and touch it lightly.

"But I am changing," Sahil says. "I am making a new shop. You must come to see it soon. It is to be the best painting shop in all of the city. I am to be . . . what is the word?"

"Let me see. Successful?"

"Yes. I like this word. Full of success. I want you to look at me and think, he is successful." He taps his fingers on the table, rhythmically, a drumbeat.

"Sahil," I say, remembering our plans. "Who will we invite to this party?"

"We invite Vijay."

Vijay, who sat silently with us through the dinner and movie date. I scrunch up my nose. "He is so young. And quiet. Not so good for a party. I know, we'll invite the French couple."

"Yes, very good. I like these people."

"Who else?"

He places his fingers on his forehead in the place where the third eye would be. "I ask Amar. He take us in the taxi up the mountain."

"Oh, yes. Amar, the taxi-driver with two wives. Maybe he will bring one of them."

"Maybe Neela. She is a very nice lady. The one who helps me heal my foot." And with that, Sahil lifts up his healed foot, now in its black sneaker. "I ask Amar to bring his CD player so we have music."

I shimmy my shoulders and give him a sexy look in imitation of an Indian dancer.

"Very nice," he says. His eyes close, then open with that deep, long-lashed look of his.

"Come," he says, touching my shoulder. "I have a plan. At three o'clock we go to buy food. Now we go to dance in your room."

"What a good plan." I squeeze his hand.

CHAPTER TEN

The Dinner Party

I'm humming a tune in anticipation of our evening. I can hear it in my head. *Tiki, tiki, tiki,* then a big swell of violins. There's a pulse, an urgency to Indian pop music that makes me feel a bit reckless. I hear it wherever I go, in the shops, in taxis, on the CD player Sahil has borrowed from Amar and set up in the rooftop restaurant.

It will be lovely to have a real dinner party. It makes me feel as if this is becoming my home and this little rooftop restaurant my dining room, my temporary home because at some unknown time in the future, I will run out of money. But that seems far away to me, now that I am settling into this life. This afternoon I picked flaming red flowers from the garden and set them in a glass jar in the middle of the table. I raided the larder and found plates, utensils, and mismatched glasses for the wine the French couple has promised to bring.

Still, I'm wondering where we will get food for our party tonight. The shops are filled with clothes and trinkets, not mounds of fruit or vats of fish. All I see here are a few vendors selling the local equivalent of fast food from their makeshift street stalls. And Sahil has warned me away from them. "Watch this one," he said one afternoon, directing my eyes to a grizzled man who was cooking his chapatis on a mini-grill at his stand. "He scratches his balls, then he scratches the food."

"You're joking," I said, rolling my eyes. But in no time at all, the vendor readjusted his lungi, reached his hand into its depths and made scratching motions, then turned over his chapatis with the same hand. I laughed, but I was glad I had only bought them from time to time to feed the forever hungry cows.

At five o'clock Sahil shows up on his motor scooter, and announces to me that Amar and Neela, wife number two, will be there. We go a long way, careening around the old road by the lake. As we take a curve, I wave to the stork who is waiting for his dinner to swim past, and I feel the shimmer of the water invading me, washing away the last calcified remains of the past. Sahil is an expert cyclist, maneuvering around the explosion of people, vehicles, animals that all seem to be moving in response to a crazy goddess's choreography.

We take the long way to the center of town, then down dim back streets. When we arrive at a dismal looking square saturated with the murky smell of dead sea creatures, I know we've reached the right spot. The fish are piled high at a half-dozen tables, wrapped in newspapers, their tails emerging coquettishly. Sahil walks to one stand, then the other, engaging in serious discussions with each of the vendors. I like watching him, the way he handles everything so effortlessly.

"What would you like?" he asks me, "a big fish or a small fish?" He makes it sound rakish the way he says it. The fishmonger smiles with pride as he opens the newspaper. Just for an instant we see a flash of silver skin before a swarm of flies moves in. He closes it quickly. "Very good one," Sahil says as he hands over the rupees. We stop at another market for a few vegetables, and with plastic bags containing our dinner slung over the handle bars, we make our way back through the streets to our rooftop dining room.

This is the best time of day here, when the sun goes down and I feel as if I'm floating in the warm darkness. Sahil is in the kitchen transforming the big sad fish carcass into something that smells delicious. I set the table for six, Western-style, with a fork on the left and a knife on the right, as I chat with the French couple. Yvette is a thin vivacious woman with an elegant cap of short dark hair. Her husband Robert is an unemployed journalist with a scraggly-looking pony tail and a quiet, self-possessed manner.

Cold glasses of wine in hand, we are having a jolly time. Our conversation has moved to the contrast between India's ideals and reality. "Here we are in the country that produced Gandhi and gave the world the idea of effective nonviolent protest," says Robert, who has spent great amounts of time in Canada and has almost no French accent. "And yet, look at all this violence between the Muslims and the Hindus, look at all the caste warfare that still goes on."

"Not to mention zee oppression of women," Yvette adds, sounding as if she were in a Paris café.

"The oppression of women seems to happen in every culture," I say. "Including our own."

"Oppressed. Yes, but this ees more than oppressed," says Yvette. "Abused. Just today, I read in the paper about dowry burnings. Abom-eenable. Are these people cras-see?"

"Impossible to understand," I say, nodding. "Maybe it started with the women that threw themselves into fires if their men were defeated. *Jauhar*, they called it. You can see their handprints on the walls here."

"There is some kind of cultural expression of death by fire," says Robert. "It wasn't so long ago that wives were expected to politely join their husbands on the funeral pyre."

"Oh, but even worse, I have read it is the mothers-in-law, conspiring with their sons, who do this dowry burning. They say it is suicide, then nothing can be proven. Then the men marry someone else for another dowry. It is nothing but grr-reeed, pure grrreeeed," says Yvette. Her throaty rrrs make her statements even more melodramatic.

I cannot even imagine the state of mind that would allow a mother-in-law to murder her own daughter-in-law. To set her on fire. It's such an unnerving topic of conversation that I excuse myself to help Sahil in the kitchen. He's whistling as he dashes bits of spices on the fish, whose eyes have turned a gelatinous white. I move up behind him and kiss him on the ear. "Let me help you."

"No, you enjoy the night," he says. "I cook this fish. You can see what cooking I learn from my mother." He is lucky he has such a mother, I think.

When I return to the guests I deliberately change the subject. "What do you think of French films these days?" I ask Yvette and Robert.

"It is sad, no?" says Yvette, "that the great French films, that marvelous period of filmmaking—do you know Truffaut and Godard—is finished."

"Long ago finished," says Robert, "ancient history. But we have many great films coming out of France. They are more . . . you know what you call action films. Relationship films. But this is what needs to be expressed. You cannot worship old gods."

"No, Robert dear, we need to worship ze old gods," Yvette says. "As they do in this country. You cannot have a new god every year, it is crazy making."

"But they do *not* worship the old gods here," Robert says. "What about the films of Satyajit Ray, the Bengali filmmaker who was so famous internationally a few decades ago. Who goes to see them now? No, they go to see the Bollywood films."

"They are the most stupid, vulgar escapist pieces of sheeet," Yvette says.

"Wait a minute, the new gods exist right alongside the old," I say, getting into the spirit of the conversation. I'm really enjoying this. I hadn't realized how hungry I was for Western culture talk. "I mean what I really love about this country is that there is a popular scene. It's not just borrowed from American pop culture. It's their own. It's not just a false preservation of something ancient or revered for the sake of the tourists."

"Tourists," says Robert. "There are no tourists. India is too big. They are swallowed up. We are swallowed up."

Sahil is standing in the doorway of the kitchen, spoon in hand, listening. "What do you think of Yvette's opinion of Bollywood films?" I ask to include him in the conversation. Immediately I wish I hadn't. For a moment, I feel part of the Western tribe, a supercilious observer and commentator. And I've embarrassed Yvette who is smiling stiffly.

But Sahil is eternally socially graceful. "I like these films," he says simply. "They are for making you happy. Is that not the most important thing?" Just then, I feel a surge of the happiness he's alluding to, or some similar indefinable emotion, that I am in this room with this sweet, amazing man. And that later he will come to my room and we will be lovers. Yet I feel sad too, because I know I can't keep him forever.

"He speaks true," says a voice from the doorway. Amar enters the room, serious and handsome in a freshly pressed shirt. He is followed by a woman in a blue and white punjabi outfit, a tunic worn over loose cotton pants fitted tightly around her slender ankles. She is probably the same age as Amar, mid-forties, and calmly beautiful. Threads of silver wind through her black hair, which is worn loose and chin length, and her big-eyed gaze is serene as an owl's. It is apparent from the way Amar guides her to a chair, as if he were touching her gently, but not touching her, his hands hovering over her shoulders as she sits, that they are deeply in love.

So this is wife number two. I envy them. They can go into a future together.

Sahil plays the host as smoothly as if he were acting a part he had seen in a film somewhere, introducing and cajoling and entertaining. "To everyone, this is Amar and his beautiful wife Neela, the best nurse in all of Udaipur, who helps me heal my broken foot," he says.

Neela smiles but shakes her head as if embarrassed at this acknowledgement. "Sahil is very kind. Of course there are many good nurses. But yes, I am very fortunate to have work that allows me to help people."

"And Amar," Sahil continues in his master of ceremonies voice, "is the finest guide in Rajasthan. And also a professor." I'm surprised. I wonder why Sahil had not mentioned it earlier. A taxi driver and a professor.

"A professor who no longer teaches, unfortunately," Amar says. He looks embarrassed.

"What a pity," says Yvette. "But what was your specialty?"

"The history of science," he says, his face lighting up. "The history of science in India. Especially the science of the heavens." He gestures to the strip of sky and stars visible from where we are sitting. "From the time I was a child, I looked at the stars and wondered. I think I come from a long line of those in India who did so. It's in my DNA, as the saying goes." He has our attention now, and continues. "If you watch the sky all night, you will see that the stars move west. But a great Indian astronomer proposed that it only appears that way because the earth rotates about its axis. Of course, we all know that now. The interesting thing is that this was about the time, you see, that the Greeks believed the heavens were constructed of crystal spheres." He shakes his head and chuckles. For a moment the sad look in this eyes disappears. "And some of the most astounding celestial observatories were constructed near here by one of the old maharajas. One of them is extant in Jaipur. Beautiful instruments."

"He can take you there," Sahil says. "As I say, he is the finest guide in all of Rajasthan."

"We would love that," Robert says. And Yvette agrees. "Tomorrow?"

"Yes, it will be my pleasure," says Amar in his perfect English and I know he is happy for the business. Everything is turning out perfectly.

I light candles and put them on the table, creating a little island of light. The conversation flows. Robert has brought up the films of Ray again.

"Yes, yes," says Amar, a frown of concentration appearing above his eyes. He turns to Neela. "Remember that film we saw, about the maharajah who spends all his money for one beautiful party."

"Yes, *The Music Room* it was called," Neela says. "We saw it together, remember, you and Sahil and me. We saw the video at my house." Sahil appears, carrying a huge platter he puts on the table. The fish is crusty and brown from tail to gills and gives off aromas of curry and lemon. A ridge of saffroned rice surrounds it and in one corner, a cup of yoghurt and cucumbers. We dig in. It's delicious. We ooh and aah in appreciation. Sahil seems pleased with our pleasure.

"I remember this film," he says. "This maharajah wants to create something fine in his hard life."

"To create something fine in the midst of the hardship of life," I repeat. "That is a wonderful thought. The mission of the artist."

"Or the mission of the chef, no?" says Robert.

"To the chef and the artist," I say, raising my glass. We all toast Sahil.

"You must enjoy," he says, sitting next to me.

Neela says, "This film you speak of, do you not remember, it is sad too, because he lost his son and only has memories in his life. Nothing else."

"Then we change to talk of happy things," says Sahil. "Just for tonight."

"Just for tonight," we echo. And so we eat Sahil's fish and rice and drink wine far into the night, talking of our favorite places we have visited. "You must go to Pushkar," says Robert. "It is a sacred town. A medieval town surrounded by the desert. And if you go, you must look up Baba. He lives in the hills in a house that looks as if it were built by Gaudi. You can visit him by camel."

"Yes, we go," says Sahil to me. "We can go to Pushkar if you like."

"I would like that." He has brought so much to my life, I think, so much laughter and joy and freedom. I am falling in love with him, and I have no idea what to do about it.

Suddenly, Amar and Neela get up to leave. "Thank you very much," she says to Sahil. "I am glad your foot is well. I must be at the hospital early tomorrow morning." She nods formally and shyly to each of us as Amar escorts her from the room.

Amar returns later, alone. The conversation is still going on. He sits back from the group, near Sahil, sighs, and runs his hand through his thick hair. He says something to Sahil in Hindi, and Sahil shrugs and replies. Later, after everyone has gone home and Sahil and I are drying the dishes, I ask him what Amar said.

"He says to me that he loves Neela, but he is worried about wife number one. He hears an American popular song. The song says many words to mean 'follow your heart.' He wants to know if I think that is a good thing to do."

"And what did you say?"

"I say songs are easy. Life is not so easy."

CHAPTER ELEVEN

A Hindi Lesson

The sun seems to take aim at this place alone, baking everything in its path. Weather that creatures with shells love. The turtle outside my window basks all day. I have no shell, so I've taken to wearing a scarf around my head for protection and carrying a big bottle of water wherever I go.

I'm spending more time with the French couple. We like to take boat rides on the lake in the morning, before it gets too hot. As planned, Amar took them to Jaipur and the celestial observatory, and to several other sights. They thought he was a charming and well-informed guide. This morning, they tell me, they were asked to go down to the police station and questioned about their time with Amar. They're not sure what it's about, and the police wouldn't tell them.

I ask Sahil and he says he hasn't seen Amar for a couple of days. "Peculiar," I say, "but then everything here is."

At the internet café, which is slightly cooler than the streets, I order a chai, buy an hour at one of the computers, and anticipate the threads of words that connect me to the world beyond this city, to Jason, whom I've heard nothing from, and to Cathy. When I log on, finally, something from Jason pops up and I click on it.

Dear Elena (aka Saraswati),

I emailed you earlier, but only in my mind. I have been thinking about you though, praying (well, meditating) for you. Remember (I know I sound like a guru, maybe I'm turning into one, scary) that you don't know who your teachers will be. Maybe an old woman in rags, or a child, or a fat businessman, you never know. In any case, I am finding I'm learning as much from the people that come here as from my teacher.

My lover has gone back to New Zealand. It wasn't meant to be. That is it was *meant to be but not forever and ever. I'll be leaving here soon. If you still want to try to hook up in Kathmandu, let me know. I'll be heading that way eventually, as you know I have the same open-dated return ticket as you do.*

Namaste,

Jason

I'm not sure how to reply. I tell him about Sahil, and the magic I'm finding in Rajasthan, and that I don't want it to end even though it felt a bit crazy in the beginning. That I will stay in touch now that I have his email but to go ahead with his plans and not wait for me. I open Cathy's email, subject line *Closing In.*

Yo Elena,

So I'm zeroing in on Grandpa. I found him fast mainly because Aussie boyfriend (he's trying to push pills from his

company to the docs here) is fairly well connected in the medi-
cal scene here. Turns out Grandpa retired a while back and
lives in a big walled estate, banyan trees in the garden, man-
sion, the whole nine yards. I send a note, "I'm your
granddaughter, don't you want to meet me?" He doesn't. No
surprise there. But I haven't given up. Plan B is to hound him.
Tough as I am (or pretend to be), that image of Grandma Rose
walking into the river because of grief just tears me up. I just
want to know exactly what happened.

But how's life for you? How's it going with your romantic
illusion? Just don't get too attached to it. You know I actually
miss you, So write,
    Cathy

I'm impressed. For all her what-the-hell persona, she is in-
trepid in her mission to get to the bottom of her family tragedy.
If anybody can do it, she can. After all, she has a set of fine-
tuned investigative and confrontational skills—including garbage sifting.

I hit the reply button, tell her I can't wait for the next install-
ment, then a little about my life here with Sahil, our recent
dinner party. It feels so undramatic in a way, like I'm writing
about a life I've lived for a long time that I've settled into. I
don't bother to tell her I've made no progress at all in finding
the master painter because that is now a quest that is rapidly
fading into the background.

The French couple told me that they are taking Hindi lessons, and that their efforts really added another layer to their
experience. Except for occasional words and phrases, I speak
mostly English with Sahil. They give me her card. "Learn Hindi

Quickly," it proclaims. And underneath "For the business and pleasure traveler."

There is a telephone number, which I have the aunties dial for me. "Come this afternoon," a woman who introduces herself as Mrs. Singh tells me in a voice with the high tones of educated Indian English, and gives me directions. I find a handsome white house tucked away on a street not far away, with the same business card taped to the door over a knocker in the shape of Ganesh, the elephant god. A tiny woman in her sixties, dressed in an immaculate red sari and gold jewelry, greets me. She escorts me into a daintily furnished parlor, then serves tea in English china cups.

I tell her I want to learn Hindi because I love the way it flows in the mouth, so many syllables, so quickly, as if your mouth was full of bubbles. She laughs at this.

"Of all the languages," she says to me, "Hindi is one of the oldest and the most appealing."

After introductions we begin with a few words and phrases. She suggests learning phrases that will be useful in the shops and restaurants. *This is very nice, but the price is too high. I would like to know where the lady's room is. My name is Elena.*

I agree. And we practice them, although my tongue has a difficult time. "I'd like to learn some beautiful words too," I say. "Not just practical ones."

"*Sundara,*" she says. "This is the word for 'beautiful.'" I remember that word from the phrase Sahil taught me. *Mera sundara bharata.*

"*Sundara,*" I say.

"*Amara prema.* Eternal love."

Suddenly, there is a commotion in the next room, pots and pans clamoring and a loud male voice. "Damn. Where is that bloody servant when we need her?"

Mrs. Singh's expression changes to a roll of her eyes. "My son Wally," she whispers. "He is very spoiled. He needs a wife to look after him."

The rest of lesson is to the accompaniment of the son's clattering and cursing.

Sahil wants me to see his new shop and new paintings. We decide to walk to it in the cool of the evening. We pass a woman with bobbed hair wearing a punjabi. She reminds me of Neela. "Neela is lovely," I say. I haven't seen either her or Amar since our dinner party. I can't seem to get them out of my mind. "So what about wife number one?" I ask.

"I do not like this woman. She is always angry."

"But to be fair Sahil, she must be hurt that he has another woman. That would make any woman angry."

"She is like Kali this wife. Kali is Hindu goddess who bites off the heads of men."

"OK, I thought she just stomped them to death. And maybe sucked their blood."

Sahil ignores my attempt at humor. "My friend Amar is a professor, as you know, but does not make so much money. She makes him drive a taxi instead."

"So taxi drivers make more money than professors?"

"Yes, of course. Because many tourists give very good tips. But this is not work he wants to do. This makes him sad. You see how he always has sad eyes." We cross the arched stone bridge over the estuary that connects the two lakes. Birds are diving for their last meal of the day.

"Yes, I do see his sad eyes. Does he have children—I mean with wife number one?"

"Yes, some children. But he does not love her."

"If he really loves Neela, what if he asked wife number one for a divorce?"

"You do not understand India."

I sigh. We step off the road to make way for a family in a donkey drawn cart overtaking us.

"In America, we like to solve problems. Not just accept the fates."

"That is good. I am also this way. But sometimes it is too big, this problem."

We take a turn up a steep street of shops. Half a block up we come to an open door. Over it hangs a hand-painted sign that says in English, French, and Hindi, *Art for all Languages*.

"Ah, welcome to the studio of Sahil the Artist." He extends his hand to me in a flourish and we walk into a big room that smells of hand-rolled cigarettes and turpentine. Painting materials fill the shelves and small easels and cloths are set up on the floor. Three of Sahil's friends, including Vijay, are sitting around on low stools, smoking, flicking their ashes onto the concrete floor. Sahil shakes his head and speaks to them sharply. They respond by getting up and leaving, looking over their shoulders at me as they go out the door.

"They help me in my new business," Sahil tells me. He explains that they are supposed to keep the shop clean, deliver orders for the paintings to his clients, fix up the shop so he can open it to tourists. But they are lazy.

He shows me some of the paraphernalia he has acquired. Shelves of brushes with very fine tips that he tells me are made from the hair of squirrels. Bottles of colors and special jars that contain silver and gold powder for finishing touches. Stacks of eggshell colored parchment paper. "I save for many years to get this shop," he says.

"Here I want to show you my latest painting." He pulls it out from a shelf. It's a miniature of a maharajah on an elephant with a jungle background. I see that it's a copy of the picture from an open book on the same shelf. "Very nice," I say. It is well executed, but I'm a little disappointed that he simply copies pictures.

"I am happy you like my painting," he tells me the next day as we are walking home from an Indian classical concert, the sarod, flute, and tabla still playing hypnotic ragas in my mind. We pass three women on a ladder, painting their house a vivid blue. "Hot," I say, fanning my face, wishing I knew the Hindi word for hot. They beam smiles at us nevertheless.

"Why don't you paint the real people of Udaipur?" I ask him. "Like those women on the ladder. They're beautiful."

"Tourists only want copies of old pictures. This is what I do."

"But if we only copy what is from the past, then nothing new would ever be invented."

He touches his forehead with his fingers as if he is considering this. "It takes a long time to be a good painter. To have your own style. Like the master painter."

"It takes a long time to be good at anything. But you're talented. You know you are."

"I want to be a success. Now I still must make paintings for other shops. But very soon I make paintings only for my shop." He keeps his head down so I can't see his expression.

"It's good you have ambition." I want to encourage him. "It's the same in America. If you're an artist often you must choose between success or money and what we want to express from our souls." Am I being a schoolteacher again? Yes, I am.

He's silent until we reach my room. Outside my window, the lake is shimmering in the afternoon heat. The turtle is sunning on the rock. "Do you see?" he says. "The rock is sometimes home to the turtle and sometimes the stork. I do not like to choose one or the other: money or art as you say. I believe I can do many things."

Now it's my turn to think about what he is saying. He pulls me to him and kisses me. "You too can do many things. You are Saraswati and now you are Parvati."

Saraswati is of the air, the realm of ideas and their manifestation. Parvati, I remember, is the love goddess. She is the goddess of the body and its sensual expression. I am enjoying getting to know my new goddess. For years, I forgot about my body. It was simply a vehicle to take me from point A to point B. Now, it's a whole new universe, with planets, stars, and comets.

CHAPTER TWELVE

A Visit to Baba

The train station is pulsing with life, and Sahil is the liveliest of all. As always, he seems to know everyone, the old men with their walking sticks, matronly women with their tins of food, even the ever-present beggars. And if he doesn't know them he still smiles and says a few words.

Enchanted by the French couple's description, I am looking forward to a four or five day trip to Pushkar. So is Sahil. Perhaps the master painter will be there, according to some information he has. Whenever I think of the painting—the shrouded, peaceful figure by the fire, the lion at its feet—I long for the peace and transcendence I felt when it was so briefly in my possession. Is this master painter truly out there somewhere? I'm not sure, but the chimera is enough to make me keep reaching.

I sit on my suitcase and watch Sahil, feeling a bit self-conscious in my sari of midnight blue silk that one of the aunties lent me for this special outing. Pushkar is a sacred city, and I want to wear this in its honor, in spite of the fact that I'm traveling in sin with my lover. The folds are tucked at my waist, curtain-like. I have to move carefully so it won't come undone.

"You look very beautiful in this sari," Sahil tells me as he returns with the tickets.

"Thank you. Somehow I feel only Indian women can wear these and look beautiful." And yet, every day I feel as if I am a bit more a part of this culture. Something has caught his attention though, and he's not looking at me anymore but out toward the street where the tuk-tuks and their drivers wait and hope for customers.

"I see my friend Amar," Sahil says. "Our friend."

I look across the street and there he is, pacing back and forth in front of his taxi, his head bowed. "He looks even sadder today than usual."

"Yes, I go to say hello. For one minute."

I watch them as they talk. Sahil reaches out and puts his arm around Amar's shoulders. I move a little closer, rolling my suitcase behind me, just within earshot but not too close. I don't want to intrude. Amar keeps lifting his fist to his face as if he is wiping tears away. His head is hanging, his eyes are on the ground. Sahil is speaking to him in Hindi, in a hushed, soothing voice.

After a few minutes, Sahil leaves Amar and walks over to me. "I am sorry. I cannot go with you." His voice is strained, almost a whisper.

"What's wrong?" I ask.

"I must stay with my friend." He closes his eyes for a long time then opens them. I can see the pain there. I wait for him to say something. I know it won't be good. He walks me back to the train platform. The train has started up, breathing smoke.

Sahil takes a deep breath and sighs. "Amar . . . ." He pauses. "Amar is a guide for the French people. The next day after our fish dinner, he takes them to Jaipur for two days. He comes back to his wife. Neela."

"Yes, Neela."

He pauses, and closes his eyes again. He wipes his mouth with his arm, and says something I can't hear because his hand is covering his mouth.

"What did you say?" I ask him.

"She is suicide."

"Suicide. Oh no. Oh no. What happened?"

"Her sari catches on fire with cooking oil. She is gone. She is dead."

Gone. Dead. It makes no sense. Why would she want to kill herself? She was a professional woman. She had a man who loved her. The shock spreads through my veins like dry ice, hot and cold at the same time. "How is this possible?"

"She is alone," Sahil says. "No one knows why. No one knows how."

"That must have been what the police were asking Yvette about, what time Amar was with them."

"Yes. Amar was with them in another city. Nurse Neela is alone. The neighbor of Neela finds her."

And suddenly I know what happened. I remember the conversation Sahil told me he had with Amar. How Amar had asked if he should follow his heart. Something he heard in a song. And Sahil had said, "Songs are easy, life is not so easy." Maybe he succumbed to the stirrings of his heart and told his first wife he was going to live with Neela. In any case, she found out about her rival. Neela did not kill herself.

"Sahil. You can't really think it was suicide."

"We do not know. Neela is alone. Maybe it is an accident."

"You know what happened. You know it wasn't suicide at all, Sahil. And not an accident either. It was murder. His first wife. Who in God's name could do that to another human being? He should have her arrested."

"No. He cannot do that. He has children with this woman."

"The police then. Will they do something?"

"They do nothing. They cannot prove. They say accident. Or suicide."

"Does Amar believe this?"

"He does not say what he believes. Because if they take the mother away from his children and put her in jail they have no mother."

"You can't just let a woman's murder . . . not only a woman, but a woman you know. A friend. You can't just let it go."

"Maybe Neela is sad. Maybe she kills herself."

"That's ridiculous and you know it." My voice is rising in pitch. I know I sound angry, but I can't help it. "I'm not going. I will stay. I will at least try to do something."

Sahil turns away from me and stares at the ground. Then he looks up at me. "I stay with Amar. You can do nothing. You only make more trouble for Amar."

"Why do you say that? I want to help."

"You help by going to Pushkar. This is a holy city. Maybe pray for Amar." Sahil takes a ragged breath and puts his face in his hands. His shoulders start to shake.

I want to say something or do something that will change things, reverse the chain of events, reverse time so it never happened. I reach out to Sahil to put my arms around him, to put my head on his shoulder. He steps back. I have forgotten for a moment that immutable law of India. Men and women don't touch each other in public, ever, for any reason. So we're stuck in this moment standing here, frozen, not able to comfort each other. I bow my head and notice how shiny his new shoes are, how much trouble he took to look good for this trip. I notice his crocodile-pattern embossed belt holding up his perfectly pressed black slacks. The train whistles behind us. "How can I go, Sahil?"

He shakes his head as if he could shake out the grief, then lights a cigarette. "In one week time is a beautiful festival of Udaipur. The festival of Shiva and Parvati. Elephants ride in the middle of the lake. Dancing and singing. Come back for this. I wait for you." Then he turns away and heads toward Amar.

In a daze, I board the train and take a seat near the back that looks out the window. Through the dust-streaks, I can see the two of them, Amar and Sahil, pacing, smoking, Sahil's arm around his friend. Will Sahil be able to comfort him? Will anyone, ever, be able to comfort him?

A small old woman wrapped in black is sitting next to me. All night, we rumble across the desert, a deep violet stretch of wasteland under the moon, gradually turning into a black nothingness.

All night, I see her life before me. Neela, a modern woman of India, her thick bobbed hair falls forward over her face, she brushes it back as she bends over a patient. Neela, the woman with a career, no children, who goes home to a small apartment, prepares dinner, and waits for the man she loves but must share. There is no question of his leaving his first family. And yet, maybe she was ambitious, maybe she wanted him all to herself, maybe she was pressuring him for something more. She usually wears loose pants and an overblouse, but that night she is wearing an orange sari; when he comes he will unfurl it. There is a knock at the door, but it is not Amar. It is his other wife, venal, thick-skinned and corpulent, her eyes narrowed, outraged because she is losing her grip on her husband. She would never confront him. That is not the way it is done. The oppressed turn on each other. She and her accomplice—her sister or her mother or her brother—have discussed this other woman. They feel righteous. She is a harlot, she must be destroyed. They take a can of cooking oil and go to her house; the sister and the mother hold her, the wife pours it, a match, and whoosh, she's in flames.

I imagine her as the flames engulf her, unfurling her sari as fast as it burns, spinning as she casts it off, like a dancer, and finally, defiantly, emerging naked, beautiful, and unharmed into the arms of her lover. I imagine that because I can't imagine what really happened. I want to cry but I can't, I'm numb, in a landscape of nothingness that goes on and on. The woman next to me must sense my emptiness. She reaches out and pats my arm.

When the dawn comes, I don't know if I've slept. The sky is filling up with light, tissues of rose and blue, and the light reveals what has always been here. This landscape has always existed in my imagination. A city rises up from the desert, a fortress of pale pink, a place where it never rains, where the wells are so deep that if you drop a coin you can't hear its splash.

Yet when I walk the streets, here is the very real mix of beauty and squalor that is everywhere in this country. I look up and see exquisitely carved windows that cast tattoos of shadow on the faces of women behind them. I look down and I see children with fly infested eyes and the thin girls who hold them with one hand while holding the other hand out to beg.

After I deposit my things in a hotel, I suddenly feel very uncomfortable in my sari. I don't want to be in a sari, it's too beautiful, too feminine. I don't want to be feminine at all when I think about it. In fact, I don't want to have a body at all. Especially the body of a woman. It all leads to love and desire that ends with pain and suffering. Look at Neela. Look at so many women all over the world under the yoke of their husbands, or their fathers, or bought or sold, or sitting in lonely rooms longing for someone who never comes, or contorting their bodies into ridiculous outfits to get the attention of a man. Even worse, it leads to women like wife number one, caught up in a furnace of jealousy, rage, evil. Turning into Kalis. I don't want any of it. I want to rid myself of all of it. I don't want to love Sahil either. It's all a ridiculous trap.

I want to rip off this sari, throw it out the window. But it belongs to the aunties. It's so hot and I can move only very slowly. I want to be invisible, I think, as I pull off the heavy silk from my shoulder, undo the tight blouse, unwrap the folds of the skirt. I want to be a spirit without a body. I want calm, I want peace.

I carefully fold the sari into a neat package and put it back in my suitcase. I put on loose pants and a long-sleeved T-shirt and a wide brimmed hat, buy a bottle of water in the lobby, and wander out into the baking afternoon. The world, amazingly, is still going on in its sacred circus way, as if nothing ever happened. People in pale pink and orange and scarlet are weaving around each other in the streets, murmuring presumably holy things and fingering their sandalwood beads. Because this is a holy town there is no meat and no alcohol. Nuts and vegetables are roasting on open coals. Humped neck cows are meditating. Even the most ragged children are chasing each other and laughing. And here I am in the midst of all this, walking and breathing even though I seem to have no feeling in my body.

Sahil said the master painter might be here. I don't really believe it, but to occupy myself I go from shop to shop to make inquiries. I don't even know his name, or what he looks like. "He makes beautiful paintings," I say, and try to describe my vision. I feel as if I am shouting and yet no one hears me. Shopkeepers squint and frown and finally shake their heads. If Sahil were here, he would distract me with a joke or a story, even in the midst of tragedy, but I don't feel lonely for him, just strangely hollow.

The French couple talked about Baba, the holy man who lives on a hillside near here. What did they say about him? It doesn't matter. Looking for him will allow me to keep moving, to keep breathing. I have a plan. I will ride to the desert on a camel and search for him.

Camels seem to be as ordinary here as cars in America. They wander through the streets or stand idly by the roadside, looking down at me disdainfully through thick long lashes, like haughty grand dames, although definitely in need of a bit of perfume. The hawkers vie for my business once they see I am interested, each saying "very nice, very gentle" about their beast. I choose the smallest. "Girl camel," her owner says. A portly man with a jovial manner, he pats the camel's nose and invites me to do the same. As I do she curls her lip and shows me her yellow teeth. I'm not sure if she's smiling or sneering.

"Do you know the holy man Baba?" I ask him. He nods solemnly. "Can you take me to see him?" He nods again. Then, in response to a gesture of his stick, the camel kneels, and the guide helps me on the saddle. In one awkward motion I'm in the air. It's alarming at first, to be so far off the ground. But I'm too empty to feel my usual fear of heights, or speed, or anything the least risky. The guide holds on to a tether and accompanies me on another camel. Soon we're back out through the city gates and strolling along a flat plain. There is an elegance to my camel's step, a graceful rolling movement that comforts me. The hollowness inside becomes a bubble that expands and contracts, expands and contracts.

As we move farther away from town, the huts outside the city walls disappear, and the leafless shrubs became scarcer until there is nothing but hard sand that stretches to a horizon of bronze hills. On one of these, halfway up, a glimmer of white beckons. "Baba house," my guide says, and begins to hum the same note over and over again.

Soon we come to a path of steps carved into the hill itself. Under a lone tree at its base, with a command from the guide, my camel falls to her knees like it was time for prayer. Her hindquarters follow. Miraculously, I'm able to slide off, the rubbery feeling in my legs distracting me from the hollow space that now seems stuck between my heart and my stomach. We leave our camels lounging in the shade to begin the long climb.

After what seems like a thousand steps, the glimmer of white becomes a strange dwelling with soft curving lines. It looks as if it's an outgrowth of the hill itself, shaped like a gourd, with rounded openings for doors. A woman emerges as we approach, gray hair streaming, a radiant smile that shows her missing teeth. She makes me feel welcome, as if she had been waiting for me.

She gestures to us to remove our shoes, to follow her inside, to a tiled room, and to sit on the floor. The room is beautiful, the floor as polished as a counter. Each tile is hand painted with a picture of a Hindu deity in vibrant colors: Ganesh, the elephant god, Shiva in his dancing pose, Krishna with his flute, Saraswati with her swan, and so many others I don't know the names of. Flower offerings are strewn before a statue of Vishnu in the corner. The rooms are shaped around openings that look out onto the desert and to the bright sky, so close here, so seamless. The woman leaves the room and in a few minutes returns with an old, old man, bent over, toothless and smiling.

My guide speaks. "This Baba," he says. "No English. This lady not wife. Helper. No English too. Baba is teacher. Guru." If he is a guru, he is definitely of the elfin variety. He is tiny. His eyes twinkle. He joins us on the floor, yoga style. The lovely old woman disappears and returns with golden pyramids of rice heaped on banana leaves. We eat with our fingers while we smile at each other. I am glad we don't have to talk. I have nothing to say. I feel the throb of the heat, the beauty of the room, the tang of saffron in my mouth, and yet I feel them as if I were a floating observer of a depressed American woman looking for redemption by sitting at the feet of a comical looking old man.

After our meal, we go outside to the terrace that overlooks the desert. Baba begins to chant *ram ram ram ram ram*. Soon the woman and my guide follow. There is something absurd and yet also soothing in the sound. After a while I join in. *Ram ram ram ram ram ram ram* we sing until our voices merge with the desert and the sky and the hawks circling overhead. In the face of such a meaningless heartbreaking world, to sit in a simple dwelling with an old man and sing *ram ram ram ram* seems to make as much sense as anything else.

We chant for a long time. Ever so slowly, some kind of feeling returns to my body, just the feeling of my breath going through me, and my mouth full of sound, which must mean I am alive in the universe now along with the hawk who is still circling looking for his food, and maybe there is no meaning beyond that. Is that giving up, or accepting?

Much later, after drifting off to a dreamless sleep in my hotel bed, I wake up to a different kind of chanting. A wheezing, agonized sound. I get up, wrap a shawl around my shoulders and go out to investigate. There, with shaggy coats that are almost white under the moonlight, are a pair of donkeys, braying desperately at the moon or each other. I wonder if it is their own kind of *ram ram ram.*

I stay in the holy city of Pushkar for four days, going to see Baba on the same little camel every day. She has no name, but I call her Aunty, for no reason except I miss the aunties in Udaipur. She lifts her long eyelashes when she sees me as if she's flirting with me. I pat her nose, she smiles at me with her yellow teeth and gives me a whiff of her badly-in-need-of-mouthwash breath, and patiently takes me where I want to go. The guide has started to play his wooden flute, a haunting melody that Aunty and I sway to on the hour-long trek to Baba's and back. The camel driver tells me he is happy for my business because his son and daughter now can have school shoes. At least I am contributing in some way.

Ram is the sound used to chant to Rama, I have learned, a blue god like Krishna, who went into exile in the forest with his wife Sita. But it makes no difference. For me, it is just the sound and the clear air and the simplicity of this ritual. I sing *ram ram ram* for Amar and Neela and Sahil and my parents in their snow-covered house and for the elegant hawk and smelly camels and braying donkeys and, finally, just for being alive in this moment. Gradually, I feel my own breath begin to flow more easily. Slowly, I come back into my body. And suddenly, I miss Sahil.

The night I leave I have an early dinner alone, with a book on Hindu deities propped in front of me, at the restaurant in the old fortress walls. There is a man at a table near me who interrupts my reading to tell me he has engraved the entire Mahabharata, the ancient epic Sanskrit poem, on a grain of rice. I am getting used to bizarre statements, and yet I frown with the effort of even trying to imagine this one. What is his hustle? He doesn't look like a hustler. He is a middle-aged, middle-class looking man with a pleasant face, dressed in a business suit. "You are leaving here soon," he says.

"Yes, that's true." Of course he could say that to anyone here in this city of pilgrims and tourists and it would be true.

"I see you are returning to the place you have traveled before. This may not be wise."

I shake my head and turn back to my book.

"Remember one thing when you go back," he says. "Remember your center."

He nods at me and goes back to his meal. Everything is so odd, so strange.

CHAPTER THIRTEEN

The Shadow

I travel all night on the train again, back to Udaipur. Fine dust from the cracked window by my seat is blowing in. I wrap my shawl around my face. I wonder if I'm doing the right thing by going back. Sahil should find someone his own age, from his own culture, and I'm keeping him from that. And then Neela. What about Neela, will her so-called suicide still be shrugged off? It's all turning dark and disturbing. And yet in the end, I'm left with the image of Sahil's eyes, his smile, and my longing. I know if my journey is to make any sense at all, I must see him again.

When I arrive early in the morning back at the hotel, the old aunties smile and nod. I hand them the neatly folded sari and thank them. I wonder what they would think of Neela's death, but I don't know how to approach such a subject.

The lively French couple is gone, the hotel is very quiet. My room is the same, the aquamarine walls, the white bed, the chair by the window, the half-built bird's nest on the book shelf. But it's darker because the shutters are closed. The shutters are closed. *The birds haven't been able to reach their nest. Oh no.* I rush to the shutters and ply them open, letting in a flood of

light. I look for them but can see nothing but the hot pale sky
and expanse of still water. Did those poor doves panic when
they saw the path to their nest cut off? Would they have been
able to build a new nest in time to lay their eggs? Did they make
it?

Later I think about how to contact Sahil. Come back for the
festival he said. That's three days from now. I don't want to
show up unannounced at his studio. I find the boy who works
at the hotel, give him a tip and a message to deliver to Sahil,
telling him I'm back. I wait. The day passes. I ask the boy if
there is a reply. He shrugs his shoulders and says nothing. I
wonder if he has even delivered the message.

Time seems to pass in a series of interminable hours, each
one a vast space. I walk the city streets. I look for Amar, but he
is nowhere to be seen either. I visit the palaces and the museums
and the shops. I talk to the aunties in the garden. I walk near the
lake, watching the turtle and the stork trade places on the rock.
After a day of basking in the sun, the turtle slides into the murky
water, and seconds later the stork flies in on his heavy wings to
perch and fish. It's their *dharma,* their work, their routine.
Every day the same.

That's what I need. Routine. Work. Focus. I get out my
notebook and call on Saraswati. She floats by but I can't quiet
my mind enough to welcome her to her satisfaction. I am the
goddess of the arts, she murmurs to me, but I am also the goddess of the river. To flow, I need calm, I need a peaceful place.
She retreats before I've even opened my notebook.

It's now two days before the festival. Where can he possibly
be? I am tired of waiting. I decide to go to Sahil's studio myself.

His friends are there—Manu, the handsome one, Vijay, the quiet one, and several others, painting, smoking, laughing. They are friendly enough when they see me. Sahil and I have had lunch with Manu several times. His English is not bad. Manu has a fiancé in Italy, and will soon leave to join her, so maybe he will be most sympathetic. I come to the point. "Where is Sahil?"

At first he shrugs and shakes his head. But I keep asking the same question.

"He is gone back to his village," he says finally.

"Which village?" I ask. Again he shrugs. It's a futile question. Every province has hundreds, maybe thousands of villages scattered in the rural country side. People don't know each others' villages any more than we know the names of streets in our own neighborhoods more than a few blocks away.

"He must go because his mother is sick," Manu offers.

"But his mother lives here, in Udaipur."

There is a pause. "Not his mother, his grandmother mother. His mother in Udaipur tells him he must go."

"Really?" I raise my eyebrows. Why do I feel like he is being evasive? "When will he be back?"

"Maybe today. Maybe one week."

They all bob their heads and talk to each other in Hindi, gesturing and smirking. They glance at me from time to time. Suddenly, I feel very uncomfortable. I am their friend's girlfriend. I am also maybe a loose American woman in their minds. I can see it in their eyes the way they look at me. One of the boys has a pack of Marlboros. He flicks one out and offers it to me. "No thank you," I say in a deliberately arch tone.

Another asks, "Do you want to go on motorcycle ride with me?"

I cringe inside and turn to go. "When Sahil comes back, please tell him I am waiting for him."

Later, near the bus station, I see Amar, pacing and smoking in front of his taxi, a lost soul. I approach him without knowing what I will say, knowing that nothing I can say will give the slightest comfort. I reach my hand out to him, and then remembering the prohibition on touching, retract it. "I am so sorry," I say. And then say it again. I can think of nothing else to say. A dozen questions go through my mind. Did he tell the police the entire story? Did the police do anything? I remember how the bully who had run over Sahil's foot bought off the cop with rupees. Maybe Amar's wife did the same. But I can't ask any of these things. I am out of my depth.

Instead, I ask him about Sahil. No, he has not seen him for days. He believes he may have gone to his family's village.

"Well, if you see him tell him I'm back." He looks at me as if he hardly knows who I am, lowers his head and goes back to pacing and smoking.

The city is oddly calm this evening, as if not only Sahil, but everyone has left. I walk and walk, without purpose, near the old part of the city, where the wall of buildings opens occasionally to the ghats that lead down into the water. I almost expect to see Sahil around every corner, his smile flashing like the sun on water, making me laugh at some outlandish tale. In front of a closed shop, I see a group of chuckling people gathered around a man with dark hair. I catch my breath. Sahil. But the crowd parts and I see I was mistaken.

A murky smell wafts up from the lake, the smell of life and death that I am becoming accustomed to. A few people sit on the stone steps of the ghat by the lake, some with food, enjoying an after-dark picnic in the cool of the night. As I slow my steps to look at the scene, a tall figure steps out of the shadows and approaches me. The light is so dim I can't see him well, but I am quite sure I haven't met him before.

He says something that sounds like "I have something to tell you." I ignore him and keep walking. He keeps pace just behind me, his heels clicking sharply on the stones.

"Please stop, madam, I want to talk to you."

I can feel the tension thrum through me, but I am determined this creep is not going to intimidate me. Near a streetlight I turn around and glare at him. He looks gaunt and shabby in the yellow light. "Who are you?" I ask him. "I don't know you. Leave me alone."

"You are friend of that Moslem boy."

It is odd hearing Sahil described in those words. He is Muslim, at least his father is, even though he doesn't think of himself in those terms. Suddenly I'm aware that here is a whole other world of categorization, of intricacy and hierarchy in social relationships that I've been clueless about.

"What about it?" I shake my head in incredulity.

"Are you looking for him?"

He seems to know about me and Sahil. A chill creeps into my throat and moves up to fill my head. "No, I am not looking for him." I have to make an effort to get the words out. "In any case he is out of town. In his village." Why am I even responding to this weird guy, except maybe he has more information on Sahil's whereabouts.

"In his village. Huh. Do his friends tell you this?" My eyes are adjusting to the weak light and I can see that he has a large Adam's apple that moves up and down when he talks.

"Who are you?" My mouth feels full of dust.

"Do you not remember me? I meet you in town with your friend. By the clock by the railroad station."

"Just go away." I turn my back on him and move into my power walk, trying to look as if I have a definite purpose and know exactly where I am going. But he stays at my side, crowding me.

"I want to tell you something. Because you are good woman. I want to help you."

"Well, what is it?" I sigh as if he is annoying me instead of unnerving me, and slow down to look at him more carefully, trying to remember if I have seen that dusky angular face, the features at odds with each other, the close set intense eyes. Was he one of the people that Sahil talked to on our walks? But then Sahil talks to everyone.

"This Sahil. He is a bad boy. He has many women. He is not in his village. He is with this other woman. I am telling you the truth."

I stop in my tracks. We are at the entrance to the tunnel passageway. A large car drives by, lights on, revealing the colors in the black and white night world, the soot on the buildings, this guy's dirty purple jacket, his black greasy hair.

"I do not believe you. Go away."

A tuk-tuk drives past, and I flag it down and get in without another word. My veins are thrumming with adrenaline and confusion. I don't believe him of course. But what if it's true? What if everything is just a pose and Sahil is really just a hustler, and I am just one of a long stream of women. This "informer," this sleazy man who stepped out from the shadows is obviously a nefarious character. But why would he lie? And if he were telling the truth what would Sahil's motivation be for pretending he cared about me? For sex? To hang out with a

Western woman to parade in front of his friends? For the possibility of going to America even though he denies that's what
he wants? For all of the above?

It's my own fault. What did I expect getting involved with
a guy whose culture I obviously know nothing about? What
was I thinking? Yet it all seems as if I had no choice, that one
event led to another and another like a string of breadcrumbs.
Does the pain I'm feeling mean I'm in love with him? My
breath comes in ragged gulps all the way home.

CHAPTER FOURTEEN

A Swollen Nose

It's the day before the festival and still no Sahil. On my way to the internet café, I pass that cliché featured on all the travelogues on India: a snake charmer. I've seen him before and ignored him, but now I pause. Indeed, in response to a few notes of a flute, the poor trapped creature emerges from a basket and flares and hisses. He has no fangs. The snake wallah motions for me to give him rupees and I do, before I move on. All anybody cares about is give me, give me, I think. Everything in this country is an elaborate façade, a deception, a toothless snake in the basket performing for anyone who is stupid enough to be seduced.

The usual cast of characters are at the café, but today instead of exotic and interesting, they look just grungy. Who *are* these people who wander around the world and whose only purpose seems to be living as cheaply as possible, to the end of avoiding any responsibility? Most of them are young, but some are older than me, some have traveled for decades, homeless, wandering the earth like modern day Ishmaels. That's what happens when the journey becomes the destination. Save me from that fate.

I buy a chai and a sweet. I'm amazed I can eat anything. In the last couple of days, I've hardly touched food. The cinnamon sweet taste of chai calms me a bit, but I'm too restless to sit still in the café. I check my email. Nothing.

Time with a capital T takes up residence in front of me, a big fat elephant that won't budge. The hours to the festival seem unending. I leave the café and walk and walk. Eventually I pass the Hindi teacher's house with its little Ganesh knocker. Ah, something to do to pull me out of my morbid self-pity. I don't have an appointment, but maybe she's free. Maybe she would even welcome the extra rupees. She answers my knock almost immediately.

"Oh yes, do come in," Mrs. Singh says. "I have no more students until this evening." We sit side by side on her purple velvet Victorian couch as we practice useful phrases for travelers. I want to have some phrases for the aunties, to tell them I appreciate their care.

"Thank you," she says is *Shukriya.*

Shukriya, I repeat.

Mrs. Singh tries more complex phrases, but I am having a hard time concentrating. My mind drifts back to Sahil, to the Shadow's ominous warnings, to my confusion and doubts. And anger. Yes, anger. I imagine how I will confront Sahil when he comes back. If he comes back. "Can you teach me to say . . . ." I want to ask my teacher if she can teach me to say "fuck off" in Hindi but I know that would give sweet Mrs. Singh great offense. I think for a moment. "Can you teach me to say 'You are a rat,' in Hindi?"

She raises her eyebrows in shock. "You must not say this to anyone," she whispers. "This is the worst insult to call a person any kind of animal. Because he or she does not want to have that past life or future life."

I am not sure Sahil believes in reincarnation, but I let it pass. "What would be an appropriate insult then?" I ask her.

"Oh my, well let's see. *Tum pagal ho.* I will suggest that. It means something similar to *You are crazy.* Whom do you want to insult?" She tilts her head and looks at me curiously.

"Oh, no one really. It's for . . . a story I'm writing." I practice saying the phrase several times.

"Come, my dear," she says, "let us move on to a higher form of language."

Just then, I hear footsteps and clattering in another room. "My son is a noisy man," says Mrs. Singh, shaking her head. "He is visiting again from Delhi on his vacation. What to do?" The door opens and the son enters, tall, broad-shouldered, good-looking, light brown hair, probably near my age. He picks up a newspaper from a table, mumbles something to his mother and looks me over, then takes the newspaper and leaves the room.

"I am sorry for his rudeness," Mrs. Singh says. "We gave him a good education. He has a very good job in Delhi as a computer specialist. We have introduced him to several quite eligible young women from good families." She shakes her head. "And with excellent dowries too, if I may say so. But as I said, he refuses to take an interest. And that is why I must work so hard." She sighs then gives me a little sheepish smile and pats my hand. "Not that I don't very much like teaching such a beautiful language. Well, let us continue our lesson."

On my way home I'm cheering myself by thinking of the shock on Sahil's face when I tell him off in Hindi when a motorcycle pulls up alongside of me. I turn to see Mrs. Singh's son. He's wearing a leather jacket, smiling as he guns his gleaming, growling piece of machinery. "I'm sorry I was rude. I am in a dispute with my mother. She tries to control my life in every way."

"Quite all right. No need to apologize." It seems in India, there is no such thing as simply walking down the street to get from point A to point B without being interrupted by men appearing from nowhere. I keep walking.

"My name is Wally by the way. My parents wanted me to have an English name."

I nod.

"Are you from California?" he asks. He's wheeling his motorcycle along with his feet.

I remain silent.

"I am going up the hill to catch the sunset. Would you like to go along?"

"No thank you," I say in Hindi.

"Very good," he says. "Good pronunciation. We could practice over a Taj beer and see the sunset. There's a very nice restaurant at the top of the hill."

"No. I really have to go home. Goodbye."

"Goodbye then."

But I walk another block and there he is again. "It will be a really excellent sunset," he says. "A shame to miss the view of it from the hill."

I glance at him, and suddenly, the sun glints off his hair and his teeth are gleaming white and he looks something like those heroes I've seen in Bollywood movies. I change my mind. Why am I making myself miserable over this player Sahil? My anger gives me energy. To get mired in misery is the stupidest possible choice. Why shouldn't I do something fun instead of stewing in my room alone?

"All right," I say. "Let's catch the sunset." I hop on. I have learned a thing or two from Sahil about being reckless.

He takes off on the long curving road that snakes up the hill. As I put my hand on the only available support, his shoulder, I see how his brown hair curves over the edge of his leather jacket. It smells like expensive leather. I wonder, absurdly, if it is all right for people to wear leather if their religion forbids eating cows.

We stop at a posh-looking restaurant with an outdoor deck that looks out to the valley below. He orders beers. The view is spectacular, but in a different way than from the mountaintop where I had been with Sahil, the mountaintop of the Monsoon Palace. There, I felt as if I was in an enchanted world inhabited by just the two of us, a world of monsoons and magic and the ghosts of maharajahs and maharanis. This feels glamorous, with its gleaming chrome tables and patrons in designer clothes, almost like being back in California.

Wally talks about his apartment in Delhi and how much money he makes and will make and how his mother is trying to marry him off to various women that he does not like. I listen politely. But the more he talks the more I don't want to be here. He asks me nothing about myself. He poses. He brags. He studies me for my reaction to him. There's something about his arrogance, his driving manner that reminds me of my ex back in San Francisco, not a memory I particularly want to have.

"Tell me. Do you like me?" Wally suddenly asks me, staring at me in a way that is blank and intense at the same time.

I don't know what to say. "Yes, of course. You seem like a nice person."

"I would like to take you the festival tomorrow."

"Oh, I don't even know if I'm going to the festival," I lie, remembering my vow that it's the last thing I'll do before I leave this crazy, beautiful city, whether or not Sahil comes back.

The conversation wanes. I try to talk about India, its history, its philosophy, and whether people really talk about each other in terms of their religious or ethnic background as the man I think of as the Shadow talked about Sahil. Are people really identified by the religion of their parents? But Wally's one topic of enthusiasm is himself. Without much of a response from me, his eyes glaze over and he falls into a moody silence. The sun moves slowly in its crystalline sky. When the sunset finally arrives, a show of corals and mauves, I tell him it's time to leave. Wally lifts his glass, "A toast to sexy American women." He smiles what seems like a fake smile, then drives me back down the mountain. "You really don't want to miss the festival," he says as he drops me in front of my place.

"I think I won't go at all. I'm not really feeling well."

"You will feel better tomorrow. You will enjoy it." I can see that whatever I say will make no impression at all, so I say nothing. "I will pick you up. Five o'clock." Suddenly I feel very tired, too tired to argue. When he looks around to see if anyone is looking, then leans in for a kiss, I turn my face away and offer my cheek.

"Smashing," he says, as he guns his motor.

In the middle of the night I wake up with a dull ache at the end of my nose. I examine it with my fingers. It's puffy and tender to the touch. I pull myself out of bed, turn on the light, and look into the small mirror in the bathroom. There is no doubt about it. It's red. It's larger than it was. Not only that, it hurts, a pulsing, throbbing pain. I'm so thirsty. I need drinking water and the bottle in my room is empty. I throw on my robe and stumble through dim corridors that lead to the kitchen. On my way, I see one of the aunties, Aunty Peaches, in her pale cream nightgown. I've awakened her.

When she turns on the hall light, she spots my problem immediately. She peers at my nose, touches it with the tip of her finger. She makes a clucking sound. "Doctor," she says.

She calls Aunty Cream, who stumbles into the hall with a shawl wrapped around her shoulders. "Doctor," she agrees. Before I know it, I'm off in the middle of the night in a taxi with Aunty Peaches accompanying me. We park on a tree-lined residential street, knock at an iron gate. In just a moment, a white-haired man in pajamas appears. They are very likely the same clothes he wears in the daytime, I think. The boundaries between day and night are different here. People sleep in the daytime and often get up to do their chores in the dark. In a way, it makes more sense in a place this hot. In any case, the doctor doesn't seem at all perturbed that he's being awakened in the middle of the night to treat such a banality as a swollen nose. He has such a kind face, a face I trust. "Come," he says, as he leads us into his dark office. "Where are you coming from?" he asks as he shines a powerful flashlight on me. "How long are you staying in India?"

As I am answering his questions, I notice more people have gathered around me. On the other side of the beam of the flashlight, faces float like balloons, peering at me. I have no idea where they've come from. They just appeared. They must be neighbors, or servants. They seem to have no sense that they are intruding; they might be medical students with the doctor instructing them on the known treatments of this particular ailment. "Yes," I imagine him saying, "we have seen very few cases of this. It's generally associated with a premonition of terrible things to happen in the future. The nose is the vestigial sense that works at a different, more psychic level that the rest of our senses."

And because they are Indians, and their minds work in very complicated and philosophical ways, the medical students offer further insights. "Just so, doctor, but perhaps noses grow when people are lying—something like the Italian tall tale of Pinocchio. Even more, if one is lying to oneself. That is when the problem gets serious. This lady is very likely lying to herself." All this goes through my mind in a second or two. I blink and see they are just curious onlookers after all, silent, shy, emerging from the shadows of the surrounding neighborhood because they sensed something mildly entertaining was happening.

After a thorough examination, the doctor turns the flashlight off and offers me some pills. "Merely an infection," he says. "These antibiotics will be clearing it up in a few days. If not, you must be coming to see me again."

He turns the flashlight off, and the onlookers scatter as suddenly as they appeared. The show is over.

CHAPTER FIFTEEN

Reunion

From my window, I can just make out a string of red-clad elephants crossing the arched bridge in the distance, weighed down in finery. It's the day of the festival. The women of the city will soon be emerging from their houses, their flickering eyes ringed in kohl, bracelets clinking, wrapped in jewel colors. I can almost hear their excited chattering.

Because of the antibiotics and the strange middle of the night sojourn in the doctor's office, I slept until almost noon. I awoke to a soft knock and there were the aunties, waiting at my door like sari-clad saints with breakfast on a tray, a pack of wet towels and murmurs of sympathy, patting their own noses in solidarity.

I touch mine gingerly. It's still tender, but no longer throbbing. I check in the mirror. Some of the swelling has subsided, but it's still red and puffy like the nose of a drunk. I think about how to disguise it, but decide it doesn't matter, really, as I'll be alone.

I nibble at my breakfast—coffee, chapatis, and a golden melon. I don't feel like eating even though I know I should build up my strength. My Hindu deity book helps to pass the

194 · JANET MARIE SOLA

long minutes while I lie in bed with a wet towel plastered on my face. The cavorting gods and goddesses are so busy with their full lives of plotting schemes of revenge, transmigrating into new forms and carrying on in general that they seem like over-inflated, angst-ridden adolescents, inspiration for a Woody Allen movie.

On one page is an illustration of Parvati changing herself from a dark goddess into a fairer one to attract the waning attentions of her boyfriend Shiva. She bleaches her skin, she doesn't quite go blonde, although if she had, she might have been more successful. No matter. He still shuns her, so she further tries to win his approval by following his ascetic diet of leaves and wind, starving herself to skin and bones. She fits perfectly into the current ideal of feminine perfection that demands beauty as the price of love, and misery as the price of beauty. Love sucks, actually. Sahil can stay in his village or wherever he is forever for all I care. So much for the love goddess.

I dress in my standard black silk dress. It hangs on me now. I add a brown sash and a strand of coral around my neck. I tuck a black silk shawl in my bag for evening. I can wrap it over my head and around my face, burka style, if I want to. I like the idea of being invisible. I like the idea of being alone. I came to India to become a stronger, more independent woman, not some slave to romance. I came to India because I wanted to experience a five-thousand-year-old culture, not hang out with a faux artist. I came to India to travel, not to be stuck in one place that is starting to suffocate me.

They all await me, these mythic places: Delhi, Agra, Varanasi, then Nepal and the Himalayas, the top of the world. Here I am, half a planet away from home, with no one really to talk to, improvising as I go along and feeling as if yes, I can do this. I've come a long way from the timid, cautious woman who wanted control over every aspect of her life. I am surviving in one of the most chaotic countries in the world. The inner goddess I want to call on is not Parvati, but Durga, eternal virgin and warrior goddess with her eighteen arms, riding on her lion vehicle. Like her, I am facing my demons and fighting them.

"I'm glad to be free of him, I'm glad to be free of him, I'm glad to be free, period," I chant to myself as I move around my room, gathering things and putting them in my suitcase. There, next to the birds' nest, abandoned now, are my few books. I pick them up to pack them away and notice an old writing notebook—the cheap, thin-papered, staple-clamped thing. I don't know why I open it, but I do.

And there, on the first page, in block letters written on blue lines, are the words Sahil wrote for me that morning when we were clowning around in the rooftop restaurant. *India is mine.* Then he had taken my hand and said: *You are mine. I am yours.* The bite of loss is sudden. Like a piranha attacking a swimmer, it tears into my body and moves directly to my heart, going for the tastiest flesh. Why is it we feel things in the heart, so physically? I toss the notebook in the suitcase and bite my lip. Tears well up, but I fight them. I know if I allow one tear to come, a torrent will follow. "I'm glad to be free," I say out loud in the direction of the half-built nest on the bookshelf. "And I don't give a damn if you birds come back either."

Unexpectedly, there's a knock, a blunt, clumsy one. "Letter from you," the house boy mutters from the other side of the door. I know he means "Letter for you." My heart starts to thump involuntarily.

"All right," I reply. Some instinct makes my fumble in my bag for my sunglasses and put them on. I don't mind onlookers seeing my red nose, but my teary eyes are a different story. I open the door and follow the houseboy to the lobby. Vijay, Sahil's silent young friend, is waiting for me, with a silly grin and a note in his hand. He hands me a carefully folded piece of heavy paper, the kind of paper Sahil sketched on. My fingers shake as I unfold it. I recognize his English block letters immediately. "I am back from the village," the note says. "Please come to meet in Blue Sky café. I wait for you."

I don't even pause. "Tell him I'll be there. In one hour." He nods. I hope Vijay understands me. I write it on the back of the note just in case he doesn't.

The Blue Sky is a rundown and lively restaurant in the center of the city. Strangely, even though it's on the lake, all the windows face the street, and on the wall is a mural of what would be the view. It's a garish painting, the lake and the surrounding hills recreated in shades of iridescent blues and neon oranges. Plato was right, I think, we'd rather watch the shadows on the cave walls than the reality in front of us. I find a tiny table in the corner and look around at the mixture of Westerners and locals—mostly dressed as imitations of each other, the Westerners in loose cotton pants and kurtas, the Indians in denim and embossed T-shirts. A haze of cigarette smoke and maybe something stronger makes my eyes water.

I know why Sahil has chosen this spot. It's one of the few places where we can feel comfortable, unjudged. No one looks at me or at my red nose, the state of which now dismays me. I wish I were younger, more beautiful, blonder, thinner, more voluptuous. Just like Parvati, I think ruefully, a slave to passion.

I order chai and while I'm waiting I take out my black scarf and wrap it around my hair and over the lower part of my face. When the waiter returns with my cup, I stare at it, trying to figure out how women who have to wear veils over their faces drink tea in restaurants.

When I look up there is Sahil. The light from the doorway creates a halo around his lean frame. I think of the first time I saw that effect, when he pressed the seed into my hand, a lifetime ago, a moment ago. He spots me immediately, in spite of my cover-up, and looks into my eyes as he approaches, holding them as he pulls out his chair. He looks frailer than I remember him, as if he's been eating only rice and vegetables. He's rolled up the sleeves of the white shirt he's wearing, which emphasizes the thinness of his arms. He's had his hair cut, a bit too high on his neck, so he looks even younger, more vulnerable. And yet he's beautiful. The way he moves is beautiful. The way he almost smiles is beautiful. Everything about him is beautiful.

"Elena, your eyes are very nice with this . . . ," he says as he sits down, and he raises his hand over his face, in imitation of my scarf. "You look like Moslem wife." He reaches one hand across the table and leaves it there, his long elegant fingers extended, very close to mine, an invitation. For a moment I pause, then extend the tips of my fingers until they touch his. The thrill is lovely and intense, but I pull my hand away. I want to be calm. I want to talk things over in a rational way.

"We must talk," I say, and pull off my scarf in a flourish.

He looks at me, tenderly, I think, and finally a smile spreads across his face. "Your nose is hurt by a fly, no not a fly . . . a bee, bee sting," he says. "Do you hurt?"

"I don't know what it is. I had to go to the doctor. He gave me some medicine. It doesn't hurt anymore, but it looks awful, I know." I shrug and smile sheepishly.

"I do not care if your nose is big or small or red or white. I only care that I see you again."

I feel him drawing me in, so quickly, so easily, as if I were a child following the Pied Piper. But there is an equal and opposite resistance to that feeling, that old voice that says *be sensible, now is your chance to walk away, and if you don't, whatever follows will be your own fault.* The words of the strange man in the business suit in Pushkar come back to me, "Remember your center." What is my center anyway? Is it what's in my heart? Or the oasis of peace that I felt on the hill with Baba? Or that state of being that I imagined was embodied in the painting I lost? Or is it just platitudes and empty words?

"Sahil, how can you say you care so much about seeing me again when you disappeared?" I try to read his eyes. He has the look of a spirit lost in the forest, a village boy in the big city, an innocent in spite of all his bravado. But I don't trust him.

I think he is going to apologize, but instead he says, "I think maybe you do not come back."

"Don't turn this around," I say. I'm determined to make my point. "We agreed to meet before the festival. Don't you remember?"

"Yes, I remember. Today is festival. I am here."

I take a deep breath. "I have been here waiting for you since I came back from Pushkar. For days. For a long time."

Both his hands are on the table now, his fingers tapping out a gentle rhythm. He closes his eyes and shakes his head very slowly, as if he is saying something I am not understanding. "I go to my village. My grandmother is very sick. Now I am back."

I try to keep my voice calm, light even. "Sahil," I say, "do you know this man who hangs out by the ghat? He's a skinny guy, with a big . . . Adam's apple." I move my finger up and down near my throat. Sahil frowns. "Anyway, this man tells me . . . he tells me you are not in your village."

"What does he say?"

I pause before I say it, but forge ahead. The mural of the lake on the restaurant wall makes me feel as if I am in a facsimile of Udaipur, a Las Vegas style India dream imitation that is closing in on me. "He tells me that you are seeing another woman. That you have many women."

"This man tells a lie."

"Why would he tell a lie?"

"I do not know why. He maybe is jealous." Part of me wants to accept his explanation, the other part of me can't let my doubts go. I look into his eyes, searching for the truth. His face is a mask of calm. He touches his fingers to his forehead and closes his eyes. It's that familiar gesture that usually means I am thinking, but now I know it means something else. I've ever seen him angry, but now I know he is angry, and also fighting the anger. "I know this man," he says. "Everyone knows him. He tries to make trouble all the time."

"Why would he do that?"

"Because this is his way, his *dharma*. He has no job, nothing better to do."

I want to believe him, I want him to present some proof to me. "Why should I believe you?" I say this in almost a whisper.

He pulls his hands from the table as if I had slapped them. His face tenses, his mouth quivers and he pushes himself away from the table. "I go," he says as he stands up. "I go and do not come back." My heart sinks at those words. I want to say something but nothing comes out. He turns to go. Then he pauses, and comes over to me. He touches my shoulder. "I am sad you believe this bad man instead of me."

"I'm sorry. I don't know what to believe," I manage to blurt out. I can't look at him. "Everything I think is true one day is not true the next day. And vice versa. And don't ask me what vice versa means." My voice comes out at a high pitch. Tears well up again but this time I can't stop them. People are staring. My nose is throbbing. I grope for my sunglasses in my bag, put them on and hurry out with as much dignity as possible through a haze of tears and smoke.

I hear Sahil's footsteps behind me, but I keep going. The street is thick with moving blurs of color and a rising crescendo of sounds, crunches, clinks, drones. I don't even have a clear idea of where I'm headed, I just keep following the familiar road by the lake. When he catches up with me, tears are running down my cheeks.

"Elena," he says, keeping pace with me. I stop and turn to face him. "Come sit."

I can't speak. I just nod. He leads me through a row of blossoming trees to a dusty little park bench that faces the lake. The overly sweet smell of flowers drifts around us. A few peahens are nibbling at the ground, oblivious to the nearby male peacock's dazzling fan of tail feathers.

Sahil sits next to me without touching me, just his arm resting on the back of the bench. He's so close to me. I breathe in his smell of grass and earth, of having been born in a village. It's that smell of the first time he put his mouth on mine on the hill at the Monsoon Palace. And so many times since. And I know then that I want to believe him. Not that he's telling the truth, but that I want to believe him because I need something to hold on to. Maybe this is what it comes down to, never knowing the truth, but simply choosing to believe in someone, in something, as the followers of Jesus, or Sai Baba, or Jason's guru do. Or believers in love do. As I have never been able to do.

"I do believe you. It's myself I don't believe," I say. The tears are coming faster now, and I start to sob. All the confusion of the last weeks, all the pain I've been holding in, for myself, for Sahil, for Neela, for Amar, for India itself, is streaming out.

"It is good that you cry. It is not good to be happy all the time." He pulls a white handkerchief from someplace and hands it to me. Even though he is younger than me, at this moment he is the parent and I am the child.

"I tell you a story," he says. "You see that palace?" He points up to a faraway building on the hill across from us, ochre-colored walls that rise into spires.

"Yes, I see it."

"In a very old time a king and queen live there. They want all the time to be happy and dance and sing. So they pay other people to cry for them. How do you say it, professional criers."

"You're making this up." But my tears are drying up and I'm starting to smile.

I take my sunglasses off and dab at my eyes with Sahil's handkerchief. It smells of turpentine. When I unfold it, I see there are smears of paint on it. "Your painting handkerchief?"

"I am sorry, I have other one," he says. He searches in his pockets. "My grandmother give me these cloths. When I visit her in the village I paint. You tell me to paint the life of India. Not just copy. So I try. I show you in my studio."

He hands me the other handkerchief. But I'm looking at the one I'm already holding. The paint flecks. The turpentine. It comes to me all at once. Of course. He was painting. He was in his village. A rush of heat spreads across my face. I'm ashamed that I was such an easy victim for that Shadow man with his menacing messages. I'm sorry I had so little faith in him. "Yes, I would love to see your paintings, Sahil." I tell him.

"Later you see," he says, as if nothing ever happened. "Now I finish my story. This is a long ago story but a true one. As I say, the king and queen are very rich and happy all the time and the professional criers cry all time. But one day, something bad comes." He lifts his index finger to the sky, then swoops it down. "Their favorite child falls from a high window and dies. Now they want to cry, but they cannot, because they forget how to cry. So forever instead of tears they have a rock in their heart that cannot melt."

"They cannot grieve," I say.

"Yes, they cannot."

We are both silent for a time. "I saw Amar. It is so sad he has lost Neela."

"Yes. Maybe he has a grief that never ends, no matter how much he cries."

"What will he do now? Will he leave his first wife?"

"He cannot look in her eyes now. But he has children. How can he go?" He presses his lips together and frowns, an expression that I know is to mask the pain he feels for his friend.

"Tell me, is there an investigation? Don't the police at least ask questions?"

"Police come. They ask questions, but there are no answers for these questions. No one sees. No one can prove. So they say accident. Or suicide. Official verdict."

Everything in me wants some justice for this horrible crime, and because perhaps there is none on this earth, I think there must be in another realm. "I'm beginning to believe that we do somehow have past lives and future lives. The Hindu belief. I have to believe that . . . that Neela and Amar will have another chance, in some other life."

"I am not Hindu. I am not Moslem. I do not believe in any religion. It makes people crazy. It makes them believe they are right when they are wrong. But yes, for Amar and Neela, I believe this. I believe she waits for him. Maybe as wind, or tree."

I think about this. How unbearable it must be for Amar, not only to lose his love but to know that her death was because of their love. "I think Amar can feel her when he feels the wind. Maybe not now, it is too soon. But some time."

"You know Elena, I cry too. Amar is my friend. Neela is my friend. I love her." He pauses. "I love you too."

He has never said that before. I want to say the same thing back to him, and yet the words won't come. Instead, I squeeze his hand.

"Come," Sahil says, smiling again, "we go to the festival to see the women who wear their husbands on their heads."

CHAPTER SIXTEEN

The Festival

Night has fallen and the streets are running with glittering streams of bright beings. The mens' huge turbans show off their sun-beaten, high-cheekboned faces. Young girls weave through the crowd holding each others' hennaed hands. Even the cows are part of the celebration. They wear the colored strings and flowers that hang from their horns with an appropriate air of indifference. Yet the women are the most spectacular. All around us their tall figures sway, a bobbing sea of shining faces and jewel-colored saris wearing three-foot high dolls fastened on their heads.

"Now you see," Sahil says, "the wives make big hats in the shape of Shiva. For all the women to honor their husbands." He tells me that newly married women fast for many days before this festival, like Parvati. The doll headdresses wear voluminous scarlet and magenta skirts and have brightly painted faces. Some look like the dashing god Shiva, and some have big, curling moustaches, looming grins with blacked out teeth, gigantic nostrils. A few have pot bellies. I wonder if they are honoring their husbands or mocking them. I wonder if they are blessed by them or oppressed.

We make our way through the crowd for a better view. Out on the water, now glimmering with reflected lights, a flotilla of barges floats slowly toward shore. Each has its own bangled and bejeweled elephant and accompanying spangled princes and princesses and musicians. It is a fantasy of old India, the maharajah's India. Children watching near us can hardly contain their excitement. They jump up and down, waving their sparklers as if this were the happiest moment of their young lives.

Then the fireworks begin. The sky lights up with gold and silver and phosphorous blue. The dark womb of the city's sky is giving violent birth to her own star children with their dazzling but brief lives. A song starts somewhere in the crowd. Sahil tells me they are saying "'our city, our city, our beautiful city, when we are gone we come back as stars in the sky, to shine over our husbands and children. Do not forget your mothers, your daughters, your wives.'"

The crippled child who walks on his hands stops and gazes up at us. In seconds, he starts laughing at something Sahil says to him. They joke back and forth as he circles nimbly around us. An incandescent smile appears on the boy's face. It's as if he had known only tenderness his entire life. Maybe each of us are allowed a certain amount of happiness, no more and no less, no matter what our station in life.

"Do you like our festival?" Sahil asks me.

"Yes, very much. I'm happy you're with me." All the anger and confusion of the past few days seems remote now, forgiven and forgotten.

"Look." Sahil gestures with his chin to a crowd on an embankment nearby.

I turn my head and pick out Amar's handsome face. He used to look sad to me. Now he looks frozen. A pouchy-cheeked woman in a hot pink sari stands next to him. I'm close enough that I can see the bindi mark between her narrowly set eyes, her yellow teeth as she parts her lips. She looks both smug and defiant.

"Wife number one?" I ask. Sahil nods. I stare at her with something like wonder. What is she thinking? *I am glad I murdered my opponent.* Or *I am the wife and she was a slut and she got what she deserves.* Or *I am celebrating my husband today now that he is all mine.* Is that what is going through her mind? I have this terrible urge to push my way through the crowd and confront her. To shout at her.

"Kali," Sahil reminds me.

"Yes, I know." Kali, the dark goddess who destroys her enemies and rejoices in it. Who drinks their blood and sucks the brains out of their skulls. If we all have the capacity for joy, do we all have the capacity for evil? Not darkness, because darkness and evil are not the same things to my mind, not at all. Just evil, the will to hurt another human being or creature we think is opposing us. I look up at Kali's manifestation again. She smiles at Amar. It seems like a false smile, but hopeful, a smile that contains equal amounts of malice and need.

Maybe she felt trapped. Her man took up with another woman, and she couldn't leave. I remember the anger I had felt toward Peter. I remember thinking, when he told me so blatantly of this new woman in his life, I am hurt, I will get even with him, even though exactly *how* I would accomplish that was vague. But I could leave. I did leave. What if I had no choice but to put up with it? Would that drive me to murder?

I remember a friend telling me, when her husband began drinking and they had fight after fight, that she would like to get a divorce but she was afraid of being alone. Did she have a choice? Not in her mind. Her choice was not to go out there on her own and discover herself, with all its unpredictable and scary challenges, but to nag and berate and even beat her husband, which prompted him to drink more and more until their lives became a circular kind of hell. Horrible to say, but in her frustration, she became a minor form of Kali.

When I think about it, we take it for granted, but in reality it's relatively recently that an ordinary woman, even an ordinary Western woman like me, can actually live this way—travel alone, have a lover for joy or pleasure instead of for necessity, pursue a creative or spiritual quest. And that's what I'm doing right now. Just that thought makes me feel as if the fireworks are landing on my skin. I am part of something new, something wonderful in society, the single independent woman. The single, independent mobile woman. Yes, it has its price in loneliness and longing, and sometimes, as in Neela's case, the price is much higher, but it's also breathtaking in its possibilities.

And then I have another thought, goddesses are the embodiment of the imagining of that free woman, and so many cultures have goddesses that create and cavort at will. The classic cultures had Athena and Diana and Venus, all embodiments of love and freedom and power. And yet Greek women were not allowed to participate in those fabulous forums with Socrates and Plato. They were barely allowed out of their own houses. And here Saraswati, Durga, Parvati, a thousand manifestations of female power in all its forms, are celebrated. They are worshipped. But the roles for ordinary women are very con-strained. Maybe I would have become Kali too in other circumstances. I don't want to look at wife number one any-more. How lucky I am not to have to *be* her.

I look around for Sahil. As usual, he's chatting away, this time with an old man in the crowd. The sky and lake are merg-ing into one thrilling burst of light. "Let's go closer to the lake to look at the floats," I say.

"We go, chalo," he agrees.

As we drift through the crowd, I'm mesmerized by the faces I see. Each is so unique, so extraordinary. I look into eyes, doz-ens, hundreds of pairs of eyes, and they seem to look back at me, tracking me as I move, like those moving eyes in portraits in museums. There are kohl-rimmed eyes, melting liquid eyes, glazed vacant eyes, narrowed eyes that seem to flash anger, eyes that pity, envy, flirt, a world of eyes.

And then, suddenly, I notice the half-closed hazel eyes, slowly sliding from side to side, that belong to a fleshy hand-some face. Wally's face. An involuntary shiver goes through me. He is just coming out of a side street, pushing his gleaming motorcycle through the crowd, forcing people to step out of the way for him. I had forgotten about him, forgotten that I half-agreed to meet him. Actually, I had not agreed, but he had in-sisted. I pull my scarf over my mouth and nose and turn away, hoping he hasn't seen me.

"Why do you cover your face?" Sahil asks. "Tonight is the night everyone should see your smile."

"I'm feeling shy. Because of my nose."

He shakes his head in that universal "who understands women" gesture.

Wally is moving in our direction although his scanning eyes show that he hasn't spotted me yet. "Sahil, is there someplace we could go to get out of the crowd? I'm not feeling well."

"My studio is close to here. We go there. I show you my painting from the village."

"Yes, I'd like that."

We leave the main road. From there, it's a short walk up the steep cobbled street that leads to Sahil's studio. One second I'm breathing in the drifting smoke from the fireworks, and then, as I step through the open door, the tar-laced smoke from the cigarettes of Sahil's friends. They look like semi-mobile pieces of furniture. I'm annoyed they're here. I'd hoped to be alone with Sahil. Nevertheless, I murmur a greeting, and in turn they offer hand-rolled bidis.

We sit down on low stools, and listen to the intoxicating violins of an Indian pop-song that's coming from the boom-box. People pass in front of the open door and nod and sometimes wave. Sahil chats in Hindi with his friends. I take a bidi cigarette, just to fit in, but after the first puff I start to cough and put it out.

"Sahil, what about the paintings you were going to show me?" I finally ask.

"Now is not a good time. Better when we are alone."

"Can't you ask your friends to leave?"

"No, they are my friends."

I sigh. "But they are always here."

He pauses and shrugs. "OK, if you want I show you now." Cigarette dangling from his lips, he disappears into the back room behind a curtain. I try to avoid the gaze of his friends as I wait, focusing my attention on the festival-goers traipsing by in their flamboyant costumes. But Sahil is taking longer than I expect. "Elena," he calls from the other room, "I make one how do you say it . . . touchup . . . before I show you." There's that playful lilt in his voice that he has when he's about to surprise me.

As I'm waiting for Sahil to reappear, a motorcycle pulls up in front of the open door. There's the growl of a motor, a *pop pop pop* as it's cut. As if I am dreaming it, Wally walks in, his leather jacket unzipped, the top three buttons of his shirt unbuttoned, a gold chain around his neck gleaming. I experience two things in quick succession: an involuntary rush of blood to my face, followed by a paralysis, as if I had been stung by a hunter's tranquilizer dart. What is he doing here?

He's wearing such a perfect smile when he looks at me. No teeth showing, the corners of his mouth turned up and the edges of his eyes creased, a kindly, patient smile. I wonder if it's one he has practiced in the mirror. I meet his gaze with what I hope is calm.

"I came to your hotel to take you to the festival. The women there told me you had absconded." Each word falls like a drumbeat, as if he were speaking a foreign language he is trying to make me understand.

"Absconded?" Then I say nothing more. If I don't speak or move perhaps he will go away. But he doesn't go away. In fact, he seems to be getting bigger. He has a way of filling up a room with his bigness and his bluster and his expensive smelling cologne that's reeking into the air.

"You actually promised to go with me." Even though I know he's talking to me, his eyes glide around the room, assessing the situation, checking out Sahil's friends who are staring back at him open-mouthed.

"How did you know the way here? How did you know I was here?"

He smirks and shrugs. "Your friend by the lake."

"What are you talking about?"

He wiggles his index finger up and down by his throat. The Shadow's Adam's apple. Of course. I had not seen him, but that doesn't mean he didn't see me.

"What is happening?" Sahil calls as he emerges from behind the curtain. Wally gives him a brief dismissive glance. "Do you know this man?" Sahil asks. His voice is nonchalant, as if Wally is perhaps a long lost relative.

For a second, I think about pretending I don't know him. "Barely," I manage to mumble. "I took some Hindi lessons from his mother."

Wally is strutting like a peacock now, back and forth across the length of the small room. Then he stops and turns to me again. "Why did you tell me you were not going to the festival?"

I gather my courage up and try to speak with authority. "I am sorry, I changed my mind. My friend came back."

"Yes," says Sahil, moving to my side. "I am her friend. So you should go."

"I will not go," Wally says. His polite smile is now interrupted by intermittent flashes of very white teeth. He zips his jacket up, then unzips it. I am so incredulous at the way this guy I barely know is behaving that I stay frozen. "You made a date with me. Come with me on my motorcycle now." He moves toward me and reaches out for my arm. Before he can touch me, Sahil moves between us and pushes Wally's chest, not hard, but enough to stop him. He appears almost fragile next

213 · THE OVERNIGHT PALACE · 213

to the much bigger Wally, and he really is no match for him. But I'm pleased he's standing up for me.

"She does not want to go with you. You must go."

Sahil's friends are all watching this raptly, their eyes getting bigger, the draws on their bidis more intense. For a moment, I think they will all rise and pummel Wally. But they don't move other than leaning forward in their seats.

"I will not go," Wally repeats and pushes Sahil back. For a second, Sahil loses his balance, but then recovers and shakes his head. Their faces are inches from each other. I can feel the energy of their anger. Part of me floats out and looks down on this scene. Two men fighting over me, two young attractive men. It's ridiculous, and yet if I'm truthful there's a certain kind of thrill in it, a certain frisson, like champagne instead of blood is running through my veins. If only my friends, who kept telling me I was Peter's doormat could see me now. For so long, I withered under his critical eye. Now I have emerged on the other side of the world, and on some weird level, I'm feeling the power of the goddess. There it is. I'm a forty year old woman with a red swollen nose feeling the power of the goddess.

They begin arguing in Hindi, Wally's more urgent drumbeat of a voice a counterpoint to Sahil's strained but modulated tone. Percussion and cello, I think from my goddess's perspective. What a concert. Through the open door I see a throng of costumed people go by, unaware of the little drama being played out here, totally ignorant of the fact they are looking at a femme fatale.

"All right, I go," Wally says suddenly to my amazement.

"This is good you go. But do not be angry. I do not believe in this fighting," Sahil says.

Wally gives his jacket a final zip up to his neck, even though the night is warm. Then he turns and leaves without so much as a glance at me. All at once I realize it's not about me after all. It's about something much more primal. I remember, oddly, a friend who had two cats telling me how exhausted and neurotic one of her cats was because he felt he had to dominate, even though the other cat gave him no resistance. Something like a bubble of amusement, of irony, is rising up in me and I want to laugh. Instead, I just look at Sahil and shrug my shoulders. Wally is gone.

But only for a moment. He appears in the doorway again. "You are right. Fighting is not good. Tonight is the festival," he says. "We should all be friends." Now he's smiling his closed lip smile again, as if he is forgiving us.

"Yes, it is bad to fight," Sahil agrees. "We are all brothers and sisters."

"I propose we all go on my motorcycle to the restaurant by the lake," Wally says. "It's very close to here. We will have a lassi and watch the parade and celebrate the festival."

I look at Sahil and shake my head, almost imperceptibly, but he does not seem to see it. In fact, he does not even hesitate. "I like this idea. The night is beautiful. We are all friends."

I sense Wally's smile is false and I know I should protest more. But somewhere inside of me Parvati rises and spins, demanding to remain the center of attention. I wrap my scarf around my neck, the boys in the shop nod goodbye to us, and the three of us get on Wally's motorcycle, Sahil sitting behind Wally and me behind Sahil. My hand rests on Sahil's shoulder. He's wearing only his thin white shirt, and I can almost feel his skin beneath it, so familiar to me now. We gun through the city, taking the dark side streets to avoid the crowds of the festival.

It seems to me we are not heading in the direction of the lake at all, but away from it.

As we begin to climb the hill the route feels familiar, the same that I took with Wally a few days ago to the posh hilltop restaurant. *Oh oh.* "Where are we going?" I shout into the wind and the roar of the motor. But the only response is a lift of Sahil's shoulder in what I interpret as a "don't worry about it" shrug. It's the shoulder of an artist, not a warrior. And yet he came to my defense. That comforts me. My moment of anxiety passes. The city spreads out beneath us, the last of the festival's procession moving in a dance of lights around the blackness of the lake.

When we round the curves I feel that inexplicable force, the force that wants to fling us out battling with the one that holds us in. As we speed up that pull gets stronger and more thrilling. The words of an Indian woman poet whose name I have forgotten come back to me: "Who knew whom then, who knew oneself, who knew of the world's wild ways?" The wind wraps around us as we snake up the hill and I think how lovely and civilized this is to let animosities and misunderstandings go and celebrate life with lassis, or tea, or drinks.

The restaurant's covered terrace is open to the night air, the moon a cold blaze in the sky. Orange-scented candles light the dozen or so well-dressed patrons. Sahil and I sit on one side of a gleaming chrome table, Wally on the other. "I changed my mind about the restaurant," he says. "This one is much nicer. I'm sure you agree."

I just smile a "who cares" smile. I'm not going to show him any concern at all. He snaps his fingers and orders a bottle of wine. I tell him I haven't eaten in a long time and prefer something a little more substantial, or at least a lassi, but he smiles and shakes his head. When the waiter comes with the wine Wally pays. It's cold and tastes expensive. We all toast the festival and take big gulps. Wally scans the dim room, as if he is looking for something. His eyes stop momentarily and fasten on my nose, as if he's seeing it for the first time. "Your nose is quite strange today, but I still like you," he says.

"Thanks a lot." I lean over and blow out the candle. "There," I say, "now you don't have to look at my nose." The truth is I am glad I no longer have to look at Wally's face, his heavy lidded eyes, his increasingly curling lips.

Wally taps his fingers on the hard surface of the table. "This Sahil," he says to me, "you don't understand boys like this. He only wants your money. He only wants to go to America with you."

"This is not true," says Sahil.

"You American women are so naïve," Wally says. His insinuating, angry tone is coming back.

I take a deep breath. Mistake, I think. Big mistake to come here. Perhaps I've had enough of being an irresistible goddess that mortal men fight over. It's time to defuse the situation. "What a lovely night," I say. "What a beautiful festival. You said we should not argue. So let's not. It's stupid."

Sahil ignores me. "What is this word *naïve*?" he asks.

"Naïve means you don't see what is really going on," I explain. The hills on the other side of the valley below us are outlined against the deeper, star-pierced black of the sky. "Like the stars out there. That twinkling star we see may not be there at all." It's kind of a desperate analogy, but the point is to change the subject. "The stars are so far away and the light takes so long to reach us that by the time it gets here the star may already be dead."

"Yes," Sahil agrees readily. "So naïve means you see stars when there are really no stars."

"Kind of."

"But we can still enjoy, naïve, not naïve, what does it matter?"

Wally stands again and runs his thumb down the zipper of his jacket. "Do you remember?" he says to me. "You rode my motorcycle with me to watch the sunset. You had a drink with me here. In this restaurant."

"Is this true?" Sahil turns to me as if he does not quite believe it. "You did not tell me this. You tell me he is the son of your teacher. That is all."

"It was nothing. He is making something out of nothing."

"Yes, it is true," Wally says. "She does do this. And it is not nothing. You kissed me. Is that nothing?"

I shake my head. "That is not true. You know that."

"Do not say things that are not true, Wally man," Sahil says. He does not move, but his voice has a deadly calm in it. Wally's eyes shift back and forth from Sahil to me.

"Now you must choose," he says.

"But that's ridiculous." I shake my head at him in disbelief.

"You must choose," he repeats. He sits down again and squares his shoulders. "I am taller, handsomer, and richer. And older. This boy is too young for you."

"Be careful what you say, Wally man," Sahil says. "These things you say are not important. She is happy with me. She cannot choose you."

He is right, I think. I am happy with him. But more than that, I am in the middle of my story with him. I have a leading role, maybe roles—Saraswati, Parvati—and I want to find out what happens next. And because . . . I think I love him.

Wally stares at me. "Choose." He presses his fists together and gives me his closed lip smile. I want to find the right words to give the least offense. "All right, I will choose. I choose Sahil because he has been my friend almost since I came to this city."

Wally looks straight ahead and says, "OK. We go back." The lights of Udaipur are beckoning from far below.

All the way down the mountain I'm waiting for Wally to make some crazy move to throw Sahil and me off the cycle. But after all, he's an up and coming professional, a man with a lot to lose. He would not do anything rash. When we reach the center of town, Wally stops dead and we hop off. Without so much as a word or a glance at us, he guns his motor and is gone.

Sahil and I make our way back to his studio. The fireworks are over, but two of his friends are still there, talking and smoking, hardly moved from their original positions. "I want to show you something," he says, and I follow him to the back room. There, on an easel, is his painting.

"This is what I paint in the village. The village market."

The scene is one of color and motion. Women are buying and selling fruit, a bespectacled man rides a bicycle, a yogi meditates, a dog barks at a fleeing hump-necked cow, a musician plays a sitar, a blue and yellow bus waits in the background. It has imagination and spirit and craftsmanship.

"Do you see someone special?" Sahil asks me. I look at it more closely. And there, in the midst of the market is a woman in a blue sari, a scarf draped over her head, blondish hair peeking out.

"Is that me?"

"I am in the village but I think of you." He looks at me almost shyly.

"I'm glad I could visit the village of your grandmother in some way."

"See this." He points to the signature. "This is your India, signed Sahil the artist. It is for you."

"It's beautiful, Sahil. It's the most beautiful present I've ever had." And it's true. I feel embarrassed that I was so imperious. "I'm sorry about Wally."

"I believe you Elena. I believe you when you say it is nothing. You believe me when I tell you I was in my village and I believe you."

"We believe each other."

"We go to your hotel to see the stars that are not there anymore." He wraps the painting in brown paper, and hands it to me.

At the hotel, we go past my room to a small staircase and then a ladder that leads from the top floor to the roof. We watch the stars for a while, then hide in the shadows of a thatched structure, where no one can see us. I unbutton his white shirt, and he slides his hands up under my dress, and there again is that smell of salt and paint and earth that make me ravenous.

When he leaves my room later that night he says "Someday I take you to the village of my grandmother." He says this with conviction, as if he sees a future for us. Could that be in the realm of possibility? What would his grandmother think of me?

CHAPTER SEVENTEEN

Escaping Udaipur

It's quiet the next morning on my way to Sahil's studio. Except for more litter than usual scattered in the streets, there is hardly a sign of last night's festivities. Just a calm blue sky and sleepy vendors selling their wares, my humped-necked cow friends, the women beating their laundry in the shallows of the lake. And the Shadow. He catches me by surprise as I pass the broad expanse of the city's main ghat.

He lifts his head to me, a cocky gesture I interpret as *come here*. "I must speak to you."

"I'm very busy," I say, barely glancing his way.

He follows me as usual. "Very important."

"What is it?"

"I have something to tell to you. Your Moslem friend is in big danger."

Something in the tone of his voice makes me think he is serious. I stop and turn to look at him. "What are you talking about?" I have always seen him in the murky shadows of twilight. In the bright light of day he doesn't look sinister. He's just a strange, awkward man with oil stains on his pants. But it's the same strange, awkward man who was happy to pass on to Wally the location of Sahil's studio. A professional trouble maker, as Sahil said.

"We sit," he says, indicating the stone steps of the ghat.

"I don't need to sit." A man with wispy white hair and a shrunken naked torso is stretched out and sleeping on the step just below us.

The Shadow's forever restless Adam's apple repositions itself. "I am not telling you truth before. About Moslem boy."

"His name is Sahil," I say, my voice icy. "Not 'Moslem boy.' Sahil is his name."

"He does not have many women. Only one before you. French woman a long time ago."

"Is that what you want to tell me? Do you think I believed your lies?"

"India is a different country," he says.

"Different than what?"

"A woman cannot have two men here."

I pull back from him and stare. "I don't know what you're talking about." I feel my face reddening. Without thinking, I bring my hand to my nose. It's still tender.

"Last night, your friend, this Wally . . ."

I interrupt him. "He is not my friend."

"This Wally with shiny motorcycle. He take a big stick— not a cricket stick but American baseball bat—and go look for this Moslem boy who is also your friend."

"Sahil," I say again, trying to remain calm. "What happened? How do you know this?"

"Very late last night, when festival finish, I see Wally man. He say you have a date with him. He say he take you and Moslem boy along on his motorcycle. He say you are a bad woman. He is very mad."

Is he telling the truth? I am trying to put this together in my head. He must have seen Wally after the three of us came down the mountain and Wally dropped Sahil and me off. Otherwise, how could this guy have known we all went on Wally's motorcycle together?

"This Wally man show me this stick. He say he look for Moslem boy and break his leg."

"Break his leg?" My voice rises in alarm.

"He go last night to do this. If he find him he break. Maybe leg. Maybe neck." He raises him arms and brings them down hard as if he had a stick.

"Why did you do this? Why did you tell Wally the way to Sahil's studio? What is the matter with you? You're a bad man." Scenarios of Wally hitting Sahil in the shins with a stick and worse are running through my mind. I think of going to the police before I remember how useless that would be.

"This is the fault of women like you," he says. "Women who do not care about our ways. Women who think only on themselves. Women who come here to have mischief with men and do not care what they leave behind."

I try to take in what he is saying. Can that be what I've done? Blood rushes to my face. Shame and embarrassment mix with fear and distress. I look at the ghat's steps that go down beneath the water, each step darker and murkier than the one above it, and wonder how far down they go. I want to go all the way down them and immerse myself in the lake. But I've got to go. I've got to warn Sahil.

It's only a short walk to Sahil's studio but I feel as if my legs are made of water. "Women like you, women like you." Those words keep pounding in my brain. This horrible man is right. I have had no idea what I was doing. I have been caught up in my own drama, as if the world were small and revolved only around me. And look at the consequences. Sahil is no match for Wally, especially Wally with a bat. If anything has happened to Sahil it will be my fault.

When I get to his studio, I pound on the closed door. There is no answer. I keep pounding. Finally, I hear a stirring inside. The door opens and one of Sahil's friends peers out. He rubs his eyes. I can see another body, sleeping on a mat, behind him. "Have you seen Sahil?"

"Sahil not here. Wally person come last night to look for him. Very late. Very loud voice. Carry big stick. I tell him the same. Sahil not here."

"When did you last see Sahil?"

He shrugs his shoulders.

On the long unpaved road that circles the lake, I look up and try to remember which house Sahil had pointed out to me as the house of his mother. Maybe he went there. I'm not sure, and even if I found it, what would I do? Go knock on the door and introduce myself to her? Tell her that someone is after her son to beat him up because of me?

When I walk into the aunties' garden though, there is Sahil, his hands afloat in the air, entertaining them with a story.

"You're all right!" He looks as if he doesn't have a care in the world.

He gives me a puzzled frown. "Yes. Nothing is wrong."

"Where were you last night after you left here?"

"I am at the house of my mother. Then I come here this morning. Do you not trust me again?"

"It's not that, it's . . . I must tell you something." The eyes of the aunties are cast down on their embroidery. "In private."

He follows me to the rooftop restaurant. I find the cold bottled water I've stored in the refrigerator and pour us each a glass. I tell Sahil what the Shadow has told me. He shakes his head at the story. "Maybe this man tells you a lie. Another lie like the one he told you before about me."

"What if he is telling the truth? Sahil, this Wally is a little crazy. I told you, he came to your studio with a stick last night after he dropped us off. He wants to hurt you. He knows this place. He could come and look for you here."

He shrugs.

"OK, brush it off. But what if he comes and breaks your leg? Or worse. Then what will you do? You don't even have insurance."

He shakes his head. "What is this insurance? The same insurance that helps me for my broken foot?"

"Please Sahil, listen to me."

He holds his glass of water, slowly rotates it in one hand, then raises it in the air. "You are right. You are always right. My idea is we go to Jaisamand. A very nice lake."

"Another lake. So many lakes in Rajasthan."

"Because the old maharajahs know people enjoy the water. They build dams to hold the water in. Beautiful. Biggest lake in Rajasthan. Many people go there on their honeymoon. But now, not so many people." He reaches out for my hand. "It is a good lake for swimming. Very nice for us."

We decide we won't tell anyone where we're going. We'll leave today as soon as we pack.

"I go to my studio first. For my paints."

"I don't think you should go there. He might be watching for you. Maybe you can get those things where we're going."

"OK. I take nothing. I need nothing."

Just to make sure, I tell Sahil to explain to the aunties that if anyone comes asking for me, especially a man on a motorcycle in a leather jacket, to say I have left Udaipur and gone back to America. While I'm in my room packing and Sahil is pacing, waiting for me, I hear a pulse in the air. A throb of feathers. There she is, the pearly gray dove, followed by her mate. They each carry a twig, which they deposit on the bookshelf before they fly out of the open window again. "They've come back."

"Ah," Sahil says, "always, birds come back to the place they love."

In less than an hour, we are on a bus to Jaisamand, after I tell the aunties to be sure not to close the shutters while I'm gone and give them an extra tip to ensure it.

PART THREE

DURGA

The goddess Durga is the manifestation of courage. When evil forces threatened the very existence of gods, she went into battle with her vehicle lion without the help of any male companions.

CHAPTER EIGHTEEN

The Bottomless Lake

I love this expanse of sky and water. Rumored to be bottom-less, and so blue it is almost black, Jaisamand Lake stretches as far as the eye can see in one direction, flanked by sparsely wooded hills. Sahil is diving and surfacing like a seal. I watch him from the steps of the gleaming marble ghat, in the shadow of the stone elephants that are the lake's guardians. He plunges down headfirst. I hold my breath along with him, count to thirty, gulp air, and try to guess where he will emerge. I take another breath, hold it, and just when I get to the end of that, and am trying to subdue my nervousness, he pops up, laughing.

"Come in, Elena. Very nice water." He swims over to the steps and playfully grabs my toe.

"No, not for me."

"Why are you afraid? You tell me you can swim."

"I only swim in pools," I tell him. It's true. When I first fell or maybe jumped into the river as a child, I was not afraid. I remember telling Sahil the story that day at the Monsoon Palace that now seems long ago—how with my six year old eyes I'd watched the green water swirl around me as calmly as if I were paying an afternoon visit for tea to my aquatic ancestors' watery habitat. And yet over and over again my parents told the story: She could have drowned *soooo* easily. If I *had* drowned, I thought, with some shock, I wouldn't be listening to my parents tell the story. What a miracle I had survived. From then on, I would be more careful about my precious saved life. I would be more cautious. Soon after that we moved to the city and then the suburbs and I became a swimming pool child, and then a swimming pool adult. I like to know that there are no slithery things to rub against me or nip at my ankles. And I very much like to know where the bottom is.

Once more Sahil goes down and comes up. The water plasters down his thick hair, runs in droplets down his smooth skin, beads on his eyelashes. He looks like a male water nymph. "No bottom, come see," he says.

I kick off my sandals, hoist my skirt up and go down, step by marble step into the water, up to my knees. "This is as far as I go," I tell him. It's hot, I would love to go in deeper, to feel his freedom, but there is something terrifying about its depth, its blackness, its mystery.

Mr. Prateek, who along with his wife takes care of the place we are staying, a former hunting lodge, will only say the lake is "very very deep." He likes to make pronouncements, his small chin nearly hidden under an enormous moustache that moves up and down like an awning when he talks. The temple ghat where we are sitting is really a dam, built only with great sacrifice. "What sacrifice?" I ask. But he continues. "Not so long ago, many famous people are coming to this place," he tells us. "Tigers at one time are roaming this forest. And lions too."

"Forest?" I wonder if this place used to be covered with great swaths of vegetation, instead of the paltry patches of trees on the hills that I can now see when I squint into the sun.

"Oh yes. Rich hunters came with their helmets and guns and whatnot to hunt. British and Indian alike. They are shooting the animals like anything else. Crack shots. Now, they are all quite gone, evaporated." He throws both arms out, palms up, to make his point. There are still plenty of wild boars and grouse that attract a few hunters, he says, although they are not the high-quality, well-dressed game baggers of earlier times. They are more of the "roughneck" variety. In fact, he is expecting a party of hunters any time.

The lodge's courtyard walls are painted with images of beasts, peacocks, gazelles, tigers, boars. I can imagine how stylish this place must have been, when parties outfitted in their arrogance and pith helmets enjoyed gins in the courtyard and regaled each other with stories of the day's slaughter. A tiger skin from those days is spread out in the lodge's entryway.

Sahil insisted on paying for the hotel. "I am becoming a successful businessman," he says. Our second floor room is enormous, the bed a floating island in a sea of black and white tiles. A glass-eyed gazelle head stares out from its perch high up on the wall. A faded photo of a pair of doves hangs over the window, a bizarre echo of the live birds' nest in Udaipur. A pair of French doors lead to a balcony that is suspended directly over the lake. The balcony is the perfect place to dive into the lake, Sahil thinks. It seems a very long way down for a dive, I tell him, but he just laughs. He goes in, his lean body arcing, feet pointed to the sky, a natural dive, not a practiced one. When he comes up, he swims the short distance to the marble ghat, climbs out, comes back up through the halls and to our room

232 · JANET MARIE SOLA

and does it again. I love standing on the balcony and watching him. I envy him his physical courage and grace and wish I had learned to overcome my fears.

I'm happy to be here, away from the maze of Udaipur, from the sadness of Amar, the menace of Wally and the Shadow. And so is Sahil. He seems even wilder here, more passionate, more impulsive, but also more relaxed. I'm feeling myself expand too. It's as if I'm a hostess in a gracious temple, with room for all my goddesses. In the mornings Saraswati wells up in me and I write while Sahil swims or wanders.

Parvati, the love goddess, lurks backstage, waiting impatiently for her turn. She is rewarded. The French doors to the balcony are open and my back is to the sun. We take turns undressing each other. He unbuttons the pearl buttons on my white blouse, one two three four, then unties my skirt where it's knotted around my waist. Then strap by strap slips off my camisole. He kisses my shoulders, my breasts, I unbutton his shirt, put my mouth on the pulse at his throat, run my hands down his smooth brown chest. I can feel each bone, each muscle. Then we lead each other to the island bed.

The first afternoon, after we make love, he tells me he would like to have a child with me. This shocks me a little. Is he serious? I can never tell with him. It's such a farfetched idea for so many reasons, just one of which is that I'm forty. In a stage of my life that seems like long ago, I had the dream of a child, but only with the right partner. It turned out not to be Peter. Sahil though, from a practical perspective, hardly seems right. "Oh Sahil, I'm sure it would be a beautiful child, but where would we live? How would we live?"

"We will have a house in the village. I will work. I will have the best art shop in all Udaipur." I notice he's using the word "will." He's speaking in the future tense instead of just the present. It's something he's never done before.

"Children cost a lot of money."

"Not children. One child. One child who talks like me and looks like you."

When he says that, something in me softens. Something in me wishes it could be true.

"Yes, like me and you," he says. "I love you."

He says that more and more often now. And now I say it back. "I love you too."

He leans over me and with one finger, traces the curve of my lips. "You see this curve." He follows the arc of my upper lip, the up and down and up curve. "This is the sign of *om*, the sign of the universe. It is everywhere this sign. "You see," he traces it again on the bedsheet. "It holds, but very gentle, hold, then let go."

I don't know what he's thinking of but I'm thinking of the vagina, the womb, the arms, the heart. Especially the heart. "Hold, then let go." The pulse of the heartbeat. It sounds easy. And yet I'm wondering if I can do that. I'm wondering if I have to do that. Maybe I don't have to let go.

In the evening, we take a rowboat out on the lake. The water is calm, the air warm. I watch the rhythm of Sahil's arms as they pull and release the oars, the soft waves of the wake fanning out until they disappear. He has given up shaving every day while we are here. His shadow of stubble makes him even handsomer. I think I would like to stay here forever with him.

From where we are on the lake, I can see the outline of a ruined palace on the distant shore, an ethereal fantasy of slender columns, blackened fingers that hold the twilit sky between them.

"This fallen-down palace you see is very special," Sahil tells me. "If you want, I tell you story of the queen who made this palace. A very annoyed queen."

"Only if it's true."

"True. Yes. The maharajah and the maharani live in a big castle. Far off, over the next mountain. They are very happy. But one day the maharajah acts very bad. This makes the maharani angry. She says, 'I cannot live with you anymore.' But he says, 'Ha, you must live here, because you have no other place to live.' And this is true, for a long way there is only forest. 'I do not care, I go,' she says. She takes only herself and goes to this place we see. In one night only she calls on her spirit friends and makes a palace that is more beautiful than the palace of her husband. A magical palace. That is what you see."

"The Overnight Palace."

"Yes, I like this. The Overnight Palace."

"Do you want to go there?"

"Now?"

"Yes, now. Why not?" He smiles his playful smile. With a few strokes of his oars, he's turned the boat in the direction of the palace. It's a very long way away. "I think it's too far and too late to go in this little boat," I tell him.

"Lose your fears, Miss Elena." But he speaks softly as he says it and reaches out and touches my hand. It's so quiet as he rows, just the slip of the oars in the water, the splash as they come out. The sky glides slowly into night, each shade of blue deeper than the one before it. A star appears on the horizon, just over the ruined palace, then another and another and another. We are suspended on this little boat between water and sky.

Both flicker with darkness, but the water, as I dip my hand into it, is wet and cold and so close, the sky so far away, now burning with stars, a million fires from distant universes. I don't remember ever seeing the sky ablaze like this.

I twist around and lie down with my head on Sahil's lap as he rows. I'm drawn in to the mystery and beauty above me, as if we're making an entrance into a great starry theater that exists only for us and will let us play any roles we like. Everything is possible.

"I remember what you say Elena. That the stars we see may be burned out already." I laugh when I recall my farfetched analogy. "But that is sad," he says. "I think the stars are forever. I would like that to be for you and me." He strokes my hair. I love that feeling. When I think about it, light keeps travelling forever, sound for a short while, but taste and touch—especially touch—can only be experienced up close.

A low moon lights the shore, but the silhouette of the ruined palace is getting smaller. The breeze, gentle as it is, seems to be keeping us from making any headway. "I think we should turn back."

"Do you remember my name meaning? The faraway shore that I wish for from the water?"

"Yes, I remember. *Sahil*. Now I wish for it too."

"Because you ask me, I will do as you say." We have only a weak light as a guide, but the light is yellow with the warmth of what must be our lodge. It takes us over an hour of rowing to reach it.

CHAPTER NINETEEN

Cathy's Email

Strung around Jaisamand Lake, like clay beads on a necklace, are a series of small villages. We're headed for one. A "surprise" village, Sahil says. But before we go, I ask Mr. Prateek if I can borrow his computer to check my email.

Mrs. Prateek, a small quiet woman, welcomes me into their living quarters just off the main lobby. Mr. Prateek takes me to his office and proudly shows me his antiquated PC. "I am able to do my bookwork and also my poems ever so fast," he tells me. It takes a while to get the internet connection going, but when I log on, there is one from Jason and a reply from Cathy, subject line *Not in Delhi Anymore*.

Yo Elena,

So you won't believe all that's happened. Finally I got Gramps to commit to having lunch with me—his own grand- child, hello!—at the most expensive restaurant in Delhi, challenged him into having a drink, which he says he never does being a good Hindu (I mean it's fine to treat your mistress and the mother of your child like shit but to have a drink might

*contaminate his holy self). Well, after using my intimidating in-
terviewing skills, plus a gin and tonic, I guilted him in to
talking.*

*The weird thing is that he has this big-toothed smile that
reminds me, I hate to say it, of me, or at least the elderly male
version of me. But here's the good news: my Grandma Rose did
<u>not</u> walk into a river. She actually went off to an ashram. He
wouldn't say how the drowning story got started but my opinion
is he put out the story himself all those decades ago because he
didn't want anybody coming looking for her, then him.*

*So that's where I found her, at this little ashram in the far
south of India. And that's where I am right now. I walk into this
garden and there she is, this kind of beautiful old lady (she's
83!) sitting under a banyan tree. She has very short hair, and
looks a little like an elf with very good posture and a perfect
British accent.*

*At first it was hard to believe she was my grandmother, and
likely she felt the same way about me. After all, I can't bring
myself to give up my khaki shorts and boots. She told me her
story. She had always been spiritual, I knew that. After all
that's what attracted her in the first place to my grandfather
(he was originally a Krishnamurti devotee if you remember the
story). A few years of misery after she sent my mother to England, she decided the best thing she could do with her life would
be to help the poor of India. So she found this ashram and she
started helping in a center they run for women, battered
women, abandoned women, threatened women, a place where
they could come and live in safety with their children and learn
crafts to make a living.*

*She couldn't explain very well why she didn't write my
mother. She knew my mom was safe, and thought she'd be better off without her. She was just in too much pain she said, too
ashamed, and wanted to forget her past. The sad thing was that
I had to tell her Mom had died. She cried naturally. And then
we talked a lot about her, and how all our eyes have the same
kind of shape even though different colors. But now Rose and I
are in each others' lives. That's something.*

*OK, here's the very best part. I'm heading back to Delhi
soon for one reason. To put the screws to the grandpa's rich
ass and get him to cough up some money for Rose's women's
project, which could really use it. I won't leave him alone until
he does. I'll walk around with my big mouth telling everybody
about his slimy behavior. I have a feeling he'll give a substantial donation. And I'll hand deliver it to Rose. And then I'll stay
for a while and help her in her projects. I think it will feel good.*

*Happy ending for a change. So tell me what's going on with
you, your relationship, your search (sorry I was so snarky
about it before, I am herewith changing my ways).*

Cathy

A happy ending. A fabulous ending, like a story in a novel.
I wonder if it's the same ashram that I started out in. I don't
remember a banyan tree though. Nor a center for abused
women. I try to imagine Cathy hanging out in a place like that
adorned in her safari outfit and her in-your-face slang. Knowing how headstrong she is, it's a stretch. But that's the thing
about India. It changes you. It's as if every moment is layered
with meaning, and you want so much to decipher that meaning,
but you can't. You just have to keep moving forward with the

wave of life and responding to it as you move. And on the way, you encounter new layers in yourself, you surprise yourself. Cathy, I think, is discovering her own hidden goddesses.

And yet, I would like to write another ending. I would like to wind back the clock of time. Neela would have escaped from the "cooking fire," Amar would have left with her for Delhi, and Cathy's grandfather would have found her a job in the medical field, far away from the evil that threatened her. Like a novel.

Jason's email is just a few lines. He's on his way to Kathmandu and planning on taking a trek. If I'm interested in going, let him know. I decide to wait to send replies. To see how it all works out with Sahil's and my story.

CHAPTER TWENTY

A Village of Clay

Monsoon season is still a ways off. I understand why people and animals alike long for the relief it delivers from the oppressive heat. For our trip to the village, I wear my floppy wide-brimmed hat and the lightest thing I own, a loose purple cotton dress with an orange scarf tied at the waist that I can also use for a shawl. Sahil tells me I look beautiful. I know, like Parvati after her fast, that I'm thinner. And my hair is blonder from the unrelenting sun. But Sahil is talking about something else. A glow, he says.

Not far down the road near the lodge, we board a bus already brimming with people, brown arms hanging out of the windows, squawking baskets of poultry everywhere, children piled on their mothers' laps, men crammed on the roof, their skinny legs hanging over the edge. The lake and the hotel seemed deserted. Where do all these people come from?

We squeeze in. I grasp the nearest rickety support as we lurch to a start. Sahil free-stands and rolls with the bumps as he chats away with his fellow passengers. There are so many bodies that it feels like we have to take turns breathing. I am eye-to-beady-eye with a scruffy-looking chicken, his beak inches from my still tender nose. And yet, somehow, it's all delightful.

Every five minutes, we stop at a hamlet. Everyone gets off to let people in the back of the bus off, then everyone gets back on again. "Efficiency is overrated," I tell Sahil, laughing, as we squeeze in again for the third time.

"What is this word *efficiency*?"

"Efficiency is . . . figuring out how to make something happen faster so you can get on to the next thing."

"The next thing is important. I will think about this," he says. Ah, the future tense again. While I am ever more in the thrall of the present moment. Maybe we're trading places. We bounce along for another half hour, while I look beyond the chicken to trade silly expressions with a little girl being held by her sister. Finally, we get off and don't get back on.

"This is village. Chalo." Sahil cocks his head toward two women in dark flowing clothes who were also on the bus. We follow them up a long path scattered with shadows of sparsely leafed trees. The village, when we reach it, is lovely. The clay dwellings have been molded into sinuous shapes that flow into one another, and are covered with intricate patterns of blue and red and black. Everything is spotless. It's as if the entire village had just been created that morning and pulled from a potter's kiln.

"The village of artists," Sahil says.

"It's magical Sahil. So this is the surprise."

He tips his head sideways in that way of his and smiles. "Wait here," he says and disappears. In a moment he reappears, accompanying a woman in a bright yellow sari. She is probably about the same age as I am. When she smiles, her face dissolves into a lavish map of lines. Sun lines, life lines. Sahil converses with her briefly, then introduces her.

"This lady is Salena."

"Namaste, Salena-*ji*. My name is Elena. *Mera nama Elena hai.*" When the words come out of my mouth, I feel as if finally I am becoming a little bit Indian. It's a lovely feeling.

Salena tilts her head and looks me over from head to toe. Suddenly I feel self-conscious.

"Lakshmi." She smiles and taps her gold tooth.

"She says you are the goddess of fortune."

"Oh. I like that. I would like to be the goddess of fortune," I say, playing along. "Good fortune or bad fortune?"

"Fortune. Goddess of wealth." He looks at me with a sly smile.

"I wish. But she's wrong, I'm afraid. You know I'm not wealthy, Sahil. Not really."

"Wealthy, not wealthy, it does not matter," Sahil says as we follow Salena on the pathway through the maze of huts. "This woman has no money, but she is happy. We can live here and be happy. We will have one child and you will write your writing and I will paint my pictures."

"And we will grow our own vegetables to eat and milk a goat for our cheese," I add. "For money, we will have a rupee tree." I bat my eyes at him, but he looks quite serious when he replies.

"Do not worry about rupees. I am now a shop owner."

"But what about your art?"

"I can be many things," he says with a touch of irritation in his voice. Again, I catch myself at being the schoolteacher. If I love this man, I must trust him. To let him become who he wants to become. I don't need to constantly impose my values on him. All I really need to do is to surrender to this moment with him, the moment that is now flowing forward so gracefully.

Salena glances at me with her bright eyes. As we weave our way through the village, I want to reach out and touch the baked clay walls, Salena's wrinkled face, Sahil's beard-stubbled cheek and feathery eyelashes. I settle for bending over and stroking the fur of a bleating baby goat. We reach a hut that is a little larger than the others and covered in a leaf pattern that looks freshly drawn in indigo ink. When I look more closely, I see the leaves are really the wings of birds connected to each other at the tips. "*Sundara*. Beautiful."

"This is house of Salena's uncle. We take tea here."

A low opening serves as a door. We have to bend to go through it. Inside the air is cool, infused with the smell of the dry earth and spices. A shaft of light streams through an opening in the ceiling, softly illuminating the room. The hard-packed floors are swept bare, shelves hold red clay pots and dishes, an old kettle hovers over the hearth. Salena beckons to us to sit down on a low bench, then busies herself making tea.

From behind a curtain comes a low hum, broken by an occasional wheeze. I wonder if this is Salena's uncle. Sahil, who can never sit still for a moment, follows Salena around and chats with her as she works. She pours, and he brings me a small clay cup and puts it in my hands. She cocks her head and looks at him with a puzzled expression on her face. I'm guessing it's in wonder that a man would do so simple a thing as bring tea to a woman. But Sahil is no ordinary man. Now I'm convinced of that more than ever.

Salena disappears behind the curtain and soon I hear voices, hers a high pitched cascade of syllables, her uncle's a cracked murmuring. A few minutes later, she emerges with an old tree trunk of a man, tall and thin and weathered, leaning on her. His full length lungi is tucked at his waist, his white hair hangs in long wisps on his yellowing shirt. He waves one hand out in front of him, feeling the air as if he were blind. Sahil rushes across the room to help. Together, he and Salena lower the man onto a cushion on the floor, where he takes a cross-legged pose and leans his back against the wall.

His features are sculpted, almost patrician, a narrow high-bridged nose, a high forehead, thin lips, palish skin. He blinks several times then narrows his eyes as if he's trying to focus—not on anything in the room, but on something he has forgotten, something important. Then his gaze settles on Sahil.

"You remember me," Sahil says. The old man doesn't react. Sahil speaks in a louder voice. "Sir, you do remember me? When I am a small boy, sixteen years old, I am your student. You are good teacher, I am a bad student."

The old man squints at him and murmurs a reply in Hindi. "He asks if I was the boy who liked to play tricks and paint on the walls." He shrugs and smiles, then comes over and stands beside me. "This is the person we seek, the master painter," he whispers. A moment passes before I can take in this information. When I do my skin tingles as if cold water were being splashed on it. I can hardly believe it.

"Are you serious? Was this your surprise?" Sahil inclines his head, a little bow to me. "I do not tell you because I do not want to disappoint you. While you are writing, I walk and talk to many country people. They tell me an old man who paints pictures lives in one village. This village. But I am not sure till I see him. Now I am sure."

He turns to the painter again. "This is my friend from America. Miss Elena."

"Namaste," I say. I rise from my bench and fold my hands and bow.

The old man nods his head. I'm not sure what to expect after such a long time. The master painter was vague in my imagination, but a genius. I remember what Sahil said about him, he was one of the beautiful hunters of the world, possessed of a spirit that sought out new realms of consciousness. As creatures in the wild use all their senses to survive, often in elegant and amazing ways, so artists use their senses to create. And so we evolve. Perhaps he was that beautiful hunter at one time. Perhaps he still is, only that part of him is hidden.

I wait. He raises his palm and brings it down, a gesture I interpret as telling me to sit. From a clay bowl at his side, he picks up a wad of red leaves and stuffs it into his mouth. He chews for quite a long time. Eventually he spits a hunk of red mulch into a nearby pot.

"Betel," Sahil explains under his breath. I've heard of it. It's used like tobacco, but its acids eat away enamel. When the old man finally smiles, he reveals red-stained stumps where teeth should be.

"Miss Elena loves your painting very much," Sahil tells him. In response, he mumbles something to Sahil, who nods and turns to me. "He says he is old. He forgets English. But this is not a problem. I speak to him for you."

"Can you describe my lost painting to him? You remember. The shrouded figure under the tree, the smoking fire, the lion reclining peacefully. The bare hills in the background. Can you tell him what happened to it, how it disappeared?"

"Yes. I do this."

Sahil speaks in Hindi and the old man listens, cupping his ear with his hand. But instead of replying, he continues chewing and spitting.

"Did he hear you?"

"Be patient Elena," he admonishes me. "You do not understand India."

Finally the old man stops chewing long enough to speak. Sahil translates. "Yes, he says he knows this painting. It is very special. It takes him a long time to make this painting. He says it is sad you have lost it."

"What?" I'm taken aback. I try to picture that day when the crowd pressed in on me. I lower my voice when I answer him. "I don't think I lost it. It was taken from me."

"I tell him," Sahil says and translates. The old man nods but says nothing. Except for the sounds of the slurping of tea, and intermittent wheezes and spitting, silence prevails. To break it I ask if it is possible to see some of his other paintings. There is more talk back and forth. "They are now in some other place, he tells me. He is very old now so he no longer paints so much."

I can't help but be disappointed. After all this time, he seems to be just a lungi-clad old man, like any other in this country, and a rather addled one at that. He's getting a far off look in his eyes as if he is slipping off. But suddenly he reaches out to the bowl, revives himself with another wad of betel, and another round of chewing and spitting. He then looks directly at me, although his eyes seem so weak I wonder if he can really see me. He makes another utterance. This time his voice seems to come up from someplace deep within him that he finds only with a great effort.

Finally Sahil turns to me again. "He says you have lost the painting."

I don't want to be argumentative by repeating that I do not believe I lost it, so I remain silent.

"He said you have lost it so that you can seek it."

"Oh." I take a deep breath and hold it, so I can absorb this. When I let it out, it's as if a drop of clear water has landed on my forehead. If I had not lost the painting, I would not have taken the path that has led me to this place right here, right now in this room with the master painter and Sahil at my side. What he said is true in some way I don't entirely understand yet. I have more questions, so many questions, but the old man is suddenly wheezing rhythmically and his head has fallen to the side.

"He has gone to sleep," Sahil says. "He is very old and tired. He must rest. We speak with him in the morning."

"In the morning? But we won't be here."

"It is not a problem. We stay the night here."

"But I don't have my things."

"What things?"

"My nightgown for one thing. My toothbrush, for another thing."

Sahil waggles his head. "Not a problem. For one night only. Sleep in your clothes. Use a twig and water for your teeth." Sahil speaks to Salena. She nods. The two of them cart the old man, the long-lost master painter, back to his room. When she returns she speaks to Sahil. "Salena has another surprise for you," he says.

Over the next hour, to my delight, Salena paints an exquisite design on the palms of my hands. *Mehndi*, she calls it. Working from my wrists to my fingertips, she swirls and squeezes a cone of henna dye as easily as my mother decorated a cake. Sahil has brought his seed and pebble game with him, and plays it with

Salena as I wait for my hands to dry. When I wash them in a bowl of water, a deep red tattoo appears, a design that is like the one on the outside of the clay hut we're in, birds and leaves that become each other, swirls and lacy patterns to the tips of my fingers. "*Sundara*. You are also the master artist," I tell her. When Sahil translates for me, she waggles her head and laughs. Then she leads us back outside and along the village path to another dwelling. Blue waves and stylized fish figures decorate its entrance. "No one lives here now," Sahil tells me. "It is for you."

"For me? You want me to stay alone?"

"I visit until it is time for sleeping," he says. "This is to be proper. We are very proper in Rajasthan," he says with an expression so serious I know he's joking.

At nightfall, a chill has set in. I breathe into my tattooed palms, warming them. My orange scarf is now a shawl I've wrapped around my shoulders. Sahil returns with some sticks he has gathered from the village woodpile, dry branches with dead leaves still attached, and starts to build a fire.

"I used to know how to do that," I say, "when I was a girl scout."

"What is this word *scout*?" I crouch near him as he stacks the sticks into a tent shape in the hearth.

"Let's see. What is scout? Someone who ventures forth into the unknown first to see what is there so she can report back to the others."

He is quiet for a moment. "I like this. Maybe I do this when I dive into the lake without a bottom. I can see if there is a big fish down there or maybe a monster and I can report back."

"Such talent as a story teller, Sahil," I say, laughing.

"I have a better idea," he says. "Maybe we are both scouts. We do not know what is waiting, but we will find out if we are not afraid."

I reach out and take his hand. "I'm not afraid," I say.

The fire catches and crackles. There is something I love about our conversations. They make me think about things like language that is part of us, yet something else too. Something that has an independent existence, almost as a living thing, a companion. I wonder if love is like that. It rises up within us, part of us but something else as well, something we want to reach out and touch.

The fire releases the aroma of dry wood into the room. I ladle water from a bucket into a kettle. When it's boiling I pour it over herbs into clay cups for more tea. So much of the world can be made from clay—dishes, cups, even houses—I think, then say out loud to Sahil. He leans over to whisper inches from my ear. "Don't forget what I say before. One child."

He keeps bringing this up. At first I dismissed it, but now—with a little shock—it occurs to me that my period is late. I didn't think much of it, because for the last couple of years, every so often that happened. What if . . . that would be alarming . . . and yet . . . . I take my tea to a stool and watch as Sahil feeds and stirs the fire. I take a deep drink. Maybe that's what he was seeing in my glow. I have this blissful feeling, as if the tea I am drinking is turning to honey in my blood. A vision comes to me: Sahil and me with a beautiful child, a late child, a child I did not even know I wanted. The child does not look like me in spite of what he said. She has Sahil's eyes, big and dark and luminous and joyous. And his playful, sometimes mischievous spirit. Sahil is chasing her around a meadow, making her laugh, as I look on. I am sitting on a stone wall, pen in hand, writing a book about all the animals of India, the cows, and the donkeys and camels, the turtles and the storks and the peacocks and especially the lions and tigers as there are so few of them left. The book is for our child.

Salena appears in the doorway. The spell is broken. She has come back with supplies: blankets for the bed, which is really just a pad on some planks, a bowlful of vegetables, carrots and potatoes. I murmur a namaste to her. "For curry," Sahil says. He tells me he will show me how to blend the spices. He takes a stone bowl with a pestle from its place on the shelf, and opens containers of spices, fiery red, earth yellow, the colors of warmth, the eye of the tiger, sun on water.

After we cook and eat our meal, he tells me he will sleep elsewhere and return in the morning. "Proper," he says, and kisses me on the nose before he leaves. As I drift off to sleep on the cot I think about him, his grace and patience in the way he brought me tea, planned this outing, his attention to every small thing, the way he enjoys making people smile, and his vision for his future. Is it our future? Yes, perhaps this is what the master painter meant, to lose something so you can find it. Sahil would be a good father. In this moment, hovering at the edge of dreams, it almost seems like a possibility.

CHAPTER TWENTY ONE

A Wild Ride

In the morning I brush myself off, run my hennaed fingers through my hair, and make my way to Salena's hut. She grins at me from her crouch by the open fire. Sahil is there too. He slept on a mat outside he tells me, under the stars, and he hands me a twig, a young and supple one, with the leaves torn off. "For your teeth." I take a cup of fresh water and go outside the hut and use it, feeling a little silly, hoping no one will walk by. Still, it works quite well. I use the rest of the water to wash my face and feel refreshed.

When I return, I ask Sahil to tell Salena I would like to help. She nods when he translates. "She needs water for washing and cooking," he says. "The village well is low. You can get this water from the lake." When he sees my puzzlement he adds, "We boil it." Salena hands me a copper pot shaped like a slightly flattened globe. I have no idea how I'll carry it when it's filled with water.

"Won't you come with me?" I ask Sahil.

"I stay here to help Salena. Here, this is better for you." He takes away the copper pot and replaces it with a sturdy tin pail with a handle. I'm a little annoyed that he doesn't offer to help, but I don't want to spoil our morning by being a bad sport. The path to the lake winds back through the village, across the road, and then down an embankment, perhaps a quarter-mile trip. Near the road, I almost trip over the baby goat, but this time the mother is here, registering her displeasure with a throaty *baaaah*. When I reach the edge of the lake, a half dozen women are filling their pots, chattering like songbirds, their children playing by pouring water on each other. A few other women are beating their laundry on flat rocks in shallow water nearby, the familiar *thwack* refrain filling the air. The morning sun catches the women's white teeth and dark eyes half-hidden under their veils of many colors. They regard me with a mixture of amusement and curiosity.

"I am a friend of Salena." I smile and hold my palms together. They seem to understand this and nod. How many children do I have? they ask me with gestures, pointing to their own children, then to my stomach. None, I signal by creating a zero with my thumb and forefinger. But maybe one, I think. They make sad expressions. I wonder how old they are, with their sun-cracked skin, their missing teeth. Probably younger than I am.

Do they beckon to me, the women in the water? I'm not sure, but suddenly I'm up to my knees along with them, someone hands me a rope of clothes, and I start pounding. *Thwack . . . thwack . . . thwack.* What had this sound said to me the first time I heard it? *Come out. Come out.* Now it says *Stay here. Stay here.* Raising my arms, lowering them, my scarf wrapped around my head to shield my face from the sun, I merge into the rhythm of the task. Time stills. I forget about who I am, where I'm from. One of the children pulls on my dress, and I remember I have to bring water back to Salena.

When I fill my tin pail and struggle to pick it up, the women laugh at me. One of them lifts her own hammered metal container to her head, so easily, so gracefully. She balances it on a kind of fabric wreath. I know that's a feat quite beyond me. I thank the women, wave to them and start back. I try carrying the pail by switching the handle from one hand to the other, until the pain in my arms and shoulders makes me stop. Then I attempt to carry it with my arms wrapped around it, the weight on my chest, a maneuver so awkward I make it only a few steps. When I reach the road, I'm already exhausted. But I have an idea. Using my orange scarf again, I loop it through the handle of the pail. I lug the pail to a high rock. Then, my back to the pail, one hand holding each end of the scarf, I stand up. Now the pail rests in the small of my back, and the weight is more evenly distributed. I make the rest of the trip relatively comfortably. I wonder, if I lived in a village, if I could find all manner of innovative ways of doing things. What a clever woman this Elena is, they would say. Indeed, Salena and Sahil seem impressed with my contrivance. Salena fingers my scarf, as if noticing it for the first time. "Very bee-yoo-ti-ful," she says in English.

When the water is boiled for tea and the chapatis are ready, Salena and Sahil fetch the old man. Our mythical master painter. He is livelier this morning, but eats very little, preferring to work on his red betel wad. I bow to him. "I want to thank you for helping me to understand my search." He listens, his hand cupped behind his ear, as Sahil translates what I say. After a while he croaks a reply.

"He wishes to tell you he can make one more painting," Sahil translates. "Very much like the one you have lost. Salena has a sister who has a son. This son can deliver the new painting to where we stay. Tomorrow or the next day."

"That would make me very happy," I say.

Then Salena speaks. "Salena asks if you can give some money now," tells me. "Not for food. Not for hand henna. That is their gift. For the painting."

"Of course." My serious money is in my pouch, under my dress, a bit awkward. "Excuse me. I'll just get my things from the other hut." Sahil follows me. "Should I ask how much, or offer something?" I ask him.

"How much do you give for first painting?"

I tell him.

"That is very much. Too much. Most is for the shop owner. A bad man. It is good I no longer have to work for this man."

"It's all right. If I can have a painting of his, it's worth it. And he's old. He needs the money." Sahil nods and shrugs. "As you wish."

I retrieve the right amount of rupees from my pouch, pack up my things, we tidy the hut and return. When I press the money into Selena's hands, she's overjoyed. "Lakshmi," she says again. She reaches out for my hand. I think she is expressing affection. She turns my palm up and traces the henna design she created yesterday. Then she turns my hand over and strokes the fingers. "Very be-yoo-ti-ful," she says again and then says something else in Hindi.

"She likes the color on your nails. They are a color like a sunset."

"Thank you. It's only polish."

"She wants to know if you have some of this color you can give her."

I like this polish, but more than I want to keep it, I want to please her. I nod and touch her sun-wrinkled hand. She smiles broadly and taps her gold tooth. "Lakshmi," she says one more time.

"I wish she wouldn't call me that," I say to Sahil. But I know there is nothing I can do about the way she sees me. To her, I am and will always be the Lakshmi of the west, the representative of a different culture, a rich culture. So be it. I put my hands together and bow to her, and then to the master painter, who inclines his head ever so slightly in my direction. Is it a gesture in recognition of our connection or a bobble of the head brought on by the shadows of infirmity? Will he really be able to pull off this painting? With no good reason, I believe he will. I will have my painting at last.

"When the boy brings the painting, you can give him the polish," Sahil says.

Everyone nods as if this is a wonderful solution. The bus will be coming soon. It's time to leave. When I say goodbye to Salena with another promise that yes, she will have the sunset-colored nail polish, I feel a twinge of sadness that I don't entirely understand.

The bus comes once a day. We're part of a throng, women laden with wares and small animals and children, men with naked stovepipe legs and hard expressions. We're all patient as trees as we wait. When the gaudily painted vehicle swerves down the road in a cloud of dust and fumes, it's a different story. Everyone tries to get in all at once with whatever advantage they have: brute force, sharp elbows, or slithering ability. "Don't push, slide," says Sahil as the doors open. Try

as I might, I can't seem to make any headway at all. And then
without warning, I'm being tugged in the opposite direction.
Sahil is scrambling up a narrow ladder on the side the bus, and
pulling me up after him.

"What are you doing?" I shout to him. But he just keeps
tugging. Before I know it, I'm sitting with him on the top of the
bus, the lone woman among grizzled old men in lungis and cal-
loused bare feet, young men in jeans and polyester shirts, giddy
boys, dozens of male legs dangling over the very narrow railing. I look around. There is no place to hold on. The railing that
encircles the edge of the bus's roof is no more than a few inches
high.

"Sahil, I'd rather wait for the next bus than be up here," I
say. I try to sound nonchalant. The truth is I am terrified.

"You are OK. Only relax." When the bus starts to move, my
first instinct is throw myself flat on my back. "You must sit up.
Hold on here." He shows me how to grip the railing with my
hands, which seems like trying to ride a horse by hanging on to
its tail. Sahil sways from side to side with the motion of the bus,
as if there were nothing to it. The lake, visible in frames between the trees, lies placid under a hot blue sky, but the tree
branches that hover near the road are moving up and down as
we bump along. The more we bounce, the stiffer my body gets.
An animal panic rises up my spine.

"Enjoy," Sahil says. "Relax. Do not be afraid. Elena, you
are too afraid."

I am not too afraid, I'm just afraid enough, I think. Every
time we take a curve my heart drops to my stomach. Then,
without warning, Sahil pushes me down onto my back. He goes
down with me. Just above us a heavy branch passes in a blur.
A branch that would have hit us if we hadn't gone down. When

he pulls me back up I see that the men on the roof are laughing at me. Sahil too laughs.

I hold my breath until the whole thing is over. All the tenderness I felt for him just hours ago is draining out and in its place absolute fury is pouring in. "There was nothing funny about that," I tell him after we are back in our room at the lodge. "I could have been killed. You could have been killed."

"But you are not killed. You are not hurt. I save you."

I look at him and see the same fine-boned face, the same luminous eyes, the same smile, the same nonchalant stance. But he is no longer the charismatic lover who is opening the windows of transformation for me. He's an irresponsible, immature brat. I try to merge these two images, the Sahil that I was falling in love with yesterday and this new person who is emerging. And yet I know that this isn't the first time I've seen this side of him. It has always been there. On the white side of the seed is his charm, his magic, even his kindness. On the black side of the seed is his casual recklessness. He appears and disappears in ways I can't predict and can't understand. I feel confused. Blindsided. Disoriented.

"I don't want you to save me." I struggle to find the right words but there aren't any. There's just raw emotion. "I want you to . . . leave me alone."

He takes a step away from me, then shakes his head as if he can't believe what he is hearing. "I am sad you are saying this."

"Sahil, I'm sad too. I'm very confused. Let's talk about it later." Right now I feel hot and dirty from our village trip. My shoulders ache from carrying the pail of water. I need to take a bath before dinner. "Right now, I want to be alone," I repeat.

"Do what you want to do," he says. He looks so out of place, so fragile, in this big room, with its gazelle head propped high on the wall, its scuffed inlaid furniture, shopworn tributes to another era, that my anger fades and I want to put my arms around him. Instead I watch him go.

CHAPTER TWENTY TWO

Another Dinner Party

I find Sahil and Mr. Prateek having drinks in the flower-filled courtyard. "Your friend tells me you are a writer lady," Mr. Prateek says to me when I sit down next to Sahil. "This is what I feel myself to be. That is, not a lady, but a writer person." He is dressed in shiny Western clothes, a yellow shirt and dark trousers. His moustache is smartly trimmed and looks as if it has just been combed, and his black eyes glisten above it.

The savory smell of cooking grouse is in the air. The hunters Mr. Prateek had said were coming have had a successful day in the scrub. The chief hunter, a bearded, gruff-looking sort who smells of alcohol, along with his "assistant," are grilling today's kill in an alcove off the courtyard. Every so often the hunter comes by and pours our glasses full of a milky alcoholic mulch. To me, it looks and tastes like poison. After the first sip I refuse any more. Mr. Prateek is drinking nothing at all. Sahil seems to be enjoying it though. In fact, every time the hunter comes by with his bottle, he raises his glass for more. Already, his eyes are taking on a glazed look and his speech is slurring. When I gently tell him I think he's drinking too much, he ignores me the first time. The second time, he looks at me in a curiously expressionless way. "You do not care about me, so why do you care what I do?"

"Sahil, that is not true," I tell him, keeping my voice low. Mr. Prateek politely ignores what is going on between us.

"Then why do you say you want me to leave you alone?" Sahil asks. "I want to live with you. To have a child with you. You do not even answer me. You come here to be part of India, I am part of India too. So why do you not care?"

His words sting me, but I have no answer, so I settle for a retort. "Why do you behave so badly?" I want to stop his imbibing. But as we don't have to drive anywhere, or even walk anywhere except upstairs, I am trying not to be upset about it. Or at least to pretend I'm not upset. I try to concentrate on the story Mr. Prateek is telling about the building of the dam-that-looks-like-a-temple that created this enormous lake, the biggest in all of Rajasthan. Each time the effort at building the dam failed, he explains. Halfway through, the construction would collapse and the river would come pouring through.

"The British did many good things for this country," Mr. Prateek declares. "I don't care what anyone else says. From them we learned engineering." But engineering could not stop the gods who were angry at the arrogance of humans. "Failure, failure, failure like anything else. 'The gods demand a sacrifice,' the people said. Just so. Volunteers were called for, a man who was willing to sacrifice his earthly life for the honor of being named in the inscription of this dam."

"So did they find such a person?" I ask. "I hope not."

At that moment the hunter appears and grumbles something, and shortly after that, the one permanent employee in the hotel aside from the manager, a short man dressed impeccably in a white kurta shirt and trousers, announces dinner with a bow.

"Our storytelling is continuing in the dining room," Mr. Prateek says. With Sahil weaving, we move from the courtyard, through the reception area with its grand staircase, into a large room where a table has been set next to long dusty windows. Cracked china dully shines on almost-white linen. I think of the opulence of the dinners that must have taken place here in the past, the guests swathed in brocade and jeweled turbans as they sat down to freshly killed and cooked boars stuffed with apples in their mouths.

We seat ourselves, and Mr. Prateek picks up his story. "You ask if they found such a man. Indeed, one was obtained. An ordinary man, a peasant, but one who believed in mighty progress." He pauses for dramatic effect. "This man was willing to give his life for the advancement of civilization and for immortality. He stood in the trench as they were building and was covered with cement and mud. And after this the dam was completed with great speed and success. He is still here, buried."

"Buried alive. So you are saying this is native ingenuity?" It would seem like another Indian legend, except for the forthright way in which Mr. Prateek tells the story.

"We in India are very much a mixture of the practical side and the spiritual or artistic side, favoring both. In fact, I have written a poem about this, it captured my fancy so much. Would you like to hear it?"

"How could I resist hearing a poem on such a topic?"

"Presently you will hear it. Just now, dinner is served." The servant appears with five or six plump and blackened birds piled on a china platter, accompanied by heaps of rice and curried sauces. Mrs. Prateek, he explains, has made the side dishes although she is not at the table. Mr. Prateek takes over the carving of the birds. A bottle of wine is opened, and the hunter appears. Indian men, even the poorest, give an air of being clean and groomed. With his unkempt hair and scruffy beard, the hunter seems have stepped out of a Russian novel. Mr. Prateek toasts him for his contribution of the grilled grouse. He growls in acknowledgement.

The hunter begins to shout and wave his fork around. Every so often he pours a bit of the mulch straight from the bottle into his mouth, and then passes it to Sahil. Fortunately, Mr. Prateek reaches out to intercept the bottle, sniffs it and hands it back to the hunter with a reprimand.

As he works on carving the birds, Mr. Prateek gamely tries to make introductions. But his ever so cheerful voice fades away as the hunter bellows who knows what jokes, followed by chortles of approval from his assistant, a gangly young man who has wandered in still wearing his hunting hat and dusty boots, his rifle slung over his shoulder. The hunter grins, wipes his mouth, grabs the carving knife from Mr. Prateek, and makes a show of cutting the birds. When he's done, his assistant picks up a drumstick before skulking off and sitting on the floor with his knees spread apart, his rifle resting beside him.

"He is not accustomed to chairs," Mr. Prateek explains.

"Is he not accustomed to leaving his guns outside either?" I ask. "I mean that's what they did even in the Wild West."

Mr. Prateek chuckles. "This is the Wild East, you might say then. I myself have a gun for hunting these very delicious birds. I have led the odd expedition or two and am a crack shot like anything else." I nod. The hunter continues at top volume. Mr. Prateek rolls his eyes in the hunter's direction. "We must ignore him."

I try to do just that, concentrating on my bird, which really is very good. I encourage Sahil to at least eat, and he does take a few bites. He is uncharacteristically quiet in the midst of the din of the competing voices of the bellowing hunter and Mr. Prateek, who is going on now about how much chairs have contributed to civilization. Sahil seems to have tuned us all out. When the bottle of wine is passed around, he fills his glass to the rim, and downs a half of it in the first gulp. "Why are you doing this?" I ask him.

Sahil looks at me in a wounded way. "I drink because I want to be happy and I am sad because you are angry at me." His words slur when he says it.

"Sahil, please stop. I'm not angry. We can talk about everything later."

"Would you like to hear my poem?" Mr. Prateek asks again.

"Of course." I smile, determined to retain the façade of a civilized dinner party. Mr. Prateek has to speak very loudly to be heard over the hunter. "And so," he begins:

They strived to build the mighty dam
But their work, alas, would not stand
The water came like anything else in a torrent
Drowning all who could not flee the current

Until one humble man came to offer
The greatest thing a man can proffer
"Cover me," he said, "with all your cement
And in your hearts do not lament"

So the work like anything else proceeded
Until the gods at long last heeded
And the mighty water crop was stopped
And so in conclusion the British were topped

He finishes his poem and waits. I think it's been so long since Mr. Prateek has had a guest who can appreciate his enthusiasm for language, if not his skill, that I put down my knife and fork and applaud him. Mrs. Prateek, sweet-faced in a pink sari, who has quietly crept into the room, and even Sahil in his stupor, clap their hands along with me.

Mr. Prateek looks very pleased. "Sometimes life is a struggle between the forces of culture and the forces of incivility," he says, casting a disparaging glance in the hunter's direction. As if he could understand and were taking offense at the comment, the hunter barks back at all of us, then gives a command to his crony. The man stops gnawing on the drumstick and springs up from the floor, gripping his rifle as he does so. They both stumble out of the dining room.

"They will sleep it off." Mr. Prateek shrugs. "What the world has come to with so much rudeness and drunkenness. We must continue the fight, we writers, with our words."

"Yes, we must," I agree. I'm glad to be rid of the hunters.

"Thank you for your wonderful company, fellow writer lady," Mr. Prateek says, standing up and bowing slightly to me. "I sadly must leave you. I must do the paperwork as always."

"I really did enjoy your poem. And the story. I hope it was only a story. Or as we say in America, an urban legend, or in this case, a Rajasthani legend."

"Quite so. Quite so," he says enigmatically, before he and his wife make their exit.

By now, darkness has settled outside, the window panes are black, the room lit only by a few oil lamps. The servant in white has cleared the table and left. Sahil's normally animated face is

flattened by alcohol or whatever else was in the hunter's con-
coction. Now his eyes are rolling and his head is bobbing on
his chest. "Time to go," I tell him. He doesn't respond. I sigh.
It's a long flight of stairs to our room, and I'm not happy about
having to support him the whole way up. "Come on. Chalo," I
say, tugging at him.

Anger is futile at this stage. I'm trying to figure out how to
lug him away from the dinner table when I hear a muffled
sound. Shuffling. Muttering. Something I know instinctively
will be very unpleasant, even before I turn in the direction of
the noise. And there they are: the hunter on one side of the door,
his crony on the other, framed by the doorway like a painting.
Their rifles are pointed upright as if they were guarding a palace. Their eyes are moving from Sahil to me, and back again,
looking both of us over as if we were grouse.

"Sahil," I nearly shout. He lets out a sound something between a giggle and a groan. The adrenaline comes in starbursts,
exploding in my knees, my stomach, my heart, my head. I feel
sure they see my fear. With newfound strength, I grab Sahil,
yank him to his feet, and put his arm around my shoulder. I hold
my head high, and move toward them step by step, looking beyond them as if they don't exist. "Please get out of our way," I
say when we reach the doorway. And they do.

I drag Sahil through the adjoining room that leads to the
staircase. I can feel their eyes on my back. Somehow, I manage
to struggle up the stairs to our second floor room, Sahil leaning
on me the entire way. Once inside, I deposit him on the bed,
slam the double doors shut, then slide the iron bolt that spans
the doors into its slot.

CHAPTER TWENTY THREE

Trapped

I move across the room and open the French doors that lead to the tiny balcony. A gust of wind from the lake blows in and the long white curtains billow in response. They look like the ghosts of veiled women. I step through the doors. Two stories below me, the dark water laps against the stone walls. The moon floats on the surface of the lake. The night is a mirror.

Then, in the silence, a thud. Then another. Sahil must be reviving. I turn to look, but he hasn't moved. There's the sound again. Muffled. Insistent. *Thud. Thud.* The sound is coming from the other side of the double doors that lead to the hallway. *Thud. Thud. Thud.* Then another sound. Sharper this time, a cracking sound, a hard object butting against wood. The sound of a rifle butt. No, the sound of two rifle butts. It's the most sickening sound I have ever heard. I can't move. I stare at the door where the sounds are coming from.

The curtains billow again. My mind stops in mid-thought, freezes, then slides through a narrow bright opening to another dimension, a dimension where everything rational, everything civilized has been left behind, like so many silly customs, and what is left is very clear. The hunter and the hunted.

I go through a mental checklist. I've bolted the double doors from the inside. It's an iron bolt. It should hold, it will hold, at least as long as the wooden frame that holds the brackets does not give. The wood is old. Maybe a hundred years old. But still it should hold, right? There is no other way out. And no telephone. I pace, looking for the switch to turn off the overhead light. The light glares down on me. It's so bright. The room is enormous, forty paces of black and white tiles. I find the switch, behind the curtain. I flick it. The light stays on. I flick it again. And again. Nothing changes. High up on the wall, the gazelle's head stares down, its glass eyes terrified and terrifying.

The sound again. *Crack.* The doors heave against the bolt. Think. What do they want? I don't know. Maybe they don't know. They're drunk. Hyped up. Mayhem. Violence. Robbery. Rape. They would probably settle for either of us. What will they do to get it? I don't know. Sahil is lying on his back, arms out, looking as innocent as an exhausted swimmer drifting peacefully on the white raft of the bed.

More cracks. More thuds. "Go away," I shout, with what I hope sounds like authority. Inside I'm shaking. Then silence. Maybe they've left. I kneel on the bed again and shake Sahil. His head flops like a puppet's. I'm furious at him for doing this to me. I want him to wake up and save me. I plead with him. "Wake up, please wake up." My voice is hoarse, desperate. But he's gone. I straddle him and peel back his eyelids. His brown irises are floating in white, like dark yolks, beautiful and blank. He's dead, I think, he's dead. The stuff he drank was poison and he's died. I put my head on his chest, listen through his white shirt. I can hear his heartbeat. I put my hand above his mouth. I can feel the warmth of his breath.

Then the sounds start again. Only now they are human voices, or inhuman, growls and rasps and howls, like wild beasts in nightmares. And the sounds aren't coming from behind the doors to the room. Now they're from the wall over the bed, an arm's length away. Scratching sounds. Scraping sounds. Behind the bed, I notice for the first time, is an old connecting door with a glass inset that has been painted over on the other side of the glass. Now I see what the hunters are doing. They are scraping the paint off. The scratches go on and on until I can see a dark spot that is growing larger. They're making a peephole. The better to see us with. They can see Sahil lying on the bed, me kneeling beside him. I know they are watching me, as if I were in a zoo or a prison cell. They're laughing. Drunken laughter. They're shouting. I can't translate, but I don't need to.

I can't stay here. I try to imagine their sight lines. If I hug the common wall between us they won't be able to see me. I get up from the bed. Sahil doesn't move as I leave him lying there. I lean against the wall and inch my way along to a corner wardrobe. It's made of a dark wood, probably wood from the forest that Mr. Prateek said used to be here. Where is that silly man? No doubt revising his ridiculous poem aloud and chuckling to himself.

I slide to the floor, press my palms together to stop shaking. The henna patterns look strange now, nonsensical. I try to connect something of what I am doing at this moment to the woman who came here a few short months ago, maybe a little naïve, maybe a little overly romantic, but a nice woman, surely, a nice educated woman with a life and friends and a career— surely that's a description of me. Will I ever get back to her? Will I ever get out of this room? Will I ever get out of India?

Now, they're tapping on the glass, as if they are summoning me to come back into view. I slide my body along the floor until I reach the bathroom. It's huge, marbled over every inch. There's a lock on the door. A safety zone. But if they do manage to break down the door and get in, I'd be trapped.

I slide along the floor back into the main room. I wish the light would burn out. It's so yellow and bright, a tiny sun glaring down on a lonely solar system, light years away from the world I lived in for so long, where there were lunches and concerts and Shakespeare and lists of things to do. The universe of this strange place I'm in has its own rules, things are born and die here, yet no one, no one at all outside it will ever know. It will take any information that leaves here so long to reach the other world, the normal world, that the event will be long over. If they react at all, people will simply shrug, "What was she thinking?"

But I am thinking, very sharply. I'm shot through with pure thought, aware of every detail of this room, of my body, of Sahil's unconscious form on the bed, of the predators next door, still scratching, still knocking on the glass. In an instant, I formulate a plan. To accomplish it I need to be invisible.

My heart is pounding as I go to my suitcase, search through my cosmetics bag for my bottle of nail polish, the color of the sunset Salena had said. I move back to the glass and stare back defiantly. I can hear their great drunken guffaws. I try not to imagine their faces. I shake the bottle, undo the cap, pull out the brush and start painting, first with small strokes, then thick sloppy fast ones until the glass is dripping with shiny coral polish. There is no more peephole. The show is over. The predators are muttering.

They do what I thought they would do. They move back to the bolted doors and attack with renewed energy. They must be shoulder hammering, body hammering. The nauseating thud of rifle butts begins again. I wonder how long it will take before they try to shoot their way through.

I take another look at Sahil. What would they do to him if they broke through? I don't even want to imagine it. It seems so long ago, when Sahil and I sat on the parapets of the Monsoon Palace, telling each other childhood stories of our mothers saving us from drowning. Now, there is no one to save us.

I step out to the balcony. I take a deep breath, close my eyes and call on one more goddess. Not those goddesses of creativity, or love, or wealth, those goddesses of transformation, of fulfillment, or happiness, all those lovely pursuits of leisure that are part of some other world. In this remote time and place where I find myself at this moment those things don't matter. What matters is survival. I call on Durga. Durga with her many arms holding her trident and conch shell. Durga who had to go it alone against some brute whose name I can't remember, but one who abused his power, like the brutes with their guns now banging at my door, like all the brutes of the world. She had to do it by herself, without the aid of any males. Were they all sleeping, like Sahil? I don't need the details, I just need her strength. Durga, goddess of courage, help me now.

I look down to the black water below. It's so far down. Fear crawls up my body like a cold, oily drug, into my legs, into my stomach, up to my heart, and through my arms. It paralyzes me. It's only my spirit, a tiny thing, floating free, that escapes. That's where Durga reaches me. It's only water, she says, only an element, indifferent, calm, beautiful even. Unlike the malevolent forces on the other side of the door. You don't have to change the whole world, but only respond to what you face in the moment. That's all courage is.

I step out of my shoes, delicate little embroidered slippers meant for that other life with those other goddesses. There is no breeze at all now. The low moon is suspended over the water, lighting a silver trail straight to me and shedding a ghostly glow on the ruined palace in the distance. I hear the low, two-noted hoot of an owl and, behind me, the cracks and groans at the door.

How far down is the water? Twenty feet? Thirty feet?

I take off my jewelry, a rope of a necklace, a twist of bracelet and let them drop. Only one step. One step. Take it. Whatever happens, Durga says to me in her soft voice, as I step over the railing and off the edge, know that you are part of this world that is lovely beyond compare.

The lake swallows me in an instant. Cold. Wet. Dark. The panels of my silk tunic float up around me, wrap around my face and arms like tentacles. Like a cold lover, the water pulls me down, down, down into its embrace. It's so strange. Like India was strange when I first arrived. Not mine. Then it became mine. Like the dark water is becoming mine. Down, down. It's so silky against my skin, no longer cold, like going back to a womb, to a place before I was born, to my natural element. I want to get to know it. How deep is it? What other creatures live here? Are they welcoming their clumsy new inhabitant? Are they haunted too by the ghost of the man buried in the dam? But I have no time for the answers to my questions. My lungs ache, and there is no air on my downward path. Breathe in, the other lake creatures say, join us in our peace.

Yes, says my body, breathe in, you will adapt like other creatures that returned to the water. You have to breathe. Wait, says Durga. Courage is endurance too.

Then, when I can't stand it another second, I'm suspended, the force pulling me down in perfect balance with the force that wants to pull me up. I rise. The lake inhabitants, the fish, the eels, the kelp, the ghost, they all expel me from their midst. I don't belong here after all. I emerge on to the glittering surface. The moon streams toward me. I open my mouth and air, sweet air, flows in. The owl is hooting its two notes, over and over again.

It's a short swim to the steps of the ghat, perhaps a hundred breast strokes with my clothes weighing me down. I search for the underwater steps with my feet and hands. I find them, slimy, but I pull myself up to my knees, and then my feet. The elephant guardians are waiting in the moonlight, their trunks stretched out in greeting. I shake myself off and make my way up the stairs, through the courtyard, and into the lodge and its halls. From faraway, up on the higher floor where I had come from, I can still hear the thumps of the drunken hunters. Light comes from under the door at the end of the hall. The manager's residence. When Mr. Prateek answers my knock, groggy but fully dressed, I put my finger to my lips. We must not give the brutes any warning.

"You said you had a gun," I say in a low voice. "Get your gun." He looks at me, his lips pursing, one eyebrow raised in a question mark. "Get your gun. Get your gun like anything else."

CHAPTER TWENTY FOUR

The Final Fight

Set on the table in our room are a pot of steaming coffee, baguettes and omelets, all on a white tablecloth with a vase of flowers. Mr. Prateek delivered it personally this morning. "Dear lady writer," he assures me, "the scoundrels are safely locked up."

I am half listening to him, half to Sahil, who is in the bathroom, retching into the toilet bowl.

"This is what I am meaning when I say the forces of civility must fight the forces of chaos. Lock them up."

"I think that fight could be more easily won if you had not left your guests with crazy men with guns and gone off to write a poem."

"I neglected to do my duty to protect my guests," he admits, hanging his head. "In the future I will have more vigilance."

As Mr. Prateek tells the story, he used his shotgun to come up from behind and surprise the drunken hunters, took their guns, locked them in a room, guarded them till their loud snoring told him they were asleep, and this morning had them carted off to the local jail. I stayed in Mr. and Mrs. Prateek's rooms, with a blanket around me, until Sahil finally, after repeated poundings by Mr. Prateek, woke up enough to unbolt the door. Mr. Prateek returned for me and escorted me to the room. I pulled off my wet clothes, took a hot bath and crawled into bed beside Sahil.

When Mr. Prateek leaves, still mumbling apologies, I pour myself another cup of coffee and pick at my omelet. Sahil ventures out of the bathroom and slumps into a chair, a towel over his shoulders. I tell him everything that happened. I walk around the room recreating the story. "Here," I kneel on the bed and tap on the glass, "here is where they scraped off the paint and I put the polish over it." I can hear my voice rising. "And here is where they tried to break down the door." I gingerly touch the splintered wood. Then I move to the balcony. In the daylight it looks less dangerous, and yet I still can't believe I did it. "And here is where I jumped into the lake."

He holds his head between his hands as if it were a melon about to burst open and closes his eyes. He refuses to take any responsibility. "It is not my fault life is full with bad, crazy people."

"You deserted me. I am in your country." I go back to my nearly untouched breakfast, look at him evenly over my coffee cup. "You brought me to this place. What if they had broken the door down? What if I couldn't have escaped by swimming? Who knows what would happen? I could have been raped. You could have been raped, for that matter. Or killed."

"But this did not happen. It is good you jump off balcony to swim. This means you are not afraid any more."

"You think this is all is a joke."

"Leave me alone," he says. "You are not my mother." He rubs his eyes with both hands.

"You are a child though," I say. "You don't care about anybody but yourself."

"I cannot help it. It will not happen again." He says this with a shrug.

I can't believe he can be so cavalier about the whole thing. "You know what Sahil, I take it back. You are not a child, you just do whatever you feel like, whatever your instinct tells you to do." I am shrieking now. "You're not a child. You're an animal."

Instantly, he is transformed. He moves toward me in a cold fury. "Do not call me that. I am not that. I am a man. An Indian man. I will show you that." He reaches out for me with both arms and pushes me back on the bed.

He has my arms pinned down over my head. I'm not moving, not trying to fight him. I want to use my will alone to stop him, to bring him back to what he was before. I stare into his eyes, trying to fathom what he is thinking. But they're black, unreadable.

"Do not ever call me an animal. That is the something you can never say." I've touched some forbidden cultural zone, the one my Hindi teacher warned me about. Maybe I should apologize, but I say nothing. He pulls himself up and turns away. "No," he says, "I do not want you. I hate you. You are driving me crazy. You do what you want to do. I am leaving."

"Leave then, yes, leave," I say.

"Yes, I leave. And I will not come back." He is still in the clothes he was wearing yesterday, his black T-shirt and jeans, rumpled now. He picks up the blue and white woven scarf I gave him from the floor and wraps it around his neck. He runs his hands through his hair, then picks up his satchel. I watch him walk across the room. He does not even look over his shoulder. He pushes opens the splintered door, goes out, and slams it behind him.

I sit for a few minutes, feeling my anger, feeling my righteousness. Taking pleasure in it, in fact. Good. It's over. I'm free. It had to be. I start to pick up my own things and pack. There is the bottle of nail polish Salena wanted, half gone now. I'll leave the remainder for Mr. Prateek to give to her if she comes. I wonder if the painting would have showed up along with it. I doubt it. I don't care now. I fold the few clothes I brought with me, the colorful silk skirts and dresses and scarves I've grown so fond of. Sahil has likely taken the bus back to town or hitched a ride. I'll have to make the bus ride alone. It will be good to wear something that hides me on the way. I opt for a loose pale blue dress that completely covers me. I take off the jeans and T-shirt I put on this morning. As I undress, I see that my period has come after all. I'm relieved. Thank the goddess, Durga it would be, who needs no man. Once I'm dressed, I sit on the edge of the bed. It's so eerily quiet. Not a sound except the faint lap of lake water. Long rectangles of gray sky press against the windows. It's as if I had made this journey all alone, as if Sahil had never existed.

Then it starts. I don't even try to stop the tears because I know I can't. I throw myself on the bed and cry, great sobs of pain, for lost love, for what I cannot hold on to—riding a bicycle through the fields and holding a lamb in my arms, for fried fish in the rooftop restaurant, and the birds building a nest in my room, and for the lovemaking at night with this beautiful man that I loved maybe simply because of his beauty, and the arc of his cigarette as he left, and the basket over my head that blanked everything out except our laughter. And then I cry for my lost youth that I will never have again, and know I will never cry for again, but today I am crying for it and can't stop. Because I know after this I will find Cathy in Delhi and Jason in Kathmandu if I can, and eventually go back to where I came from, to the other side of the world, I will have another relationship maybe, surely, but it will never ever be as wild and as beautiful and as heartbreaking as this one. Is there a goddess for angry, forlorn women? For women who make bad decisions? For women who are leaving their youth behind? Maybe, but I don't know who she is. I'm alone, with just me, or the shell of me.

There's a sound mixing in with my tears, a soft pattering. I get up from the bed and go to the balcony. Rain. A million tiny pellets turn into a net of jewels as they hit the lake. In the distance I can see the gossamer outline of the ruined palace, the Overnight Palace. It will be a good place to cry.

CHAPTER TWENTY FIVE

The Overnight Palace

The road to the ruined palace is strewn with rocks. Here and there stacks of mud bricks have been left on the side of the road near half-finished huts. The rain is warm, fine, a shower that is over in minutes, leaving the trees, the rocks, even the hard clay dirt glowing with a fine sheen.

My guide is the palace's profile against the gray washed sky. The road narrows and finally gives out entirely. I follow a pebble and leaf strewn path into a woodland and through a mile of wet trees and shrubs and thickets, inhabited by flashes of feathers and fur.

And then it's in front of me. Three stories of twilight-colored stone, blue and gray, a fairy skeleton of the palace that had been. Without walls, its arches and columns and staircases are open to the elements—the rain and the sun and the field mice. One scurries in front of me and disappears. I climb over the knee-high wall that surrounds the grounds. Wild grasses are growing on the palace floor, and a sunken pool stands in the center of what used to be a courtyard. I bend over and splash my face with clear water, then wash my feet.

Gradually, I'm aware of a scent in the air, a spicy, acrid smell like burning sandalwood. I look around to see where it's coming from. A puff of smoke rises from behind a gap in the ruined wall on the far side of the courtyard. I move quietly in a wide arc, skirting around loose stones from fallen walls. Through the gap in the wall I can see the back of a shrouded figure, wrapped almost entirely in blue cloth. I can't tell if it's a man or a woman, but he or she is settled under a tree, in front of a smoking wood fire, tending it with a stick.

I call out hello, namaste, but there is no response. Maybe it's a pilgrim, or a homeless person who is camping out. As I move closer, I see that it's an old woman, with strange blue eyes that match the pale blue of her garment, absorbed in stirring the fire. Namaste, I say again. Without looking at me she nods toward the fire. As quietly as possible, I fold my legs underneath me and sit down next to her. After a time, she reaches into a cloth bag, and pulls out a handful of seeds and nuts. She offers some to me, and the rest she scatters around her. Birds appear, tiny birds in cloaks of yellow and brown. They peck up the seeds and fly off again.

I think about fear and courage. Was I courageous last night? Maybe courage is not about taking undue risks but necessary risks. To do what is needed to move on with life, to find out what we are capable of. When I had jumped into the river the first time as a child, it wasn't courage, it was impulse, or curiosity, or something I can't name really. It was a jump of innocence. But in our life, something called experience comes in. It teaches us about disappointment, and having things and losing them, and wanting things and not being able to get them, and seeing that the world is often beautiful, but just as often unjust, and that wrongs go unavenged, and that a search for beauty or joy in the midst of that uncertainty is a good way to live.

Maybe what I have found is not the courage of resolution, but the courage of response, just to respond to a call in the moment, knowing that in the next moment it might change, and that it might change because of my response. What call to courage does that little child have, the one that walks on his hands because he is crippled? Only perhaps to find his own joy in whatever way he can, moment by moment. Maybe that is why his smile spreads out to the world. And what call to courage did Sahil and I have? Only to reach out to each other across the divide of cultures for love or for some other reason we don't even fully understand. Because if we hadn't reached out, we would never know what our story could have been.

Then my mind empties of words entirely. Or of ideas. The moments flow by seamlessly. Minutes pass, perhaps hours. At some point the old woman turns to me and hands me the glowing stick, bows slightly to me, stands up and disappears into the woods. She has gone to look for more firewood, I think. I trace the embers of the fire with the stick and watch the pattern of light through the arches of the ruined palace. I close my eyes, and listen to the sounds of the forest. It all feels eerily familiar, as if something is tugging at the edge of my awareness. I have no more tears, I have no more sorrow, only the peace that comes at the end of a storm. When I open my eyes again, a figure is at my feet. For a moment, through some trick of light or imagination, it looks like a large cat curled up, tawny, sleek, with a contained feline calm. In that breath of a moment, the image comes from somewhere deep inside: the swathed figure tending the fire under the tree, the lion at its feet. No, not *its* feet. *Her* feet. *My* feet. Everything is suddenly illuminated. I understand. I have become my lost painting. The image I sought was my journey. Or maybe our journey, Sahil's and mine. A sense of peace and transcendence that comes with completion invades me. Then the illusion goes, I am looking at a crown of dark hair, a lean body in black clothes. He sits up, gently takes the fire stick from my hand and stirs the fire.

"You must forgive me," Sahil says. "I want to protect you but I do not. I am weak. I am still learning how to be a man."

I look at him. The downward tilt of his head keeps his eyes in shadow.

"We are all weak," I say. "Me too. But we can learn from each other, and become stronger."

I know my words sound like a platitude. He nods. "Will you go?"

I pause for a moment. "Yes."

We gaze into each other's eyes. His face changes like the weather: clouds, then, by great determination, the sun. A smile. An innocent smile, now tinged with experience. A smile that breaks my heart now and always will, when I remember it. With the fire stick he traces a curving line in the dirt. "The sign of om," he says. "Hold, then let go."

"Yes. I think I am learning how to do that."

"I wish I can write like I talk, I could tell my story."

"I will tell your story for you," I say. "And my own. Our story."

"Come," he says, "leave the fire for a moment." I get up and follow him back into the ruined palace, through rooms that are defined only by fallen walls, onto a stairway that leads up and down and up again to the very top story, lined by columns that support nothing but the sky and arches that frame the view that looks out to the lake, to the far shore. The gray skies are gone and the sky is infinitely blue.

"You see," he says, "over there is the sun," he nods toward the west, where it is just beginning its descent. "And over here the moon," and I look to the east, where the rising moon is a circle of white. "Both in the sky at the same time."

"Like you and me, here."

"You must come back at monsoon," he says, "and we will have a picnic in this same place, with the storm all around us. It is very beautiful at monsoon."

"I would like that," I say, and some deep part of me wants it to be true.

Janet Marie Sola is a fiction writer and poet living in the beautiful Rogue Valley of southern Oregon. After a professional career as a news reporter and magazine editor, she earned an MA in Creative Writing from San Francisco State University. Her poems, fiction and articles have appeared in diverse publications including *Forge, Painted Bride, Poetry Flash,* and the *San Francisco Chronicle.* She can be reached through her website janetmariesola.com

Made in the USA
San Bernardino, CA
29 June 2015